Girl at the Window

**A Dark Psychological
Crime Thriller**

DECLAN CONNER

SCORPION BOOKS
THRILLERS WITH A STING IN THE TALE

Copyright

This book is a work of fiction. Characters, names, places, and incidents, either, are products of the author's imagination, or they are used fictitiously. Any reference to actual locales, or persons, living or dead, is entirely coincidental.

Girl at the Window

**A Dark Psychological
Crime Thriller**

US English - First Edition.

.

For information on subsidiary rights, email in the first instance.

declanconner@hotmail.com

ISBN-3:978-1976245497

ISBN-10:1976245494

Contents
Title page
Copyright
Contents

Chapter 1

Clara's Dilemma

If I'd have died there and then in the bitter cold of my bedroom, no one would have shed tears for me. Only maybe Pa, but I wouldn't have missed him, and that's the God's honest truth. He would likely have mourned that there'd be no one to cook and clean for him to his command, and little else. I wondered if death could be the freedom I needed. But then as I thought about it, freedom to live a life of my own choosing would have been preferable to anything death could ever have provided me with, unless it was his death.

A deep-felt craving to venture out ate away in my chest with every breath I took. That's what hurt me the most. Maybe if the world outside wasn't my enemy as Pa had taught me, I could have tested fate out there. He told me that it was a world full of sinners who would do their best to harm me now that I was a woman. I shivered at that thought and rolled my shoulders. It was as if a spirit had walked through me.

Even in the daylight, I sensed darkness through my bedroom window. I fought with the not knowing what was out there every day. Pa said it was dangerous on the outside. I was only to go out with him by my side to protect me. I had my doubts about his preaching, and yearned for the independence to find out for myself before my mind would implode.

1

The glass misted with the steam from my coffee. I drew HELP with my finger on the windowpane. None was coming. It was a cry to myself. No one would be out there waiting to rescue me. There was no white knight ready to whisk me away, and that's the truth. Maybe it's because only I could read the word that faced me. Especially when there weren't any neighbors as far as my eyes could see. With a flourish, I wiped my sleeve across the letters at the futility.

A fresh blanket of snow covered the landscape. It taunted me, for it would have left witness, lest I had dared to sneak out and leave tracks for him to find. The flakes were heavier now. I had an urge to dance in the snow. To scoop up a handful and throw it in the air. To make a snowman like I did when I was a child.

Pa was asleep, snoring. He sometimes slept light. A creak on the stairs would surely have wakened him. Strange how he ignored his own honking, yet he had a second sense when I attempted freedom to be alone, even if it was only to the porch out front. I yearned to overcome my internal fear. If only I would have had the courage to defy him. To be able to make my own way outside with no one watching my every move. To feel the warmth of the sun's rays, or the cold of a winter breeze, bathing me without his shadow following my every move.

The few times I had dared to venture out alone, I had been torn inside out with guilt. Tightness in my chest would consume me as our house disappeared from view. Short breaths. Leaden legs. Then the tremors for if Pa caught sight of me.

He guessed all my excuses to venture out alone. Kept my shoes under his chair, or he took them to his bedroom. I thought it would be different in our new home. He promised. It was a lie. I didn't know why we had to move around so much. Every move always seemed to be in such a hurry. I didn't even know why he always had to choose isolated locations, except, he said it was better to live off the grid. All I did know is that I wouldn't have had a clue what to do if he were not there.

Movement outside distracted my train of thought. A

2

blackbird took flight from a pine tree. It swooped and landed on the ground. Ruffled its feathers. Dug its beak in the snow. Moved on, hopping, then stopping and digging some more. It took flight, landing back in the cover of the pine tree. Its claws had left arrow tracks in the snow, but only for a short while. They were soon covered by the flakes as if it had never been there.

Maybe, I thought, that's what would happen to me if I defied him and tried to escape. I could have died in the freezing air. No one would have known if a fresh blanket had covered my tracks. Only the blackbird would have borne witness, but then who would he have told? Birds can't speak. But then neither could I. Even if I had had the nerve and the strength to carry life's breath beyond the confines of our house, I wouldn't have dared to speak. Not that I knew anyone. I knew no one, only Pa.

I wished Pa dead. It's not that he hadn't treated me well as long as I had obeyed him. He provided sustenance and I wanted for nothing in the material sense. Except I did want. There were people out there my own age. Experiences I had never had. All I knew was from the books he had provided over the years for home schooling. Then there was his Bible, The Old Testament. He used passages to prove he had the rights over me that God gave him. I had a deep urge to taste a different life that I would never have while ever he lived. That was another truth I couldn't deny. There was no doubt in my mind that the sooner he breathed his last breath, the better.

Chapter 2

Hunter's End

The following morning Pa was outside, fixing the chains to his pickup tires. He glanced my way. I shuddered at the rattle of the links clinking as I washed the breakfast dishes. I reckoned that he gave them an extra rattle to remind me. My ankles itched at the memories.

It would be our first journey into town for provisions. He bent over to secure the last of the chains. Elbows on the worktop, I held a carving knife with both hands and closed my eyes. A vision of Pa instructing me to slice his hunting knife across a goat's neck crossed my mind. "Empty your head," he'd said. "It's God's will." I couldn't help but wonder if God was putting the images of me grasping Pa's hair and slicing the knife across his neck when he stooped at the tire. He rose to his full height and held his back as if pained.

Pa hollered, "Clara, get out here now."

As I reached the front door at the porch, he stamped his boots, then he shook his coat, powdery flakes cascading to the wooden flooring.

"I'll get my coat and boots," I said.

"No need."

"But it's cold and snowing."

"The engine's running. It'll be warm in the pickup soon. Forget your boots. I don't want you wandering off."

There was no point protesting. He picked me up and carried me to the open pickup door. Launched me onto the seat. My teeth chattered as he opened his door and slid onto his seat. The tires spun, and with a lurch, together with a crunch on the crisp snow covering, we set off. My entire body trembled at the cold air blasting through the ducts. Even with the short distance to the pickup, the flakes that had settled on me now melted into my cotton dress and hair. Spider webs of cracked ice covered the side windows. Staring ahead, I flinched as clumps of snow dislodged from the hood and peppered the windshield, swiped away by the squeaking windshield wiper. At last, warm air began to circulate. The wind picked up, swirling and blowing drifts across our path.

"It's a blizzard out there. Are you sure we'll make it back?"

"It's now or never. We have to eat, child."

Child! I hated Pa calling me a child. It was his way of being condescending. His way of wishful thinking that I would have remained so. He'd stopped putting candles on the cakes this past seven years since I had my eleventh birthday. That was around the time he lost interest in me after my first bleed. His attitude changed. Pa gave up the right that he preached The Old Testament bestowed on him, but still demanded complete obedience.

It stopped snowing. The clouds gave way to sunlight. Ice on the side window turned to pearls of water droplets, streaming across the glass as we picked up speed on the main road into town. The streams of melted ice reminded me of the tears I'd shed the night before when I'd cried myself to sleep.

Pa turned off the wiper. The sign for the town flashed by. Hunter's End, it had read. Under that it had, 'Population 786' but that was struck through with a line and changed to '491.' That in turn was struck through with another line, and under that someone had scrawled '299.'

The town looked picturesque. Like a Christmas card image. A wooden church spire dominated the far end of Main Street. Wisps of smoke plumed into the sky from the chimneys. The smoke mocked me with images of families warm in front of their fires. I knew about families, and their begetting, but I had none, except for Pa. That's not exactly true. I had cousins when I was younger. At least I knew that much. Quite a few really, but I hadn't seen any of them for many years. They'd only come for the day and sometimes I'd catch a glimpse of them before being sent to my room. Pa said they weren't cleansed enough for me to meet them. We pulled over and stopped outside the grocery store.

"Wait here."

"Can't I come with you?"

"No, I won't be long."

He reached over me and removed the handle for my side window. His breath reeked of chewing tobacco. I retched at the repulsive smell. He was wheezing. I'd noticed him being short of breath lately and talking with a rasp. Maybe it wouldn't take a knife to see the back of him, I thought.

He labored up the wooden steps to the porch outside the store. There were three young men around my age, sitting on a bench to the left of the entrance that I'd noticed when Pa opened his door. They'd been laughing and passing a cigarette between them. I drew my knees up to my chest. Wrapped my arms around my legs. Rocked back and forth. Closed my eyes and dreamt of a better place. A rap on my side window and I near jumped out of my skin. My chest tightened. I opened my eyes. A dark patch danced outside the side window. Praying to God, I hoped it wasn't one of the demons paying a visit that Pa talked of.

"Roll the window down."

It wasn't Pa's voice. The windows were fogged up again. All I could see was a shadow.

"C'mon, don't be shy. Only we don't get many gals around these parts. We only want to jaw."

"Go away," I wrote with my finger on the misted window, then tugged at my ear. I pulled the sleeve of my dress over my hand and wiped the words away at realizing they'd need a mirror to read the message. It was one of the youths from outside the store. A mop of black hair and white teeth loomed large as he bent over. It was the white teeth that held my gaze. I was used to seeing Pa's toothless grin, surrounded by his long white facial hair. Well, not exactly toothless, just his top two teeth were missing. The rest were twisted and stained with the tobacco he chewed.

"I'm Jordan, what's your name?" he said, and smiled. "You moved in around here, or just visiting?" he said, not waiting for a reply to his first question.

Pulses of shivers ran through my body. I noticed my hands shaking, unable to stop the tremors.

"I... I'm Clara. Listen, I can't open the window, please go away."

His features distorted as the moisture on the window fogged again. Maybe Pa's preaching was right and it was the demon in him I could now see.

"Hey, watcha doing hanging around my pickup?" Pa called out.

"Just being neighborly."

"Well, just skedaddle."

"Screw you, old man. Just trying to be friendly."

"Screw you! I'll show you who's gonna screw who."

"Whoa there, put the gun away."

Chapter 3

Mixed Feelings

Pa grunted when he climbed into his pickup. He put the provisions behind his seat, then spat tobacco-stained saliva on the snow.

"What the hell ya think ya doing talking to those punks?"

"I wasn't. They did the talking. I ignored them like you'd taught me."

He broke wind as he fired up the engine. He didn't even say excuse me, but then he hardly ever did. "Whether in church or chapel, let the damned things rattle," was his usual wisecrack, followed by a belly laugh. All that followed this time was the smell of rotten eggs.

"Can I have the handle to open the window?"

He turned the fan on full blast to clear the mist.

"It'll pass. Don't want you catching your death of cold."

Pa's nose was dripping. His cheeks flushed. He coughed, then wiped his coat sleeve across his nose. I wasn't sure if a cold could kill. I'd survived all my sniffles. If colds could kill, he was starting with one. Maybe that could be my salvation. The mist cleared from the windows.

"Sheriff. Keep your hands where I can see them. Step out of the car."

I turned to see a woman crouching and pointing a gun at Pa.

"Damn," Pa said.

She pulled the door open. Pa shuffled off of his seat. She was middle aged, with a red bulbous nose, and a stout figure. A dour expression rolled over her face.

"Turn real slow to face away from me, and keep your hands where I can see them."

Pa obliged. I saw her hands frisking him, then pulling his gun from its holster.

"I have a carry permit. Clara, pass it here. It's behind the sun

9

visor."

"No, you stay where you are and put your hands on the dash," she said.

She reached inside and retrieved the permit.

"What's all this about?" said Pa.

"Jordan over there said you pulled a gun on him."

"Oh, that. Sorry, I thought they were trying to break-in and I had my daughter in the pickup. The windows were fogged and I thought they might not have seen she was in there. Just wanted them to back off. No harm done as it turns out. Misunderstanding. If you don't believe me, look at the footprints."

The sheriff dropped the clip from Pa's gun, then walked around the hood. I wiped the side window. Even I could see Jordan's footsteps in the snow and them leading off across the road to where he was standing. She stroked her chin, then ambled back, took out her notebook and wrote down Pa's details.

"Holster your pistol and put the clip in your pocket until you're out of town. Just be careful not to be so jumpy next time. We don't want no shooting accidents," she said, then called across to Jordan and his friends, "Misunderstanding that's all. It won't happen again, but you need to stop hanging around the vehicles." She turned and walked into the store shaking her head.

Pa climbed back onto his seat, then did a U-turn. He rolled down his window as he approached Jordan and his friends.

"There'll be no misunderstanding next time if I catches you talking to my daughter again," he called out, then rolled up his window. Just as well he did as they pounded his side window and the windshield with snowballs. Pa jammed on the brakes. They must have scooped up dog dirt in one of them and I watched it slide down the glass.

"Damn town jerks," he said. They ran down an alley at the side of a house. "See what I told you about the outsiders. No good sons of bitches. Good thing I was with you or they'd be up your skirt by now, taking turns."

The Sheriff appeared at the front of the hood. Pa rolled

down his window again.

"Did you see that?" he said.

"Yeah, I saw them. They're at that rebellious age. Don't pay them no mind in future. I have enough problems with them dicking around town as it is without a feud developing."

"Yeah, well just tell them to stay away from my daughter and me, or else."

She walked from the hood to his window, then leaned over.

"Or else! What does that mean? Don't go making threats. I think it's you who needs to stay away from them. Listen, seeing as how you've just moved into the farmstead over at Hunter's Lodge, I'll drop by and we can chat about security. We've had a few break-ins lately at some of the outlying properties."

"No need. We don't need no visitors and I know how to keep things secure. Now step back. We need to get home before it starts to snow again."

She looked directly at me.

"You okay, hon?"

"She's fine," he said, and rolled up his window, then stamped on the gas pedal.

"What the hell does she mean, 'you okay, hon'? You'd better not have been giving off vibes."

"I was shook-up. Worried she was going to lock you up that's all," I lied.

"That's my, girl. We gots stick together. They're all tainted with the Devil out here."

As we drove on, Jordan appeared, peeking from behind a bush at my side of the road. He waved and smiled, baring those white teeth of his. I sensed a hot flush in my cheeks, not daring to look at Pa, but raised a smile back at Jordan. There was no doubting Jordan had the Devil in him. But then didn't I with the thoughts that ran through my mind. If only Pa had his window down instead of the crap hitting it when closed. Emotion flooded through me. My eyes moistened. I couldn't be sure why I felt tearful really. Perhaps the fact that Jordan and his friends were running around as free as a pack of feral dogs, while I was tethered. It could have been that I had a desire to run free with them. Maybe it was that he had the courage and defiance that I didn't possess. I know that I'd felt admiration at Jordan's sass when he had bad-mouthed Pa.

I sighed and pushed back in the seat. Closed my eyes and prayed to God that He would deliver me to freedom. Asked forgiveness for my bad thoughts. Especially for lying when I'd said that I didn't want the sheriff to lock him up. He never answered me. I hoped that one day He would before I had to do something drastic without His help. A tear escaped and ran down to my cheek.

Chapter 4

The Proposition

Driving along the road from town there was a sudden clunk, followed by a second jolt. The pickup skidded sideways, then stalled.

"Damnation," Pa said.

He fired up the engine again. The front had plowed into a drift. The more he tried to reverse, the further it slewed sideways, making matters worse. He gave up trying and elbowed his door open, then climbed outside. Pa walked back a ways and picked up two broken tire chains. I heard the chains land in the back of the pickup. The next thing I saw was Pa digging at the snow with his shovel. A snicker escaped my lips at the sight of him having to labor. He stopped, took off his Stetson and wiped his arm across his brow, then started to wave his hat. Throwing my arm over the seat, I turned to see what he was waving at behind us.

An SUV pulled over back a ways and stopped. A young man climbed out of the cab and walked over.

"Looks like you're having problems, sir," he said.

"Yeah, thrown two tire chains."

"Morning, ma'am," he said, as he passed my window and smiled at me. His hair was fair, and he sported a neatly trimmed beard. "Nathaniel, sir," he said, by way of introduction. "But Nat will do. Looks as though you need a tow. I have a cable winch. Give me five minutes."

For a young man, his hands showed the signs of hard work. Pa followed him to his SUV, not giving him the civility of returning introductions. He glared at me, running his fingers across his lips as though fastening a zipper as he passed by. Nat had seemed pleasant enough and polite. Not the sort to be cussed at as having the Devil in him. Pa stood back and left Nat to it.

"We're all hooked up," Nat said. "Let's give it a try."

The door opened and Pa climbed inside.

"Nat seems like the good Samaritan," I said.

"Yeah, well looks can be deceptive."

With the transmission in neutral, Pa released the handbrake. I felt the cable tugging, followed by a violent jolt, then we slowly backed out of the drift and stopped.

I sneaked a look over my shoulder. Nat climbed out of his SUV and ambled over. He had something of a swagger about him that oozed confidence.

"You'll not get far with the tire chains on one side. Best thing is to take the one from the front and put it on the rear. More grip that way with the drive at the back," Nat said.

"Thanks, I'll do that," said Pa, and struggled to climb out of the cab. He straightened up and held his back.

"Problems with your back, sir?"

I hoped Pa's back pain was caused by him carrying me to the pickup. It would serve him right as retribution for not allowing me to wear my boots. The more excruciating pain he suffered, the better.

"Yeah. Old age setting in," he said, and started to cough into his hand.

"Best leave it to me. I need to unhook the cable first."

"Don't wanna put you out."

"It's no problem, really, sir."

I half expected Pa to argue and to stand his ground out of pride and his usual stubborn obnoxious attitude. I was surprised when he left Nat to it. Nat unhooked the cable then walked over to his vehicle and wound it up with the winch. The next time I glanced over my shoulder, Nat had bent over to chain up the rear tire.

"Does it usually snow in the fall around these parts?" Pa said.

"Not often, and not this bad. We usually expect this in January. Still, climate's gone to hell. Saw it on the news this morning. Torrential rain's caused floods and mudslides in California and broken the drought. I'm guessing it's thrown up a weather front that's drifted over the Rocky Mountains.

14

Usually we just get snow dumped on the high elevations on the mountains close by, but it's missed its mark this time and hit the town and the surrounding area. Not seen you before. You live around here?"

"Just moved in," Pa said.

"I hear Jed O'Leary has just rented his Hunter's Lodge homestead. Is that the one?"

Pa was backed into a corner. He didn't like to give out where he lived, but Nat had guessed right.

"Yeah," he said.

"Listen, I work as a handyman. If you need any help fixing things, especially with you having a bad back, give me a phone call," Nat said, then rose and handed Pa a card. "My telephone number is on there."

Pa grunted a reluctant thank you, and then climbed alongside of me. Nat leaned inside and he looked right at me. I'd not seen eyes like that close up. They were an amazing pale blue, almost mesmerizing.

"We have a get together in the church community hall on Friday nights. We're having a Halloween dance night this week. You're welcome to come along. I could pick you up if you phone me."

Pa almost choked, and replied for me, "We're away on Friday. Right now we have to get going." Nat took a step back. Pa closed his door a little on the heavy side.

Our pickup juddered as he set off along the road. I pulled down the sun visor. In the vanity mirror I noticed Nat take off his hat and scratch his head as he watched us drive away. Pa reached over and pushed the visor back.

"Good Samaritan, bah. More like the Devil in disguise."

"But he was nice to us," I said, then sighed.

He reached into his pocket. Rolled down his window, then tossed Nat's card outside.

"They're all nice until they gets what they want. Don't you dare doubt my word, child. Halloween is the night when the demons show themselves."

More than ever, I wanted him to die. Not in his sleep, but a horrible death for him to feel the pain that I felt inside.

Chapter 5

Wishful Thinking

Staring out of the kitchen window, I craved to know more about Halloween. I tried to imagine what the meeting at the community hall would be like. All I could grasp at were images of being encircled by a crowd of demons, and them tying me to a chair for some ritual, with Jordan and Nat fighting over the right to cover my body with theirs.

We'd had children calling at our door dressed in all types of costumes in the past at Halloween, many of them with pointed hats and their faces painted. That was way back in the day when we had neighbors on a trailer park. Pa had said not to open the door and told me about witches casting spells.

A wish circled that I had the knowledge to cast my own spells as I stirred some crushed garlic into the pan of boiling water on the stove. I added the glycerin oil, then sprinkled in some bay leaves. Pa stamped his boots out on the porch. Using a cloth, I picked up the pan and poured some of the liquid through a strainer I'd set over a cup. Setting the pan back on the stove, I ground out some phlegm, then removed the strainer and spat into the cup, then dropped in some lemon slices.

"Is it ready?" Pa said, and took a seat at the table.

A tingling sensation ran through me as if my soul had leapt from my body. I prayed that he might not have seen what I'd done, avoiding looking in his direction.

"Y... Yeah. It's ready. Just need the water to cool in the cup before you take a drink," I said, and carried the pan over to the table with my hands shaking, half-expecting a slap for spitting in his cup.

My prayer was answered. It felt as though a great weight lifted from my shoulders. He pulled a cloth over his head and bent over to take in the vapors. Hands held out in front of me,

17

palms down and hovering over his head, my fingers trembled. A part of me wanted to push his face into the scalding hot liquid and I had to fight the urge. I curled my hands into fists and shuffled back to the stove. A sideways glance at the cup and I was horrified that my phlegm had settled on the top as a green slime. Taking a spoon, I sprinkled in some sugar and stirred it, then stirred it some more, but the slime wasn't for dissolving. Just about to spoon it out and an arm reached past me. Stepping out of his way, I raised a hand in front of me, just in case he had seen it floating, and he'd pour it over me. Pa picked up the cup, and not looking, he swallowed the contents in gulps. He set the cup down, and then walked over to the cabinet. He took out a bottle of whisky and poured some into a glass.

"Why are you blushing?" he said.

"Didn't know I was. How do you feel?"

Pa belched, then said, "Tired and my back aches. I'll take a nap in my den."

"You do that. I'll go to my room."

I took the cloth from my shoulder as he walked into his office, stuffing the whisky bottle into his pocket. His key scraped in the lock. Pressing the cloth to my face, I stifled a snicker.

Chances were that he'd drink himself to sleep. At least I hoped he would. I took a seat at the table, deciding to give him twenty minutes to be sure. There was an attic room I'd not explored yet and I didn't want him looking over my shoulder while I discovered what could be up there.

Chapter 6

The Attic

Gazing out through my bedroom window, I was blind to all outside. The thought of being invited to join Nat at the Halloween dance still consumed me. Goodness knows why I couldn't let go of that thought and move on. What had me confused was that Pa said that the church was probably a front for the Devil seeing as how it was hosting a Halloween party. I had no recollection of Nat saying it was a church hall. Maybe he had, I couldn't remember exactly all he'd said. Understandable really, considering the warmth of his eyes had mesmerized me at the time. Anyway, one thing I could remember was when Pa had said, "No God fearing religion would pay homage to the work of Satan by holding a pagan dance event." Satan or not, I had a desire to find out for myself.

My vision turned inwards as I closed my eyes. Scenarios ran through my mind of different ways to ask Pa help me gain a little freedom. Sure, he'd taught me to drive, but only after he'd sprained his ankle when we were in the forest picking mushrooms. That was a case of necessity. It was how we had earned a living before we moved. We picked mushrooms in season and sold them to restaurants, then trapped game in the winter. Ate the meat and sold the pelts.

The occasion he went over on his ankle was the only week he let me out of his sight. Well, that's not strictly correct. He'd sometimes lock me in the cabin when he went out hunting and trapping back in Alaska, but that was hardly freedom to roam. Even then, when I was in the woods collecting mushrooms during spring, he sat in the SUV we had at the time, constantly calling me on a two-way radio. I recalled wishing I had the pluck to kick away his crutches back then.

I opened my eyes and tiptoed over to the open door. All was quiet as I craned my neck and listened. I struck a match, lifted the glass on the oil lamp and lit the wick, then dropped the glass. My entire being trembled as I crept along the hallway toward the attic doorway. A sudden loud creak as I stepped onto a floorboard and I stopped, glued to the spot. My heart pounded. It was so loud, I was sure he would hear it thumping. Part of me wanted to dart back to my bedroom, but something else spurred me on as if I had a demon on my shoulder whispering in my ear. Fingers shaking, I reached out, turned the handle and slowly pushed the door open, then scurried up the stairway.

With the lamp out front of me, guiding my way, there didn't appear to be anything interesting at first. Then I saw it. A large chest off to my right the previous occupants must have left behind. In my eagerness to get to it, my face caught a spider's web. Then another snagged me. I shuddered and wiped them away, brushing them from my face with my fingers. The top of the chest was covered in dust. There were just two clasps. I took a deep breath, then set the lamp on a hook screwed into a truss.

Luckily, it wasn't locked. Can't say that I knew what to expect as I unfastened the clasps and lifted the lid. At the top there was some clothing. I rummaged through the items. The top one was a red dress. I held it up against me, surprised that it was my size. It had no sleeves, and it was low cut at the chest, with the hem above my knees. Pa would never have let me wear anything like that. It was understandable really. I couldn't imagine doing the house chores wearing it, especially chopping logs for the fire. There were other dresses, but they were smaller and ranged in sizes down to a child's size.

I set the clothes to one side, then worked my way through a pile of paintings. One of them was obviously of the homestead and painted with the hand of a child. It displayed a stick man, a woman, and a young girl, all holding hands. At the bottom corner was scrawled, Kate, Mom, and Dad. I placed them on top of the clothes, then picked up a stack of photographs.

As I shuffled through the photos, tears welled in my eyes. They depicted the life of a child with her family that I assumed was Kate, from the cradle through to womanhood. Kate seemed to have a permanent smile etched on her face on the images as she transformed over the years, from her riding a pony as a child, to skiing with the mountains as a backdrop, and to pictures of her around my age at a rodeo.

My thoughts turned to my own life without a mom. I had no recollection of her. Pa said she died in a car wreck. We had no photographs. Pa insisted they were the work of Satan collecting souls to take to hell. With the smile on Kate's face, it didn't look as though having her picture taken had troubled her in the slightest. I wiped my sleeve across my eyes, then putting the photos to one side; I delved further into the chest.

Near to the bottom, there were some magazines with pictures of women on the front, scantily dressed. Flicking through the pages of one, there were images I hadn't seen before that talked of fragrances and face coverings, from creams to powders. Cosmetics I think was the word they used. One image stopped me turning the pages. It was a picture of a man and a woman entwined, their lips touching. I rolled it up, and lifting my dress, I stuffed it under my waistband. That was when I noticed the red shoes and a purse. They weren't like the shoes Pa bought me. It defied reason how anyone could walk in them, with pencil-thin heels around three inches long. I pushed them to one side and came to some books. I picked up the first one and flicked the pages, surprised that none of them had been removed. I couldn't recall any book that Pa gave me for studies that didn't have at least one or two ripped out from the spine. That included my dictionary and my Bible, which were always at the side of my bed on a nightstand.

It was a worry that Pa would stir and catch me rummaging. I placed everything back in the chest, but kept the book. Lifting the lamp from the hook, I had one last scan around. There was a tarp to the left of me. I lifted the corner. Underneath the tarp there was a small suitcase fastened with padlocks. It was Pa's case. I couldn't imagine why he would want to hide it there.

"Clara, where are you?" Pa called out.

I hurried down the stairway, then along the hallway and into my bedroom.

"I'm in my bedroom."

Despite the cold air, sweat poured from my brow and stung my eyes. I heard his boots on the steps. My body trembled. I stuffed the book under my mattress, then rushed back to the dresser to douse the lamp. His footsteps were now along the hallway and I felt my chest tighten as I stepped back to my bed. The door opened.

"I need a massage. My backs playing up," he said.

Even with him standing at the doorway, I could smell the whisky on his breath.

"I'll go and get the oil."

His eyes narrowed.

"What's that dirt doing on your face?"

Heat rose in my cheeks. I felt the magazine slipping at my waist, catching it with my knees and sat on the corner of the bed.

"I've been cleaning while you were asleep, now go to your room and I'll get the oil."

He turned just as the magazine dropped between my legs to the floor. I kicked it under the bed as he turned back to face me.

"What's that smell?" he said, then touched the glass on the lamp. "Why have you been using it in daylight?"

"My hands were cold."

He grunted and stepped outside.

"Use gloves in future, we don't have money to waste on lamp oil."

"Good thing I did warm my hands if you want me to give you a massage."

He gave me a sideways glance, his expression saying 'don't give me any sass, child.' I prayed he wouldn't look down and see the magazine.

"Whatever. Hurry up and get the rubbing oil."

Rising from the mattress, then stepping over to the doorway, I ushered him along to his room. He closed his door behind him. I bent over and held my knees, taking a moment to compose myself. I wasn't sure how long I could carry on with his controlling ways. Without any doubt, I knew that I'd have to stand up to him and put an end to his hold over me.

Chapter 7

Unexpected Guest

I'd not slept much during the night. Too much of an active mind after reading that magazine, and then the romance book. It didn't help that I kept having visions of Jordan and his devilish grin, and the warmth of Nat's blue eyes. When I had finally fallen asleep, I'd only awoken and rushed down the stairway after I heard Pa's pickup drive off. I picked up a note from the kitchen table Pa had left for me.

"Back around noon," It read, nothing more.

It didn't mean diddly-squat. For all I knew, he could be out in the woods watching the house through his riflescope lens. He'd done that before and returned early. Knocked the living daylight out of me for daring to go outside. At least this time he'd taken the key so I couldn't be tempted by the Devil to go wandering. I scrunched the note into a ball and tossed it into the wastebasket, then sighed.

He'd want his dinner when he returned. A hot stew. It was expected. Especially after a morning setting traps in the freezing cold. He'd not said so the night before, but I knew that's where he'd gone. When I'd glanced out of the kitchen window and around the room, I'd noticed the traps had gone from the porch, and his snowshoes, together with his hunting rifle from the wall.

My head was still buzzing with the magazine articles and the love story I had read. I skipped breakfast. Instead, I set about making the stew. I used the last of the venison together with mixed vegetables and set it to simmer on the stove. One article that I had read about a supermarket kept circling through my thoughts. It had blown my mind. Never knew there was such a thing as readymade meals you could heat up in a gadget called a microwave. It would have sure made life easier. But then I could hardly ask Pa to buy a microwave. He'd want to know how I found out about them.

With everything prepared, I decided to go and take another look at the chest in the attic. Collecting the book and the magazine on the way, I entered the attic. Over at the chest, I opened it and exchanged them for two more books. Back in my bedroom it was freezing, despite wearing a thick wooly sweater and jeans. I wrapped my blanket around me and started to read. Halfway through the story and I heard a vehicle outside. My heart thumped at the thought that Pa had arrived early. I tossed my blanket to one side, then placed the books under the mattress and peered through the window.

"Oh, no."

Nat was standing at the side of his SUV. He looked up and waved. I ducked from the window and sat on the corner of my mattress, hoping I was imagining that he was there. The repeated knocking on the door told me he was there all right. My insides knotted at not knowing what to do. I covered my face with my hands. All I did know was that I needed him gone before Pa arrived. I imagined he'd swear blind I had somehow encouraged Nat when we were stuck in that drift. Can't say what spurred me into action as I leapt from the bed, shuffled along the hallway, and ran down the stairway. I grasped the handle, then sighed. It would be locked and Pa would have the key.

"Pa's not here. What is it you want?"

"It's Nat, remember me from yesterday? I didn't get your name."

"I'm Clara. Sorry, I don't open the door when Pa's not here."

The last thing I wanted to tell him was that I couldn't open the door, much as I wanted to.

"No problem, just in the area and thought I'd drive by to make sure you arrived back okay. Started to worry when I saw the pickup wasn't here. Thought he might have gotten stuck again. When will your dad be back?"

"Later today, why?"

"Scouting for work, that's all, and I have some spare tire chains I can sell him cheap. Or maybe barter if he has something I need. Listen, about Friday, sorry you couldn't make it. We have a dance night there every week. I could pick you up any Friday if you want to get to know the others in town?"

"Thanks, but it's difficult just now."

"Well, your dad has my number. Phone me when you have a mind to go for a night out."

I leant my forehead against the door, fighting the urge to head butt it at a vision of Nat's card disappearing out of Pa's window. But then I thought, what good would it have been. Only Pa had access to a cell phone.

"Thanks. Look, sorry but I have to go, I have something cooking on the stove."

"Sure."

Relief washed over me when I pressed my ear to the door and I heard the sound of his footsteps on the porch stairway, then his door opening. Darting over to the kitchen window, I peered out as his door closed. He turned and saw me, then waved. My return wave was a little on the half-hearted side. More of a curling of fingers really. Mindful that Pa could be watching, I snatched my hand to my side, then dodged out of sight until I heard him drive off. A hot flush rose in my cheeks and I darted up to my bedroom, then dove onto the mattress. Pulling the curtain to one side, I watched his vehicle until he was out of sight. I rolled over and stared at the ceiling. My chest heaved and I blew the breath out slowly through pursed lips, forming clouds of misted air in the crispness of the cold room. I reached under the mattress for the book I'd been reading, then wrapped the blanket around me.

At the end of the story, I realized that I still had the stew on the stove. Panic set in at thoughts that it could have boiled dry. I sat upright and tossed the blanket from around my shoulders. The story had left me with tears streaming down my cheeks. I hid the book under the mattress, then ran out of the room and scurried down the stairway. Luck was with me, when I caught the stew just in time for it to be ready and moved the pan to one side on the stove. I hoped the gas in the bottle would last forever. I doubted Pa would change it when it ran out of gas. The owners had left it behind with the stove. It sure was easier to use than the wood burner with far more control.

My fingers were numb and I ran them over the flames until I could feel them again, then turned off the gas. The wood burning stove was down to its last embers. I placed some more logs inside, then sat at the dining table. Overwhelmed with emotion, I sunk my head into my hands and began to wail as visions of my life passed before me. I was all cried out, when I heard a vehicle outside. Dashing over to the sink, I grabbed a towel and dried my eyes. There was no mistaking Pa's pickup outside the window. He climbed out of the cab and walked over to the door. The key scraped in the lock, then the door creaked open.

"I need a hand with a deer," he said, as he entered. "Back's playing me up again. Help me get it hoisted in the barn and you can skin it and gut it there."

He tossed a pair of rubber boots over to me.

"Don't you want to eat first? The stew's ready."

"Time for that when we've hung it up to bleed out." He walked over and put his rifle on its wall mount. "What are you waiting for? Hurry up. Go to the barn and wait for me, while I back up to the doors."

At the back of my eyes to my forehead a thumping pain dug at me. I arrived at the barn and dragged open the doors. Pa reversed inside as I stood to one side. I dropped the tailgate on his pickup. He climbed out of the cab and joined me.

"I'll need you to get it on your shoulders and carry it to the rope pulley."

"What, me?"

"Yes you."

I looked at the rope, then back at the deer. Pa doubled over, coughing and spluttering. When he stood upright, he wiped his sleeve across his mouth. I noticed his beard stained with blood.

"Are the keys in the ignition?"

"Yeah, why?"

"Go sit down. I'll back it under the rope. That way I don't need to lift it on my shoulders."

With a little maneuvering, I backed under the rope dangling from the ratchet pulley. Climbed out of my seat, walked around to the tailgate, then tied the rope at its ankles. A little heaving in fits and starts with the ratchet holding and I tied off the rope on a hook. Back in the cab, I slung my arm over the seat and looked over my shoulder, then pulled forward until the deer's head dropped off of the back. Pa tossed me his hunting knife as I climbed out of the cab.

"You do the honors," he said.

I held the knife and looked at him. He looked so frail. Like death warmed up. For once, I felt as though I held all the power and he was the weak one. I knew what he meant by doing the honors, but wished he meant me to put him out of his misery, so we could both be at peace.

"Well, get on with it, child. It won't freakin' bite."

I grabbed it by the ear, and then sliced the knife across its neck. It wasn't the deer's neck I imagined that I was slicing, but Pa's gullet.

Pent up anger raged inside my mind. The internal fury bubbled to a point that all reason as to the consequences eluded me. I turned, stamped my foot, and wagged the bloody blade at him.

"You keep calling me Child. I'm not a child. I'm a woman."

Chapter 8

Pa's Decision

Pa didn't say a word when I'd flipped in the barn. I'd turned away from him, sticking the knife in the deer's gut, and then marched back to the house. Him not saying anything worried me. I'd have rather taken the beating than experience the torture I felt at wondering what would happen when he joined me. The least I could have expected at the time was the back of his hand. Maybe I'd misjudged just how ill he felt.

By the time Pa hobbled back from the barn, the stew had started to bubble. He ignored me as I ladled some into a dish and set it on the table with a spoon and some bread. He limped over to the table and took a seat.

"You not joining me?" he said.

"Not hungry."

He put a spoonful to his lips, then with the contents untouched, he dropped it back in the bowl. By the look on his face, I expected being chastised as a delayed reaction to what was said in the barn.

"Who's visited us?" he said, and thumped his forearms onto the table with such force, the dish bounced, and catching the spoon with his sleeve, it did a somersault, landing back on the surface with a tinkle. He drummed his fingers. Narrowed his eyes.

I shook from head to toe. He had to have been watching when Nat arrived. I took a step back and bowed my head.

"I… I was going to tell you, honestly. How did you know?"

"Fresh tire tracks in the snow. They're wider than mine."

"Oh, yeah. It was that Nat. The one who gave us a tow. Said he wanted to see if you had any work for him. He has some tire chains he can sell or exchange. Said he'd call back."

"And you talked to him?"

"Not really. Only listened, then told him to go away. Said he'd have to speak to you. Had to say something. He was banging so loud and he'd seen me at the window."

He picked up his spoon and waved it at me.

"I'm going to tell you this once more. If anyone else knocks… don't freakin' answer when I'm not here. Do I have to bang it into you?"

He dug his spoon into the stew and stuffed a spoonful into his mouth. His eyes bulged and he spat it back into the dish, followed by a bout of coughing.

"Was it too hot?"

"No, my throat's sore." He pushed the dish away. "We need to talk. What was the lip about back there in the barn? I also don't take kindly to you pointing a knife at me. Sit down."

I took a seat at the table opposite him, wondering why he didn't say anything back at the barn. I dug deep. It was time for some honesty.

"I'm eighteen. I'm not a child anymore. You keep calling me a child and it bugs me. I pull my weight around here."

He rolled his eyes.

"Why are your eyes red?"

"Been crying, that's all."

"Crying! Give me any of that lip again you gave me in the barn and I'll give you something to cry about."

That same uncontrollable rage surfaced again, and I rose to my feet, leaning forward with my clenched fists on the table, then with my face close to his, I exploded.

"I hate you," I screamed, through gritted teeth.

There was no taking the words back. The floodgates opened. There was no doubting my head was messed up. Tears streamed from my eyes. I couldn't stop them and I backed up to my chair. Kicked it away. Ran to the stairway and up to my bedroom and bolted the door.

Leaning with my back to the door, I prayed to God that he'd carry on with his meal and let things settle down. I should have known better, when I heard his boots stomping up the stairway, then along the hallway. The door handle twitched.

"Open this door now, or I'll tear it from its freakin' hinges."

"Not if you're going to hit me."

Stepping away from the door, my eyes darted around the room, I didn't doubt him. I'd be trapped once he entered. I had it in mind to climb out of the window onto the porch roof, but then recalled he'd nailed the frame. He coughed and spluttered again, then called out, "Shit, no."

It sounded as though he had fallen.

"Pa, you okay?"

"Forget all this nonsense. I don't want a fight. Help me up. It's my back again... please."

I slid the bolt and opened the door. Pa was holding his back and on one knee.

"You're too heavy. What should I do?"

He sprang to his feet and grabbed me by the hair, forcing me to bend.

"Get back down those stairs. That's what you can do."

He dragged me all the way to the kitchen by my hair and forced me to sit at the table.

"I'm going to let go. Don't you dare run off, child. I won't hit you, I just want to talk."

"Okay, okay, okay."

He let go of my hair. My scalp hurt like hell. He used the table surface for support as he made his way around to his chair, grimacing all the way until he took a seat.

"Listen, my back really is bad, that's what I want to talk about."

The pain was evident in his eyes. I doubted he was lying, but I couldn't be sure.

"What about it?"

"I'm not sure I can carry on providing for the two of us."

I pushed back in my chair.

"And?"

"We need to find someone else to take care of you."

"What does that mean?"

"It means it's time to give you your wings. I've been waiting for the day you might give me some sass. Time you took a husband."

"What!"

All of a sudden I was torn. Torn between being excited at the prospect of him giving me the chance to strike out on my own, and fear. The fear of how I would go about finding a partner. I began to wish I'd read all the books in the chest.

"Say that again," I said, rising from my chair and took a seat next to him.

"Not now. I need to take some medication. I'm going to trust you to work outside alone. I can trust you?"

"Have I ever done anything different for you not to trust me?"

"Okay. Go out to the barn. My boning knife and the others are on the wall there with the saw. I need you to cut up the deer, and then we'll talk. There's a sack in the cabinet. You can use that to bring the cuts up here for processing

I couldn't remember the walk to the barn, nor did I feel the cold. I had to wonder if the quest would start with him allowing me to go to the community hall dance.

Chapter 9

Hot Flushes

I'd skinned the deer, then set about removing its innards into a bowl, when I heard a vehicle crunching on the frozen snow in the driveway. I wondered if Nat had returned, and took off my bloodstained apron. Over at the water barrel I turned the faucet, but it was frozen solid. There was water in the barrel, but the surface was covered in ice. I smashed the thin layer of ice with the saw handle. Dipped in a rag, then wiped away the blood. Stepping over to the door, I dried my hands on the back of my jeans, then ran my fingers through my hair. I looked through a gap at the doors and took a step back. It wasn't Nat, but a police SUV, followed by a red pickup truck. I couldn't make out who was in the other vehicle hidden behind hers, but I recognized the sheriff right away.

Pa appeared at the door, cradling his rifle in his arms.

"What is it you want," Pa said, and spat on the porch boards. Then carried on chewing his tobacco.

The sheriff walked behind her vehicle and reached in to the back of the red pickup. She walked over to the porch and dumped some traps on the boards.

"These yours?"

"What if they are?"

I stepped away from the opening out of sight and listened.

"Trapping isn't allowed around here. These are Federal lands."

"Since when? This is Hunter's End, right?"

"Yeah, well, that may be. The town's name came from the settler days. There ain't been no trapping around these parts since the wildlife dwindled and the Feds took over the land. Is that the rifle you used to shoot the deer on Jake's private property?"

Pa didn't answer.

"Just so you know, the only hunting for deer you can do around here is with a permit and permission from the land owner. And then you're given a quota. Not to mention that you have to wear an orange viz vest. Jake here heard a gunshot and found a blood trail."

"I don't know about no deer."

A side door behind me creaked open. A toothy grin greeted me as I turned. He put his fingers on his lips. The last thing I expected was Jordan to be there.

"So he doesn't know about my dad's deer," he whispered, then punched the carcass, leaving it swinging. "What's it worth not to snitch?"

Panic set in at the thought of the sheriff taking him away. Much as I hated him, I wasn't sure I could survive without him. I dreaded him digging a deeper hole by lying about the traps, especially as I'd need his help in finding a husband.

"Please, don't tell. We've just moved in. He wouldn't know it was illegal, or that he was trespassing. It won't happen again. I'll swear that on the Bible," I said, and crossed my fingers behind my back.

"Don't make me laugh, they'll hear us," He walked up close to me. "I won't tell about the deer if you don't," he said, and planted a kiss on my lips, catching me by surprise. I reared away. Touching my lips with my fingers, my body tingled, unable to say anything by way of rebuke, and I watched as he turned and strutted back over to the side door. "He's in trouble now. Dad followed his tracks in the snow. Saw him setting the traps." Jordan stepped out of the door.

I drew my hands to my chest and took a deep breath, then slowly exhaled through my lips with faltering breaths. Closing my eyes, I wrapped my arms around me, with my hands caressing my upper arms and imagined Jordan holding me, just like I read in the love story.

"Hey, watcha doing over there?" Pa called out.

I opened my eyes and shuffled over to the barn door.

"Keep your shirt on, old man, just stretching my legs," I heard Jordan say.

"Yeah, well stretch them right off of my land."

I opened the door and rushed over to Pa.

"Just give us a minute," I said, and tugged Pa's sleeve. We

stepped inside the house.

"What is it?" Pa said.

"Why do you think they're here? Someone must have seen you setting the traps. Put your rifle on the wall and be civil. Try eating crow for once."

Pa huffed, but did as he was told. The first time ever. He picked up his Bible and I followed him out to the porch. He held up his hands.

"Okay, ya got me. Those are my traps. Well, not mine exactly. Found them in the barn when we moved in. Owner said I could make use of the furniture and everything else he'd left behind when he rented us the property. Just assumed with him having traps, it was the same as back home. I swear on this here Bible, I didn't know the law in these parts. It won't happen again. I promise."

"Yeah, well, many townsfolk still have traps laying around from the old days. The parks and wildlife rangers have an office in town. If you call in, they have a map showing where hunting and trapping is restricted. It's a day's travel to where there are no restrictions. Where have you come from that allowed trapping?"

"Alaska. Lived out in the wilds. Off the grid."

"Why move here to Colorado?"

"Bears. Went out to get one last moose to add to our winter supplies of meat. When we came back, damn things had eaten all our meat supplies and ragged all the pelts. Can't survive the winter up there without enough meat. One moose wouldn't cut it. With the pelts destroyed, I couldn't sell them to buy provisions to last us till spring."

I couldn't believe his lies. Not when he was holding his Bible. He nudged me with his elbow.

"Isn't that right, Clara?"

I looked down at my boots. "Guess so," I mumbled.

When I looked up, the sheriff seemed to be sizing me up. She stroked her chin. Jordan was sitting in the pickup with his dad. He winked over at me, kissed the tips of his fingers, then blew on them as if sending it my way. I sensed a hot flush in my cheeks, recalling him kissing me on the lips. The sheriff walked over to their pickup, leaned in at the window and spoke in a low tone. The red pickup reversed, did a turn and headed out of the drive.

"Okay, I've had a word with Jake and he said to let it pass, so I'll not press charges, but just so you know, keep away from Jake's land. If I catch you setting traps again, I'll report you to wildlife and game. You're lucky you brought out the Bible, Jake's a God fearing man, and I can understand you didn't know the law having come from Alaska. Just heed my warning this time."

"Amen to you, sheriff. May the Lord be with you," Pa said.

The sheriff climbed into her cab, turned in the drive and drove away. Pa glanced at me.

"Maybe you're not a little girl anymore, smart thinking," Pa said. "It worked eatin' crow. Still, it's all the more reason to be shot of ya now you're acting all grown up like a woman. Better hurry with cutting up the deer. Bring the joints here, then dig a hole around back and bury what's left."

"Why lie to the sheriff?"

"Oh that. It wasn't a lie. It's called trickery. See, when you're dealing with the Devil's disciples, they use trickery, so you throw it back at them. They can't handle it. God fearing... huh. There's some of the trickery right there."

I didn't buy his explanation. He never gave me a reason why we had to move. One thing was sure. There was no way a bear could have gotten into our outside food storage area, or his pelt shed. He'd sold all his pelts before we moved.

Setting off to the barn, I couldn't help but wonder that his sentiments were bitter sweet about letting me work in the barn. On the one hand, he'd given permission to work outside and alone, together with hope of a better life away from him. There again, he'd still be the same old Pa until I was wed. Whatever, I still had a spring in my step as I stepped into the barn. Even more so with that kiss on my lips. Now I had the hot flushes for two possible husbands. But then thinking that, I doubted Pa would accept Jordan into the family.

Chapter 10

Under Attack

When I'd arrived back at the house, Pa said he wouldn't even discuss with me finding a husband until I'd finished preserving all the deer cuts. That threw me into a sulk. I still sulked as I rubbed the last cut with salt and pepper, then rolled the webbed stocking over it and took it to hang in the pantry. I had a million questions, none of them I wanted to ask Pa. I wished I had a mom like Kate who once lived there. It would have been so much easier. He'd been in his den this past two hours. I'd heard him talking on his phone, but it was muffled, so I didn't know who he had talked to while he was in there.

We had a rule. I was never to enter his den. His sanctuary as he called it. I washed my hands and hung up my apron, then took a seat at the table. I'd not eaten all day, but my stomach was tied in knots. I wondered if Pa was the same with his decision to marry me off. All he'd eaten was the bread dipped into the stew. Nat hadn't called back. I wished that he had. He could have asked permission to take me to the dance one Friday, though it was a given that Halloween would be out of the question for Pa.

His den door opened. He gave me a stinky-eyed look. That look I'd seen a thousand times, with one eye partly closed. I could never work out what it meant, or what could be on his mind when he did that. I started to breathe short breaths, wondering what I'd done wrong.

"Can I make you some soup?"

"Not now, maybe later. Did you bury the bones?"

"Yeah, all done. Everything is hung in the pantry, so we can talk now."

"Later. I'm waiting for someone to phone me back first. I'm going to my room to rest and to think it through. One thing's for sure, we can't stay here if we're not allowed to trap."

My jaw dropped as he walked past me to the stairway. Leaning over, I placed my elbows on the table and held my head in my hands. I didn't think my emotions would take much more anxiety. Much as I wasn't hungry, I needed something to do. I walked over to the stove and heated up the stew. As soon as it steamed, I laded some into a dish and took it to the table. All I could do was to pick at it, draining the gravy onto my spoon and sipping at it.

Lost in my thoughts, the only consolation I could take for him saying he'd talk later was that he said he needed to think it through. At least he had sounded as though he was going to look out for me. All I knew about meeting men was from the two books and some of the stories in the magazine I'd read. They were all about feelings, betrayal, and overcoming all that was thrown against you, then finding happiness. Pa would be thinking more about suitability, their ability to provide, and if they followed the ways of the Bible. I doubted he had any feelings in his bones. Hell, I didn't even think he'd recognize them if they were displayed right in front of his nose.

I tiptoed up the stairway, then along the hallway to my bedroom. Pa was snoring. I stooped and pulled out the second book, another love story. Sitting on the mattress, I faced the window in case Pa came to my bedroom so I could slip the book under my pillow. That's when I noticed someone moving about in the tree line at the edge of our property. Recalling the sheriff saying they'd had robberies lately, I had it in mind to awaken Pa. Whoever it was stepped out from behind a tree and waved. I squinted. It was Jordan. He waved again, not in the sense of recognition, but a beckoning wave.

"I can't," I mouthed. Not that he was near enough to work out what I'd said. He crept over to Pa's pickup, and then ducked. Guess he was looking out for Pa. He rose to his full height and beckoned me again. I shook my head and mouthed, "No."

He crept back to the tree line. That's when I noticed he had his friends with him skulking behind the trees. Pa's cell phone rang. The next thing I saw was a hail of snowballs heading to our house. They had to have stones in them with the racket they made as they hit the fascia boards. I ducked away from the window and slipped the book under the mattress.

"What the hell?" I heard Pa shout. Then his door opened and his boots hammered down the stairway. I wasn't far behind him. He'd grabbed his rifle and he was heading out of the front door when I arrived at the bottom of the stairs.

"Pa, don't," I screamed.

He scanned the tree line through his scope. I grabbed his arm just as he pulled the trigger, letting the round loose in the air. There wasn't time to see it coming, when I felt a searing pain and hit the decking. He picked me up by the neck and dragged me inside, then slammed the door.

"Next time I'll shoot you instead of giving you the back of my hand if you ever pull that stunt again." He locked the door. Walked to his den, pulling out his cell phone on the way.

"Don't phone the sheriff, Pa," I said, and used the table surface for purchase to stand.

He turned.

"Why?"

"It's those boys from town goofing around. They weren't on our property. Sheriff will likely lock you up for firing on them. God forbid if you'd shot one of them."

"For your information, I wasn't phoning the sheriff, and I wouldn't have shot any of them, just put a bullet in the tree next to where they were. Now put the stew on to heat it up. I'm starving. I'll be out in a few minutes. I have a phone call to return."

He pulled his door to as usual so I couldn't see what he was doing. I could hear him talking, but not what he said. I ladled out his stew and placed it on the table. His den door opened and he walked out with a smile on his face, then took a seat at the table.

"I'd wait for it to cool a little if I were you. It's hot."

Studying him, I wasn't sure why I had protected him from the sheriff, and then with Jordan in the barn. And now this situation, when all the thanks I had was the back of his hand. Then thinking about it, he had offered me the chance of an unfettered future. Last thing I would have wanted was to be left alone, unable to pay the rent. The venison wouldn't last forever. He caught me looking, the smile disappearing from his lips and he scowled at me.

"So if you knew it was those punks from town, did you invite them here when we were at the grocery store?"

I backed off.

"No, I didn't."

"But that ignorant son of a bitch talked to you at the barn earlier. Didn't he?"

I moved to the opposite side of the table out of harm's way.

"We owe him. He saw the deer in the barn but promised not to tell."

"He did, did he? A promise for a promise was it? Good thing we're moving then since you've started to socialize with the heathens. Especially now I've found you a husband."

"What! Who?"

Chapter 11

Passing the Parcel

Pa didn't answer my questions as to the, who, why, what, and the wherefores. Instead, he slurped one spoonful after another, but struggled swallowing the solids.

I rose to my feet, placed my hands on my hips and pouted. There was no point in not saying my piece. I stamped my foot on the floorboards.

"How do I know I'll fall in love with him, whoever he is? I can't just be wedded to a stranger."

He pushed his empty plate to one side. Showed me the palm of his hand while he struggled to swallow the last of the potato. Finally he gulped it down, wiped his mouth with his napkin, then blew his nose.

"Where did that talk come from? Who told you about love? You don't get to choose. God has blessed many an arranged marriage, you should know that. You've read the Bible and your history books. If it was good enough for the kings and queens of old, it's the way it was meant to be. For goodness sake, have you forgotten that the priests arranged for Joseph to marry Mary? You'll grow on him. Learn to cherish him. Bear children like the good Lord intended. You'll be too busy to worry about love. Besides, he'll pay a sizeable dowry. Give me a place to live. Put food on your table."

I stamped my foot again. The thought that he was selling me like a basket of mushrooms angered me.

"Well, who is it?"

"You'll see. You already know him."

"I don't know anyone, only you."

"Yes you do, but it was from years ago."

My backside dropped on the chair as my legs weakened. I didn't have a vision of anyone from our past, only brief encounters with the odd woodsman and hunters.

"When you say he'll give you a place to live, do you mean with us after we wed?"

"No. He has a cabin in the woods near the Sierra Nevada Range he doesn't use. I can live there as long as I like. No problem trapping and hunting. Not a town for miles around. You'll have your own home. I should have my disability claim approved by then. If not, the dowry will keep me going until they decide."

That revelation came as a relief.

"Is he my age? What does he look like?"

"It doesn't matter. You'll find out in two weeks when we get there. He might come here for the ceremony if the snow thaws before then."

"You mean at the church in town?"

"No, at the table here. I'll marry you off with all our hands on my Bible. Good as any preacher could do. You'll just have to say the words to obey him until either of you die and you'll be married."

Obey him.

I couldn't take any more. It felt as though I was being passed like a parcel of meat from one ogre to another. More drudgery. More control.

He started to cough and put a napkin to his mouth. He looked at it before stuffing it into his pocket, but not before I'd seen the blood.

"Stop sniveling and go to your room. I need more stew and I can't concentrate on my meal with you slobbering at the table. I've said what's happening. That's everything you need to know. Now go, child. Skedaddle. I can ladle my own stew. Read your Bible and pray for forgiveness for doubting I'm not doing what's right."

"I... I." This time I didn't dare utter the words that I hated him. I'd seen that look before. I could see the agitation in the way he fidgeted on his chair, ready to pounce if I didn't do as I was told. I stormed out of the kitchen, palming a carving knife on the way. Ran up the stairway and into my bedroom. Slammed the door behind me, then slid the bolt. If he tried to knock the door down, I decided to drag the bed in front of it for if he tried to enter and I wandered over to the bed head.

I wanted to stay in there forever, or to at least only to surface when he was dead and buried. The way he was coughing up blood, it was looking as though it could be anytime soon. Still, knowing him, I knew that he'd prob'ly get through whatever was ailing him. That's when a thought struck me as I stared out through the window. I didn't have to wait for him to die, or to be wed to a stranger for me to escape and to find freedom. Holding the tip of the carving knife to my neck I closed my eyes. Took a deep breath. Slowly exhaled. Asked God to give me strength. One quick slice and I could end it all.

Chapter 12

Deception

My vision focused as I awoke. The bolt was still in place on the door. God hadn't answered me the night before when I'd asked for help to end it all. I'd not found the strength to slice the knife across my throat. But He had taken heed when I'd prayed for Pa not to come to my room. I stared at my Bible on the table next to me and wondered if maybe He had given me an answer to my request for courage after all. Not having the guts to see it through could have been a sign. A sign that He had a purpose for me to remain alive.

Pa's footsteps creaked on the boards along the hallway. My shoulders hit south. There was a tap on my door. I pulled the blanket over my nose, and glared at the door. It wasn't like him to knock, which threw me. He'd normally barge right in. I half-expected him to shoulder charge the door and bust the fastener holding the bolt. I scrunched my eyes and sucked in some air.

"Hi, Clara. Thought I'd let you sleep in. I've rustled up some scrambled egg."

That was a first time in ages. At least since I was nine. Not only that, his voice had raised an octave and sounded sickly sweet. I opened my eyes and let my breath escape.

"I'll be right down, Pa," I said, with an equally childish voice.

I'd slept in my clothes. I tossed the blanket to one side. Threw my legs over the side of the bed, then tiptoed to the door. I heard him walking to the end of the hallway, then his boots clomping down the stairway. At first I unfastened the bolt, then hesitated, before deciding to open the door and to follow him. The smell of coffee greeted me as I entered the kitchen. It looked as though he'd used up all the eggs with the pile I saw on the plate.

"I've eaten. Tuck in. I made it especially for you," he said, an insincere smile curling on his lips.

It must have pained him to smile. Something was afoot, that was for sure. He never let things pass in this way. He pulled out a chair for me then wandered into his den. A quick glance around the room, and I wondered if it was some kind of trap he was setting. Taking a seat at the table, I felt as though I was an insect venturing into a spider's web. The scrambled egg was steaming. I lifted up the plate and sniffed at the eggs. Setting it back down, I picked at the eggs with my fork. Apart from some shell fragments and a little pan burn, it looked and smelled okay. After picking out the shell and the burned bits, I wolfed it down, then took a sip of coffee.

Pa was talking on his phone again. I rose, and then stepped over to his door and listened. Caught part of his conversation.

"It will be cash? Ten thousand in tens and twenties." There was a pause. "Good, that's all agreed then. It's all down to the weather now."

It couldn't have been his pickup he was selling. He only paid twenty-five hundred for it when we crossed the Canadian border to the US. That was after he'd sold his SUV, generator, and snowmobiles in Alaska. The only other things we carried through Canada were our backpacks, tents, and that padlocked case of his.

I hated it that I had had to leave all my books behind, but he'd said we needed to travel light through Canada, where we sneaked over the border at both ends under cover of the forests on the mountains. I stepped away from his door, picked up my plate and took it to the sink. My heart sank. The pan he'd used to cook the scrambled eggs was toasted. Egg shells everywhere.

Pa stepped out of his office, when his phone rang again. He pulled it from his pocket and answered with it pressed to his ear.

"Got it. Why Denver, isn't there a medical center nearer? It'll be a three day journey for me." He didn't look pleased and paced around the room in a circle. "Yeah, I have the X-ray. So, have I got that right? This Friday at ten in the morning."

46

Pa hung up with a stab of his finger.

"Bastards."

"What's wrong?"

"My disability claim. I have to take a medical in Denver of all places. They want to see the X-ray I had done in Canada to prove I have that hernia between my discs."

"That's good isn't it? Once it's approved you won't have a problem with money and we can stay here."

"That may be, but it could take forever, so it changes nothing. We're still leaving, and you are getting married."

That dashed my hopes that he'd forget the idea of an arranged marriage, and that we could stay at Hunter's Lodge.

"So what's the problem you having to go to Denver?"

"Oh, it's a problem all right. It'll mean a two-day stay over. Can't afford for both of us to go."

"When?"

"I'd have to set off tomorrow."

"Oh, no?" I said, trying my best not to look pleased.

Pa grimaced and rubbed his back.

"Here," I said, and pulled out a chair at the table. "You take a seat and I'll pour coffee for you."

I poured his coffee from the pot on the stove, then set his mug on the table and took a seat opposite. My mind churned over the situation. I was thinking it was nothing to do with his tightfisted ways that he didn't want me with him, but rather he didn't want me in a city where I could wander off. Picking up my own mug, I took a sip. The way he looked at me it was as if he was trying to look into my soul through my eyes. I knew what the problem was.

"Listen, sorry about last night. It was all a shock. I feel better about it now. Excited really."

I could see the tension drain from his eyes. He picked up his mug, took a gulp, then caressed it as if warming his hands.

"I knew you'd come around to the idea. You have a great life to look forward to with him. He's a good man."

He took another sip.

"I wish Ma was here. What was it like when you first met? Was it arranged for you?"

He choked and spat the drink back into his cup.

"Err... yeah. Didn't set eyes on her until the day we married. Cause it was arranged. God put us together, just as He's doing the same for you. He gave me you didn't He?"

From the way he said it and from his expression when he'd taken his eyes off of me, I knew he was lying. And why mention me when he treated me the way he did as if I was a trophy?

"Amen to that, Pa."

"That's my girl."

"Don't worry about me, when you're in Denver. It's only like you going off trapping on your snowmobile and leaving me back at our lodge."

I could see him churning it over. Of course it wasn't the same. I wouldn't have survived the distance in the freezing temperatures of winter in Alaska alone to get to civilization, whatever survival skills he'd taught me.

"Come to think of it, we've plenty of provisions to keep you in food. I'll dip into my savings while I'm there seeing as how I have the dowry coming. I'll buy you some new underwear and a dress for your wedding day. How's that?"

We were playing each other. He'd taught me well. The clothes were his carrot.

"Aw Pa, that's great. Can't wait to see the dress. Now I'm really excited."

He set that deceitful smile again, thinking he'd pulled one over me. It was time to plant my own carrot.

"Got plenty to think about while you're away. I could make a cake for if he arrives here."

I beamed a smile at him, but really I was laughing inside.

"You do that. Do you have the ingredients?"

Pa saying that planted a seed.

"Oh, no. I have everything but the flour."

"Don't worry. I'll pop along to the store in town. I'll leave you here to put some of my clothes to one side for my journey. Can't go like this for a medical."

"No problem." I rose from the chair. "Best I wash the dishes then." I wandered into the pantry. Moved around some provisions and hid the flour.

Over at the sink, I stared out through the window. Fear of what lay out there and how to survive on my own without Pa took a backseat. I had my backpack and tent. All I needed was a plan of action. It wasn't just the freedom of the house that I wanted while he was away. Especially after I'd worked out who my intended was prob'ly going to be.

Chapter 13

The Stalker

I'd been handed a test with Pa leaving the key in the lock. His game was obvious, seeing as how he would have been panicking at leaving me alone for two nights, so I guessed he'd be watching the house. He'd need to protect his dowry. Saying that, Pa calling it a dowry confused me at first. He'd not torn any D pages out of my dictionary. When I'd looked it up, any payment was supposed to go in the opposite direction to the husband and not to Pa. It confirmed what I thought, and he was selling me. Pa saying it was a dowry was nothing but a lie.

Second only to my Bible, my dictionary was a Godsend. I would need it with me on the outside. One time we had a woman call at our door. Said she was from child protection. Pa wouldn't let her inside. She looked over his shoulder. Said our home was *spartanly* furnished and she wanted to see me. He closed the door in her face. She hollered that she'd be back with the police. We were gone within the hour. When I looked up the word *spartanly*, it explained what she meant. I'd read about the Spartans, but I would never have guessed the connection with the word she used to their harsh plain lifestyle. I slipped the dictionary into my jacket pocket that was hung in the closet.

He hadn't locked the door when he set off to town to buy the flour. I pulled my backpack out of the closet in my bedroom. The binoculars that I retrieved from a side pocket weren't as powerful as his were, but they were better than nothing. I breathed on the lenses, then wiped them with my bed sheet.

Standing back and to one side of my window, the sky had cleared of clouds and the sun was out. The snow was already melting and dripping from the branches of the pine trees. Pa's pickup tracks had turned to slush in the drive below. At around ten in the morning, I knew the sun would be behind the house, midway from the horizon to its noon position overhead. He'd not taken his rifle, and the scope was still in place. From the bulge in his jacket pocket, I guessed he had his binoculars with him. All I could hope was that by standing back from the window, he wouldn't see me if his vision flared through his lenses from the sun's rays.

The coat he was wearing when he left was black, but that's not to say he couldn't have changed it for his white hooded waterproof that he kept in his pickup. It was the one he had used when hunting moose in winter. Scanning the area, I caught sight of a blackbird in a pine tree, preening his wing feathers. He stopped, then swiveled his head before taking flight. Something had disturbed him. I lowered my vision. That's when I saw the old dog, moving from trunk to trunk in the wood. He had changed his coat.

Stepping away from the window, I smiled. It wasn't in my plan to go just yet. First I had to gain his trust, and to show him some more that I was excited at the prospect of him arranging the marriage. The time to go was when he was in Denver for his medical assessment. There hadn't been time for him to get to town. Perhaps he wouldn't go to the grocery store, and say they'd sold out when he returned. Whatever, I wasn't for going wandering outside.

I tipped everything out of my backpack and moved the items around. "Be prepared," he always said. Guess that's why I had a box of hurricane matches, a lighter, and a flint with a scraper. Moving the first aid kit to one side, I picked up a flat piece of wood and a pointed stick, charred at the end. My mind drifted back to Pa teaching me to make a fire with nothing but those pieces of wood, together with some tinder from slivers of wood I'd shaved, and the lining from a bird's nest. I'd kept the pieces of wood as a memento. I could still recall the aches and the ever weakening of the strength in my arms, together with the blisters forming on my palms and fingers after trying for ages to create enough friction and failing. Pa didn't show any sympathy, standing over me and telling me to suck up the pain. Almost at the point of giving up, he showed me how to make a bow with a thin branch and some string to twirl the

GIRL AT THE WINDOW

pointed stick. First there were the tears from me, then the joy on both our faces, and the hugs, when the first ember smoldered, and with a little blowing we had a fire.

I enjoyed those times around the campfires, playing checkers with Pa under the stars. Then there was him instructing me how to make a simple snare to catch rabbits and other small game. Then his praise for snagging my first critter. Or the times he spent teaching me which mushrooms were poisonous, and the ones that were edible. He'd taught me which plants you could use for medicine, and what berries you could eat. There was much more I could be thankful for as I recalled. Teaching me to read and write took hours of his time. I began to wonder if I was acting unkind with the bad thoughts I had of wanting to escape. I wouldn't have been able to lose myself in the books he brought home without his devotion to teaching me.

When I was younger, I would have done anything to please him. It was his insistence on him having the rights the Bible bestowed on him that I hated at the times when he came to my room. But then, he hadn't come near me for seven years, but the pain of those times still haunted me. There was that, and the times he fettered my ankles with chains. He'd said it was normal when children acted headstrong. Said I was like a wild filly that needed breaking in. He sure broke my will.

Later, I often wondered if he was scared of me coming to some harm, or losing me after mom had died. At least that's what I convinced myself for me to remain compliant as an excuse for his treatment of me. Thoughts of defying him had only surfaced again this past two years, but they had grown in intensity, and that's the truth. What had really got me to thinking was the trek back from Alaska and the sights in some of the towns. Women pushing babies in strollers, or holding hands with their children as they walked along the sidewalk. Youngsters playing in the street with no one watching them. Then there was the odd young couple, holding hands and sneaking a kiss or a hug.

I sighed, then checked off the contents as I placed them back in my backpack. The only things I didn't stow away were my

53

hiking boots. Pa had forgotten all about them. Back at the closet, I hid them under my tent and placed the backpack in front of them. All I really needed was some supplies of food, and to get those fond memories of him out of my head. Especially now that he had mentioned that cabin he was going to live in over at the Sierra Nevada Mountains after I was wed. Him saying that had given me a clue of who it was likely to be.

We'd only ever been through that area once on our travels. Pa worked for a week at an old sawmill in a forest clearing. Said the owner was rich and we needed the money and rest. We sure needed to eat, and that was the truth. We'd only eaten berries and grubs for three days when we arrived. Pa knew him from when they'd both lived in a commune when they were teenagers and they shared the same religious views. He let us stay in an old miner's cabin that he owned away from the mill. I shuddered, recalling the owner calling by when Pa was working. He was old then, and I was only ten. The door was locked, but he had a spare key. Said Pa and me would have starved if he hadn't given him work and I should be nice to him. A shiver ran through me. I shrugged at the recollection.

It had to be him. Not only that, but I'd worked out what the ten thousand dollars was likely for. Pa told me that women had no rights and that they were the chattels of men, to do as they commanded, without question. I knew he was telling the truth, because I looked up the word chattels in my dictionary, and I'd read about it in a history book. Those love stories with independent women free to choose their path told a different story. I was Pa's only chattel, and as he'd said, the guy was rich. He was selling me like a wild animal pelt. There was no doubt about it, I had to go and strike out on my own. Problem was, I would encounter outsiders, and it was those thoughts that scared me to death. It was the not knowing if I could hack it with them that kept circling.

Chapter 14

Close Shave

Bereft of emotion waiting for Pa to return, I experienced a strange sense of purpose. I guess folks would think me weird if I told them it was akin to standing outside my body looking down on my surroundings, then watching myself walk out of the door with my backpack. There was nothing more to do, only to wait for the time when Pa would leave for Denver. The pit of my stomach ached, prob'ly the only sign my body showed of the nervousness I felt, when Pa's pickup pulled up outside. I'd have to look him in the eye I kept reminding myself. One glance away at any question he might throw at me, or to display a shy disposition with reddened cheeks, and he would have sensed I had been up to no good. I had his pants spread out on the table when he walked inside.

"Make sure you get the crease right. Don't want to be looking like a homeless bum when I turn up for the medical," he said, and dumped the bag of flour on the worktop next to the sink.

It was easier said than done ironing his pants. Back in Alaska we had an old settler's iron. The type made of cast iron you'd fill with a hot stone using tongs and it held the heat. Not that we used it much for ironing, but it came in handy for warming the bed sheets. We'd had to leave that behind. Rubbing the saucepan bottom over a damp cloth covering his pants was proving troublesome, with it not keeping the heat long enough, even though it was filled with boiling water.

"It's not working, Pa."

"Put the pan back on the stove to boil the water again and don't use the damp cloth this time."

"But it'll shine the cloth."

"Just do as you're told, child."

I showed him my palms, not wanting to create a bad

atmosphere. He dragged a chair from the far end of the table, and sitting, he warmed his hands at the stove with his back to me. Glaring at the back of his head, I often wondered just what the hell was going on in that brain of his. He must have had the same ability as me to recall his childhood and growing up. He had to have gone there at times as I did. Really, all I knew of him was from his time with me. Said he lived with the heathen outsiders, right up to God visiting him and then he'd been reborn. According to him that's when his life had started. Anything before then was off limits. He refused to talk about family or anything about his past life as a sinner, apart from the occasional slip when whisky loosened his tongue. But even that wasn't enlightening.

When I'd finished pressing his pants, Pa inspected the crease.

"They're fine," he said.

I hung them over the back of a chair and placed it next to the wood burning stove.

"All your clothes are ready. Did you bring some polish for your shoes?"

"Oh, yeah, nearly forgot." He dug a hand in his jacket pocket, then tossed the shoe-polish can at me. "Make sure you can see your face in them."

With luck, I hoped these were the last chores I'd ever have to do for him.

"Don't throw the hot water away in the pan. You can use it to give me a shave."

I wondered when he'd get around to changing his appearance. All he'd done on this move was to change his red and black plaid trapper hat for a white Stetson he bought from a thrift store, and to tie off his beard under his chin with an Indian bead chain. I decided to have a little fun with him to see his reaction.

"What took so long in town?"

He coughed and spluttered, but I could see it was for effect while he came up with an excuse. I hardly expected the truth and he'd admit to watching the house.

"Shoes. I stopped by the store to buy you some ribbon. Your

intended said he'd like you to put your hair in pigtails and tie them with ribbon. They had shoes, so I bought you some for your wedding day."

"Great. Where are they?" I said, knowing he'd simply have walked into the store, pointed to some shoes and given them the size. Ten minutes at most.

"They're in the pickup. You can have them when I return from Denver with your new clothes."

"What if they don't fit? Can't have me hobbling around in front of my intended."

"Okay, you can try them, but first the shave." Pa settled in his chair. "Just trim my hair and beard, then shave it at my neck."

"We need to wash it first. It's all tangled and matted."

"I don't need a running commentary, just get on with it."

He rose from his chair and walked over to the sink, then leaned over. I dropped a towel over his shoulders and turned on the tap water. It was freezing to the touch as I rubbed his hair with a block of soap. I knew he wouldn't complain, but he'd feel the icy water, so I dallied with the rinsing. My skin crawled at the touch of his scalp with my fingers. It was a relief when he called out.

"Enough."

He dried off his hair and took a seat at the table.

"You forgot to lock the door when you went to town," I said, as I laid a dry towel around his shoulders. "Don't worry, I locked it, then opened it again when I saw your pickup arrive," I lied, casting out my line with juicy bait.

"Oh, yeah. Did it on purpose. Like you said. You're not a girl anymore, you're a woman. Better get used to it. I doubt your intended will lock the door."

There he was, throwing me another carrot. I dangled my own bait in front of his nose.

"I doubt I'll want to go out alone once I'm married, only to hang out the washing. I'll be too busy keeping house. Make sure you lock the door when you go to Denver. I'll close the curtains and keep away from the windows."

"That's my girl."

Now I had him reeled in. If only he could have seen my ear-to-ear smile. I could have simply snipped away his matted locks. Instead, I tugged at them with the comb, tearing out chunks to the sound of him grunting and groaning. A final snip around with the scissors and it was on to trimming his beard.

A thought crossed my mind that I could have it wrong as to who my intended was. From Pa talking at the time, I recalled that the guy at the old sawmill had two sons living with his ex-wife in the nearest town. I wondered if my intended could be one of them. It was hard to remember, but I think Pa called him Tex, or maybe Rex. I lathered up the soap, and tilting his head back, I used his shaving brush to spread it over his neck. With the cutthroat razor held over his neck, a question burned inside my brain.

"I can't keep calling him my intended. What's his name?"

"What, and spoil the surprise? Nah, you'll find out on the day."

I spread my fingers out to stretch the sagging skin under his chin and started to scrape. His artery pulsed under the touch of my fingertip. I dipped the razor in the pan of water, then poised the blade to scrape some more. That's when I noticed his aging spots. There were black blotches around his windpipe and small lumps that I hadn't seen a year ago when I'd last shaved him.

"I've spoken to him. With the snow clearing, he'll meet up with me on Sunday and I'll bring him here."

With one finger on the soft spot above his Adam's apple, and the other on his artery, my other hand holding the razor, my fingers trembled. It would have been easy to end it there and then. One quick slice. We both snatched our heads in the direction of the door as a vehicle pulled up outside. Pa grabbed my wrist and pushed my hand away.

"Damn it, girl, you've nicked me."

"Sorry, Pa. You moved."

He took the razor from me, then pulled the towel to his neck.

"Go to the window and see who it is."

Chapter 15

Grave Doubts

Pa was already at my shoulder when I looked outside. Nat climbed out of his cab.

"Shit, what does he want? Get me some paper from the john," he said, dabbing the cut on his neck with his towel.

By the time I returned, they were out on the porch dickering the price of the tire chains. With the negotiations in full flight, I didn't like to interrupt. Pa was gaining the upper hand with a low-ball offer, and pointed out that the snow had all but cleared. Nat fired back with a laugh and told him there was another weather front on the way and to expect more snow. Pa scratched at his beard.

"You say you're a handyman. Would you have use for a set of chisels?"

"Sure. I'd have to see them."

"Wait here."

Pa ambled down to the barn. Nat caught sight of me and winked.

"Your dad strikes a hard bargain."

I didn't like to tell him they weren't Pa's tools he was bartering.

"Yeah, guess so."

"Pity you're going away, most of the town around our age will be at the dance, what with the snow clearing. It would've been a good time for you to get to know everyone. You really must phone me for the next one."

Not sure where it came from, but I blurted out, "Don't tell Pa, but I'm not going with him. You could pick me up if you like. You really can't say anything to him though."

"Sure. How about seven?" His cheeks flushed.

"Okay, seven. Got to go."

I stepped out of sight, placed the toilet paper on the table and ran up to my room.

"Stupid, stupid, stupid fool," I said, then dove on the bed and thumped my pillow.

Perhaps it was Nat saying that I'd meet others of my age that tempted me to want to go with him. The last time I had mixed with anyone a similar age to me was as a child. I envisioned Pa taking me to different local parks whenever we moved house. He would lighten up, pushing me on the swings, or helping me on the climbing frames. It was the only times I recalled him smiling. He'd help the other children without parents and share out my candies. It was as though he came to life with the laughter of children. As soon as we were home, he'd be back to the same old Pa, mean and commanding, as if he'd done his duty for the day in the eyes of God.

I pulled the pillow over my head, wondering if I should go anyway as planned and to forget about the dance. Maybe Nat had used the demon in him to hypnotize me with those eyes of his, using the trickery Pa talked about. I thought it stupid to think that. He'd been nothing but polite to the both of us. The way his cheeks blushed after asking me out, he seemed every bit as bashful as I felt in his presence. Whatever, I tried to convince myself that I'd only lose a day. It changed nothing only the timing. Besides, I needed to overcome my fear of what it would be like to mix with the outsiders to stop it screwing with my mind. I threw the pillow to one side. Having Nat with me would at least provide me with some protection from harm. At least that's what I hoped.

"Clara, where are you?" Pa called out.

When I arrived in the kitchen, he was sitting at the table, giving his neck a last stroke with his razor. He stuck the toilet paper on his cut.

"Did you agree on a price?"

"Sort of. Exchanged some tools."

There was a box on the table with an image of a shoe on its side.

"Are those the shoes?"

"Yeah. Try them."

Eager to get at them, I pulled off the top and moved the

packing paper to one side.

"What are these for?" I said, and held up a pair of long white socks.

"They're to go with your wedding outfit. He was very specific as to how you should dress. The ribbon is in there for your pigtails. When you plat them, do them at the side of your head, not the back."

I pulled out the shoes and tried them. They were slip-on style with false buckles and they fit perfect.

"They're very tight. I'll be struggling wearing the socks with them. Can you leave them here so I can break them in?"

He huffed and puffed, then said, "Okay, but don't you dare scuff them."

"I won't. Trust me. I want to look my best for him." I walked over to where he was sitting and threw my arms around him. "Thanks, I'll make you proud of me on the day, you'll see."

"Get off of me, child, don't fuss." He grabbed a hold of my wrists and inspected my hands. "While I'm away, you can get that dirt from behind your fingernails. Soak your hands in hot water to soften your skin. God won't take kindly to you getting married in His name with grubby fingers."

I took a seat next to him. Spread my fingers out on the table palms down, then turned them over. They were nothing like the images in the magazine. I doubted bathing them would heal the dirt-ingrained cuts and get rid of the calluses. Pa had never said they were other than normal. Those images I had seen told a different story. It was hard to believe that any of those women ever did a day's work.

"If you leave out your clothes that need patching and darning, it'll keep me busy while you're away."

"I'll do that. I'm gonna take some more medication and rest up in my room for a few hours, then I'll be on my way. Don't want my back playing up on the drive to Denver." He took a pill container from his pocket and popped an oxycodone tablet in his mouth, then swilled it down with cold coffee. "Just got a few chores to do first."

He pushed back on his chair, rose to his feet and ambled over to his den. With the door ajar, I watched him dip into his drawer and take out his moneybox. He unlocked it and put some bills into his pocket, locked it again, then stuffed the box under his jacket. I looked away as he locked the door to his den. He picked up his Stetson, put it on, then removed it and sighed

"Damn thing doesn't fit me now. Cut up the shoebox and use the cardboard to line the rim," he said, and tossed it at me, then he walked past me and out of the front door. Stepping over to the window, I watched him hobble to the barn. I took a seat back at the table. When he returned, there wasn't a bulge under his jacket. Why he'd decided to hide his moneybox in the barn eluded me. I could hardly ask him. Then I recalled the sheriff's talk about break-ins. The sneaky old dog was protecting his money.

"What should I do if someone tries to break-in while you're away?"

Pa scratched his head. Maybe he hadn't thought about protecting his so-called dowry.

"Take my rifle to bed with you like you did when I was away in Alaska. I'll leave a round in the chamber. You know how to use it. There are some nightlight candles in the pantry. Leave one burning in both our bedrooms. Push your bed over to the door at night."

I had more to worry about than break-ins. Colorado had its share of black bears and mountain lions. Sleeping in a tent out there in the wilds without Pa there to protect me made me wonder if my plan was half-baked. If I took his rifle, one round might not be enough.

"I'll be fine, Pa."

With my elbow on the table, I covered my eyes with my hand and rubbed my brow with my thumb and forefinger.

God, I hope so.

Chapter 16

Unwelcome Attention

It wasn't just me that sighed when Pa drove away on his journey yesterday. It was as if the entire house had sighed with me, then silence. My sleep had been fraught with nightmares which carried on with fleeting recollections when I awoke. But now the sun was shining. The creepy shadows cast from the nightlight in my bedroom had long since extinguished, yet the uncertainty remained. A feeling that Pa's eyes were watching me was ever present.

A blackbird was out in the yard. It could have been the same one that had the area staked out as his territory. He'd been joined by his sparrow friends, digging for earthworms and grubs in the soft sun-kissed dirt. The sparrows were ever alert, with the odd ones stopping scavenging and exchanging posting sentries on a rusting plow. Prob'ly on the lookout for predators. The flock suddenly took flight, leaving the blackbird pulling at an earthworm. It was clear why they had taken off. A yard cat was stalking along the hedgerow. I rapped on the kitchen window. One final tug at the worm, and he flew away just as the cat pounced, missing his target, then it skulked off into the woods.

I didn't know why the blackbird was alone and not with his own flock, but I felt an affinity with him. I'd soon be out there with him, tasting freedom on my own, trying to survive, unaware of the dangers that I could face.

A shake of the head and I turned, then set off up the stairway to Pa's bedroom. His clothes he had changed out of were strewn on the floor. I toed them out of the way and opened his closet door and pulled out his backpack. From a side pocket, I retrieved his maps. There was nothing else of his I needed, so I set off back down to the kitchen.

I spread both maps out on the table. The map of the US and

Canada made the distances seem so small, considering it had taken two months to travel from Alaska to Hunter's End. Pa had marked out spots in some of the states with a felt tip pen, then a series of numbers. I was more interested in the map of Colorado. One thing was certain; I'd need to steer clear of the routes to the Sierra Nevada Mountain Range and any roads leading to Denver. With my pen, I marked off a route south to Santa Fe, for no other reason than I recalled that we lived near there at one time. It didn't matter where I ended up as long as I was free to do as I pleased.

A shadow passed over the table. I turned and let out a scream, then felt foolish when I saw Jordan at the kitchen window.

"What is it you want?"

"Noticed your dad's pickup wasn't here. Why don't you come and join us?"

"Go away. He'll be back any moment," I said, and walked over to the window.

His two friends were standing by the plow, drinking bottles of beer. One of them saw me.

"Hey. Girl at the window. Jordan's gotten the hots for you. We don't mind sharing if you don't. Know what I'm saying." He put his thumb over the opening to the bottle, shook it, then put it at his crotch with the froth bubbling out. His friend pushed him and they rolled about laughing.

"Cut it out, guys," Jordan said. "Ignore them. I'll send them away and we can go for a walk and do some jawing. Get to know each other."

"In your dreams. You'd better skedaddle before Pa gets back."

"What, that old fart? Missed us by a mile the other day. He couldn't hit a barn from ten yards."

I stepped back and grabbed Pa's rifle from its mount. Pointed it right at Jordan.

"I can't miss from here. Take you and your heathen friends off of Pa's land, or I'll put one between your eyes."

"Whoa, steady on."

He held his arms high. That's when I noticed a large

64

screwdriver in his hand.

"Git," I said, and racked the slide with the bolt.

"Okay we're going. Look, all I really wanted was to get to know you. You're mighty feisty for a skinny gal, I give you that. Just don't get so nervous with that rifle in your hands."

"Do I look like I'm crapping in my pants? If you come this way again, don't be thinking 'cause his pickup isn't here that he won't be at home. He's taken it for repairs and getting a ride back. Now git."

I closed one eye and looked down the barrel, then moved my finger from the guard to the trigger. His eyes popped as if they were on stalks. Never seen anyone run so fast. I had to laugh. The bullet was still on the mantle over the fireplace where I had left it after I'd taken it from the chamber earlier. Still, Jordan turning up had been a warning. Especially as he was carrying a screwdriver. Pa once lost his keys and used a screwdriver to pop open a window.

I doubted they'd be back and placed the rifle back on its mount. There were more pressing things to think about as I folded the maps and stuffed them in a side pocket of my backpack. All I had to worry about now was what to wear for when Nat called. I should have asked him. Panic set in, recalling some of the outfits the women wore in the magazine. I had hoped my jeans and sweater would do for a small town dance. Now I had my doubts. Then I remembered the dress and purse in the chest. I wondered if it was worth the effort to get ready to go to town. The plan I had was to use a screwdriver to take off the catch on the door that held the locking bar and I could be out of there with my backpack. I had a decision to make. Either to go there and then, or wait for Nat and to see if I could cut it socializing with people my own age. The free will to decide what to do on my own made my head ache.

Chapter 17

Halloween

I'd gone past the point of no return. There hadn't been time to wash and dry the red dress. I'd spent hours using a damp cloth and the saucepan on it to try and steam out the musty smell. It still had a faint odor to it when it had dried in front of the stove, but it was better than it was. No amount of scrubbing and bathing my hands could heal the cuts. I had given up on the red shoes with the high heels. Almost twisted my ankles trying to walk in them. Pa would be furious if he knew I was wearing my wedding shoes. Still, it was six fifty and I was ready. I'd left nightlights burning in both bedrooms and removed the screws from the lock catch. My chest tightened as I heard tires scrunching on the gravel outside. For a brief moment, I thought Pa might have returned early. I dashed to the window, relieved when I saw Nat climb out of his cab. I closed the curtain, then lit the nightlight on the table.

Over at the door, I grasped the handle and took a deep breath. Nat was about to climb the steps when I walked outside and closed the door. He took a step back, looked me up and down and blushed.

"You look...erm, wonderful."

He took my fingers as I walked down the steps, let go, then opened the cab door for me. It made a world of difference walking to his vehicle and not being carried and thrown inside. The first thing I did was to press the button to roll down the window, if for no other reason that I could. Nat climbed inside, settled on his seat, and we set off. Turning on my seat, I poked my head out through the window like a puppy dog I'd seen doing the same, letting the passing air whip my hair across my face. I had plenty to ask him, but the thoughts stuck in my craw, unable to say anything. I turned back and rolled up the window. My dress rose above my knees. I thought they looked ugly and put my hands on them.

"Where are you from?" he said, breaking the silence.

"Last place we lived was Alaska."

"What made you come here? Most of the folk our age move away from here."

I didn't have a clue why we moved to Hunter's End, but I felt I had to say something.

"Pa's back's bad. He was struggling hunting, I guess."

"Did you have a boyfriend in Alaska?"

I was tempted to make one up, or use a name from one of the love stories I'd read, but chickened out.

"No. Didn't have anything of anything. We lived out in the wilds."

"How old are you?"

"Eighteen. How old are you?"

"Twenty-one."

"How long have you lived here?"

"Lived here all my life. Most of the townsfolk are retirees. Town's gone to crap since the furniture factory closed and moved to Mexico. Most of the youngsters never come back after they finish college. Town's dying. I never went to college. Dad taught me enough to work as a handyman, but work's thin on the ground."

"Then why not move away? What's to stop you?"

"I have to look after my mom since dad died. She'd struggle to put food on the table if I wasn't here."

I couldn't help but wonder how Pa would cope without me cooking and cleaning which made me smile. He pulled over and parked. I couldn't recall the journey, but we'd arrived. The entrance to the hall was at the side of the church. There were people walking inside, greeted by a preacher wearing a dog collar. Thankfully they were not wearing costumes. Nat opened the door for me and we walked to the entrance. "St Mary's Catholic Church Community Hall," it read, on a sign fastened to the fascia boards.

"Who is this we have here, Nat?" said the priest.

"Clara. Just moved in over at Hunter's Lodge," Nat said.

"I'm Father David. Please to make your acquaintance," he said, and reaching out, he shook my hand.

I gave him a faint smile and walked on through into the hall. The deafening sound of the music thumped my chest with rhythmic explosions of the bass. Nat leaned over, his lips brushing my ear. The hairs at my neck prickled.

"What will you have to drink?" Nat asked. "They only serve soft drinks."

What he meant by soft drinks, I couldn't be sure.

"Whatever you're having. Is there a bathroom?" I asked, only for refuge from the loud music.

Nat pointed. "Over there," he said, and left me to my own devices.

All eyes seemed to be looking at me. People were huddled together in groups around the darkened room, with more people arriving. At the far end was a raised area with curtains drawn back and someone center stage, bobbing his head to the beat coming from stacks of boxes, and surrounded by flashing lights of all colors. His face was alternately bathed in red, blue, and green patterns, distorting his features. He held out both his arms, one finger on each hand pointing to the dancers and he wagged them to the beat. As if paying homage to him, they returned the gesture. I wondered if he was a warlock, or the Devil himself, and shuddered. One of the lights shone on a mirrored ball, rotating in the center of the roof, spinning white diamonds shapes all around. They made my head spin all right. What I thought was more ominous were the pumpkins hanging from the roof beams. The faces cut into them looked evil, with the flames of candles dancing in their eyes. At the sound of a hiss, I gasped and put my hand to my mouth. Clouds of fog shot out from under the guy's table on the stage and engulfed the dancers. I began to think I'd made a mistake and Pa had been right. Maybe they were all the Devil's disciples.

I hurried to the bathroom, closed the door behind me and leaned against it. I closed my eyes with relief that the sound was reduced to a faint thumping. Someone pushed on the door and I stepped to one side. Five girls around my age hustled on through. They surrounded me. One of them with blonde hair stepped forward. I thought my dress was short, but her skirt hardly covered her backside.

"Saw you arrive with Nat. Who are you?"

"Clara."

"Clara!" she repeated, and looked around at the other girls who snickered.

"What's with the white virgin socks?"

The girls erupted with laughter. I pushed her to one side and walked over to the sink, then glanced in the mirror.

They came up behind me.

"You gone mute or something? I asked you a question."

"Leave me alone."

"Leave me alone," she mocked, shaking her head and rolling her shoulders as she'd said the words, and with her hands on her hips.

"What's that smell," one of them said. She leaned over and sniffed at my dress. The blonde took out a can from her purse and sprayed me with clouds of fragrance.

I felt a rage welling inside, turned and pushed through them, then hurried back into the hall. Nat walked over to me and handed me my drink.

"What is it?"

"Coke."

I sniffed at it, then held it away as bubbles tickled my nose. For all I knew it could be some sort of heathen potion. I set it down on a table.

"You look shook up. Is everything okay?"

"Not really. Can I ask you something?"

"Sure."

"Do I look stupid wearing these socks? Only some girls in the bathroom were making fun of me."

"Well, I didn't like to say, but it's usually the younger girls who wear socks. You look fine to me. Who was it who made fun of you?"

The blonde girl walked out into the hall with her pack of hangers on.

"That's her. The one with blonde hair."

"Oh, Clarissa. Don't pay her any mind. She thinks she's the permanent homecoming queen of the town."

I didn't like to ask what that meant. Glancing around, the hall had filled up quickly. Most of the girls were moving around to the music in the center of the room, flailing their arms around, gyrating, and puffing out their chests in some sort of ritual. All the guys were seated on the chairs surrounding the room watching them dance. There were more males than females that were for sure.

"Can we sit down?"

"Sure, there are some spare chairs over there."

We took our seats. Clarissa kept glancing over at me. I kicked off my shoes, removed the socks and put them in my empty purse. My shoulders sagged when I looked over at the door. Jordan and his cohorts strutted inside. Clarissa hurried over to him and threw her arms around his neck. With her draped all over him, he looked right at me and winked. The priest walked up to them and separated them, then wagged his finger at them. I turned away. Nat must have seen him wink at me.

"How do you know that idiot?"

"He's had a few run-ins with Pa."

"That doesn't surprise me."

With the scowl on Nat's face, I guessed there was no love lost between them. I prayed Jordan would keep his distance. He didn't. When I looked around he was walking directly towards us.

Chapter 18

Ambushed

I looked away as Jordan approached, wishing for a hole to appear and devour me. Nat rose to his feet.

"What do you want?"

"Who rattled your cage? Just wanted to say hi to Clara here."

"Yeah, well, she says hi back at ya. She's with me, so go and play with yourself."

Clarissa grabbed Jordan's hand.

"Come and dance."

As she led him away, it was as if his head was on a pivot, not taking his eyes off Nat.

"He's trouble that one. Been a pain in the butt for me right from first grade. Never done a day's work since he'd gotten himself expelled from high school. I wouldn't worry about Clarissa and her friends. They're all leaving town for college. I doubt they'll ever come back."

Nat took a seat beside me again. I was thankful he didn't see Jordan blow me a kiss from the tip of his fingers, or I guessed they'd get to rutting. Clarissa saw him though and grabbed his hand, then looked daggers at me. Jordan pulled her hand away, then walked off of the dance floor and joined his friends.

The priest was walking around the hall, nodding at some of the groups and stopping to chat with others. His attention was drawn to a young woman who sat on a guy's lap. He marched over, exchanged words, doing that wagging the finger at them again. The woman rose to her feet and inspected her shoes at the priest chastising them. Some of the boys were now walking around the room, looking over at the girls dancing. Every now and then they would stop and nudge shoulders as one of the girls would grind their backside in their direction.

"Do you want me to introduce you around? They're not all like Jordan and Clarissa."

73

"No, it's okay. Can't say as I'm used to mixing. In fact, I could do with some air."

That was about as polite as I could make it. I'd seen enough to slake my curiosity. What I really wanted was for him to take me home, but I thought that would be rude.

"There's a porch out back and some benches. We could sit out there. But not for long. It's not exactly freezing, but there is a nip in the air." He rose to his feet and took my hand. "This way."

It took me by surprise that he didn't let go of my hand as we made our way to the porch until we reached the exit. Somehow, I'd felt comforted by his touch. I took a seat on a bench at a table. He draped his coat over my shoulders, then took a seat opposite.

"Look, It doesn't bother me none if you put those socks back on. I noticed you had scars on your ankles when you took them off. If you were wearing them to cover them up, don't worry about what anyone says."

That wasn't the reason I wore them, I just did. I really didn't know what to say to him, so I smiled.

"Listen. I'm not much good at chatting with women on a sort of date. Also, I don't dance. You're going to have to help me out a little."

Even in the half-light from the lamp on the wall, I saw his cheeks redden.

"I'll let you into a secret," I said. "I've never been on a date and I've sure never danced, so it's going to be like the blind leading the blind."

We both laughed. I placed my hands palm down on the table. He reached over and took a hold of my hand and turned it over.

"Those look like they're used to hard work."

I snatched my hand away, embarrassed with how they looked.

"Hey, no problem. Got to admire a girl that's used to hard work. I didn't mean anything bad."

Looking into those eyes of his, it was though they were sucking me inside of them. I wanted to tell him that I was going away. If only Pa hadn't gone and arranged that stupid marriage. My chest heaved and I let out a sigh. There was no doubt that Nat was polite and attentive. It didn't seem right to use him in this way, just to see what it would be like to mix with others. Truth was, surrounded by the people in the hall, all I had longed for since the place filled up was to be alone, especially after the welcome from Clarissa and her pack. Still, there was no getting away from the fact that I enjoyed being with him, and the touch of his hand had made my body tingle. I began to wonder if I was lying to myself that I was there out of curiosity. A part of me deep down wanted the evening to develop with Nat as it had done in those love stories. My eyes moistened. I felt a tear run down my cheeks.

"Hey, what's wrong?"

"Nothing," I lied, and wiped the tear away with the back of my hand.

"Not joining in the fun?" I heard the priest say, then he walked over to our table.

"Just getting some air," Nat said.

"Clara, isn't it? Will you be joining us for the Sunday service?"

"Er... Sorry, no. Pa arrives back on Sunday. I don't know what time and he'll expect me to be there. But I have my Bible at home."

"Good, good. Perhaps next week. And what about you, Nat? I've not seen you attend this past few weeks."

"Yeah, it's difficult with Mom."

"How is she?"

"You know how it is. She has good days and bad days."

"Tell her I'll look in on her."

"Sure."

"What about your father, Clara? Are we likely to see him at church?"

A middle-aged woman popped her head around the doorframe.

"We've run out of orange juice."

"Oh, very well. I'll get some from the storage cabinet."

It was such a relief when he hurried away. Pity Pa hadn't

been there. I'd have given anything to see them lock horns to discuss the good book and the Catholic religion. The first thing he would have banged on about was the inquisition.

"Sorry about Father David. It isn't often he gets a chance to try and add to his flock. Hardly any of the pews get filled these days. Are you Catholic?"

"I know the Bible if that's what you mean, but Pa doesn't hold with the different religions. Says they twist God's words to suit their own interpretation and way of doing things."

"So I guess you won't be taking him up on his invite," he said, and laughed. "Listen, I need another coke. You didn't drink yours. Can I get you something else?"

"I'm fine."

"Won't be long."

The tables started to fill up and the foul smell of cigarette smoke polluted the air. It reminded me of Pa smoking before he discovered a taste for chewing tobacco. Six tables down, I noticed Clarissa and her friends. Jordan and his friends were standing close by them. They were passing around a brown paper bag and taking turns in drinking whatever the bag was hiding. I turned away from them, thankful I had Nat's jacket wrapped around me and hoped they wouldn't recognize me.

The next thing I knew, Clarissa was standing next to me, with her friends lined up behind her.

"What's all this making eyes at Jordan?" Clarissa said.

I put a hand to my forehead and shook my head. I could see this ending badly.

Chapter 19

Cornered

It was beginning to look as though I'd made a bad decision going to the dance. I prayed that Nat would return and intervene. Clarissa reached over the table and prodded me with her finger.

"I asked you a question. Why have you been looking at Jordan all gooey eyed?"

"Don't know what you mean."

Clarissa placed her hands on the table and leaned over, putting her face close to mine.

"Yes you do. Don't give me any of that that 'I'm Miss Innocent' look. My friends told me you've kept ogling him. You're welcome to my cast offs like that nerd Nat, but leave Jordan alone, bitch."

More people crowded around me, chanting, "Bitch, bitch."

I felt trapped and rose to my feet. Clarissa started to edge around the table and raised her arm as if to hit out. In a blind rage, and part self-preservation, I grabbed a hold of the table and tipped it at her, then turned to escape. I was stopped mid-flight with someone tugging at my hair. The next thing I knew I was rolling around on the floor with Clarissa. She had me pinned down and was raining blows about my face with one hand and grasping my hair with the other.

"Cut it out you two," I heard Jordan shout.

He dragged her off of me with the help of his friends prying her fingers from my hair, but not before I managed to strike her nose. It exploded instantly, with blood dripping all over her white top. His friends struggled to hold Clarissa while they called out for everyone to stand back. I staggered to my feet and fell back against the wall. My legs gave way and I was about to collapse when Jordan stepped forward and took a hold of me.

"Get off of her," I heard Nat shout.

It all happened in the blink of an eye. Nat dove at Jordan and they both hit the boards. It was frightening to watch them striking blows on each other. All around me started to spin, and then I blacked out.

When I opened my eyes, I was laid out on a bench in a small room. The priest was holding my hand. A woman dabbed a cold damp cloth on my forehead.

"How do you feel?" he said. I let go of his hand, pushed the woman's hand away, and throwing my legs off of the bench, I sat upright.

"I'm fine."

Truth was, I wasn't fine. Nat was sat over in the corner holding his arm and sporting a gash under his eye. His eye was almost closed with the swelling surrounding it. I was annoyed with him. All Jordan had tried to do was to rescue me. Blood trickled from my lip and I licked it away.

"Where's Jordan?"

"I don't know why you should be asking after him. He ran off with his dumb friends and the girls when Father David came out. You okay?"

"I think so. Just sore. What about you?"

"Sprained wrist."

"I'd better take you home, young lady," said the priest. "Nat won't be able to drive with one eye partly closed and a sprained wrist."

The woman was busy bandaging Nat's wrist. It wasn't how I expected the night to end, but I was pleased with the offer. At least it saved the worry of a passionate kiss at my doorstep that I'd been dreading. I'd tried practicing how to do it on my pillow, with the magazine open showing the couple entwined, and the words spinning around my head from those love stories. It hadn't been worth the anxiety that had been burning at my brain all evening. I'd had enough of the town. Pa was right; they were nothing but demons in disguise, Nat included.

I didn't waste any time in following the priest out to his car. Still angry with Nat, I didn't even say goodbye. All I had on my mind was that the sooner I could get home to bed, the sooner it would be morning and I could get on with making my own way in life. The whole experience made me wonder if Pa had been right for us to live in solitude and I should follow his example by living off of the land. Steering away from civilization seemed to be the best option for me. My lip stung on the drive home and seemed to have doubled in size.

"I'm sorry you got tangled up in all this," the priest said. "Unfortunately, when there is an imbalance of genders like you have in town, the sin of jealousy rears its ugly head."

I didn't reply, but asked him a question.

"Are there many arranged marriages in town?"

"Goodness, no. Not in our community. Some religions still accept them as the norm. It's more common with the Mormon and Muslim communities. Why ask?"

"No reason. Just curious."

"Is there more you want to ask me on the subject?"

"Do you know if any of these arranged marriages work out?"

"Well, I wouldn't really know, but if you want my opinion, it's better if people come together naturally."

"It's the next left," I said.

He turned into the drive and stopped, then flicked on the vanity light and turned sideways.

"Are you sure you'll be okay?"

"I'll be fine. Thanks for the ride."

By the expression on his face, he'd looked to be genuinely concerned. His features changed from displaying concern to a sort of quizzical look and he stroked his chin.

"You're welcome. Listen, if there's anything troubling you at any time, I have a good ear for listening. You could say it's part of my calling. You'll find me most days in my cottage at the rear of the church. You don't have to be of my faith to confide any worries you might have. I would never break a confidence."

"Thanks," I said, then pushed the door open and climbed out

of my seat and closed the door, then watched him drive away.

As I walked up to the steps to the porch, I grabbed my chest and let out a gasp.

"What the hell."

Jordan was sitting in the shadows on the bench.

"Don't panic. I only came to say sorry?"

"How did you get here?"

"My friends dropped me off. Our house isn't far. It's just through the woods over there."

"Don't you dare come near me or I'll call Pa."

He rose to his feet.

"Go on, call out all you like. He isn't here, is he?"

I glanced around looking for anything I could use to protect myself.

"Yes he is."

"No he isn't.

"Is so. I'll scream."

"Go ahead. Empty your lungs. We only have one garage in town, and your dad's pickup isn't there. There's no need to lie, I only wanted to be sure you were okay and to say sorry. That was some beating you took and I felt like it was my fault. I'll go now. Maybe I'll see you around town and we can start over?" he said, then vaulted the balustrade and strutted toward the woods.

I hurried inside. All fingers and thumbs, I re-screwed the lock catch back into place. Feeling secure, but breathing rapidly and with shivers of relief running through me, I leant with my back to the front door.

Stepping over to the table I took a seat. My head throbbed. I put my fingers to the source to find a lump on my forehead. A vision of Nat and Jordan fighting flashed through my mind. Tears formed in my eyes at the realization they had been fighting over me. Their jealousy aside, I was confused. If that's what finding a husband meant, I wanted none of it. I began to wonder if it would be better accepting Pa's arranged marriage. I rested my head on my arms on the table. I pictured my intended husband; his aged body writhing over mine and felt sick to the stomach.

I opened my eyes to the daylight trying to break through the curtains, and I was sitting on the armchair by the wood stove. Confusion set in, until I vaguely remembered moving from the table to the chair in a stupor. The deliberating I'd done before falling asleep was replaced with a sense of purpose. I rose from the chair and walked unsteadily over to the sink, turned the faucet, cupped my hands and splashed the water on my face. I rushed to my bedroom, changed into my jeans and thick wool sweater, and then grabbed my hooded jacket and hiking boots from the closet. Kicking off my wedding shoes, I noticed they were badly scuffed with the fight. He'd have a fit when he found them, I thought. I sat on the corner of the bed to fasten my laces, and then dashed back to the kitchen.

Dragging my backpack from under the table, I heaved the straps over my shoulders. Over at the door, I removed the catch and opened the door. I took a deep breath, then slowly exhaled and closed the door behind me. There was a thin covering of snow all around and small flakes drifting from the sky. It could have been raining heavy for all I cared as I slipped my gloves onto my hands.

I set off marching along the drive, head down, not knowing what my future held. I glanced back at the house as I reached the road. Then it started as I turned to walk along the road and the house disappeared from view. Leaden legs. Tightness in my chest. Short breaths. I gritted my teeth and powered on.

Chapter 20

Thwarted

N at had told me there was a thirty-three percent chance of there being snow on the ground during the fall in Colorado, but only a sixteen percent chance it would snow on the day at Halloween. But that was yesterday. As it happened, the snow had all but cleared on Friday, which had been comforting. What I had forgotten to ask him was, if he had been telling a white lie to Pa when he'd said there was another snowstorm front on the way. For now, it was just small flakes, but the wind was biting at my face, and my jeans were getting moist.

Under the cover of a tree, I slipped off my backpack and retrieved my waterproof snow pants and a scarf. I pulled the pants over my jeans and wrapped the scarf around my face, then pulled up my hood. Just as well I did as the flakes started to get thicker.

With a route I had marked out which would take me through town; I had hoped to make a further fifteen-mile trek to thick woodland where I could make camp. I had my doubts that I'd make it that far as I slipped my backpack straps over my shoulders. I must have been carrying at least sixty pounds, and I cursed under my breath that I had not set off yesterday when the sky was clear of clouds.

Pounding ahead, the snowflakes were swirling around on the road. Just past a wooded area, I walked on by a driveway and a sign for Hunter's Farm. It was the only drive I had seen since leaving home and I wondered if that was where Jordan lived. The church spire in the distance gave me some motivation to walk at pace and to put some distance between the house and me. But then the spire disappeared as the falling flakes became denser. The car tracks that had been visible in the slush on the road now had a white covering. Head down, I carried on, hoping that I would soon reach the sign for the town. A semi-truck rolled past, throwing a spray of slush all over me. I wanted to weep. It was as if I was destined to fail.

Finally, I reached the sign for the town. A vehicle pulled up beside me. I carried on marching, ignoring the vehicle. The car's horn sounded and it pulled up beside me again.

"Can I give you a ride, fella?"

Pa had said never to get into a strangers car alone. This was no stranger. I recognized the voice and turned.

"Oh, it's you" he said. "Get in."

"No thanks."

"Don't be stupid," Jordan said. "I can at least give you a ride into town. You can take shelter there. Throw your backpack on the back seat."

He reached over and opened the back door, but I stood my ground.

"Don't be an idiot, get in the back. I don't want the front seat wet. I have to pick Mom up in town."

The heavy snowfall made the decision for me. I dumped my backpack on the backseat, pushed it over and climbed inside. He was right. It would be better to take shelter in town and to wait for the snowstorm to subside.

"Where were you going in this weather?" he said, as I closed the door.

"That's my business," I said, shaking my head to stop the melted snow now dripping onto my face.

"Where do you want dropping off?"

My mind raced, thinking how to reply. Then I remembered the grocery store and the bench on the porch.

"The grocery store."

His eyes met mine in his rearview. That was when I noticed he had a black eye. Prob'ly a trophy he'd picked up from his fight with Nat.

"The grocery store? Is that like some kinda romantic gesture, seeing as how that was where we first met?"

He crunched the transmission as he changed gear, his eyes still watching me in the mirror. The snow was blasting the windshield, the wiper losing the battle to clear the relentless flakes.

"Just keep your eyes on the road."

Jordan laughed.

"They sell coffee in there. I could keep you company until Mom is ready for picking up. My treat to make up for last night."

"Whatever. Just concentrate on driving."

It was such a relief when we arrived and he pulled up outside the store. At a guess, visibility had only been around six feet and the ride had scared the hell out of me. He climbed out his side and walked around to open my door.

"Take my hand, or you're likely to slip."

"I can manage," I said, then wished I had accepted his offer as I slipped and fell on my backside.

"Stupid, feisty, and stubborn. Will you take my hand now?"

I held out my hands and he hauled me to my feet.

"Thank you," I said, ignoring him bad-mouthing me.

He reached inside the open back door and grabbed a hold of my backpack.

"What the hell have you gotten in here? It feels like everything including the kitchen sink stacked inside."

"Ha, ha, very funny."

"Age before beauty," he said, then ushered me through the store door before him.

"How do you like your coffee?"

"Black," I said, and took a seat at a table next to the window. He dumped my backpack next to me, then went over to the counter. I pulled down my hood then wound my scarf from around my face. Jordan arrived at the table and set down the coffees, then took a seat opposite.

"Thanks," I said.

"You're welcome, just as long as you buy coffee next time we meet."

It was just as well he was buying. I didn't have a penny to my name. I'd never given a thought to money. It was something I had never had a use for before.

"More fool you. There won't be a next time."

"Fool am I? We'd make a good pair then, seeing as how

you're stupid and I'm a fool. C'mon, seriously, where were you going? You can't be going shopping with a tent bag and snowshoes fastened to your backpack."

"As far away from here as possible, so you can forget about me pairing with anyone."

"What, just because Clarissa was jealous of you being with Nat?"

I wondered what trickery he was using to come out with that odd statement.

"That's not what she said."

"Of course she wouldn't say that, but then you don't know the history between them. Here, let me show you something."

He took out a cell phone, touched the screen, and then showed me the display. My eyes must have looked as though they were on stalks.

"I took the photo this morning when I dropped Mom off at the butchers. She works there part time until she goes to college."

It was a photo of Clarissa with cotton wool attached to her nose with two Band-Aids, and wearing a scowl on her face. Under the image was a list of comments. He snatched it away, held up the phone to a flash and I blinked.

"What was that?"

He tapped the screen with his fingers, then turned the screen to me. My image was on there, showing my cut lip and the lump on my forehead. Under it he had typed a caption. "The new girl in town who battered Clarissa."

"Get my photo out of there now. I don't ever have my photo taken."

"Okay, but only if you give me your cell phone number."

"I've never had one. Just get it off of there."

"Don't be a wuss. It's only a bit of fun. See, ten people have liked the photo already."

He showed me the screen.

"Who are these people? How can they see my photo?"

"God, where have you been all your life. It's called social media. Okay, I'll delete it… later."

His mischievous eyes danced about me. I didn't believe him

for one second. Reaching out, I tried to grab his cell phone, but he slipped it in his pocket.

"You're not leaving here without you do," I said, half-heartedly. It wasn't worth the effort to fight with him. I'd need all my energy for the trek ahead. "So this Clarissa and Nat, what's the history?"

Chapter 21

Frank Discussion

Jordan took a swig of his coffee, then did some huffing and puffing. It wasn't looking as though he wanted to tell me about Nat and Clarissa.

"Listen, it's complicated. It would take forever. Besides, I'm not interested in them. I'm more interested in what you were doing out there in the snowstorm with that tent and a backpack. Looks like you're leaving home."

"Like I said, I'm going to get as far away from here as possible, and it's got nothing to do with last night."

"Had a falling out with your dad?"

"Sort of."

"You could have picked some better weather. I wish I had your guts to go it alone."

"What makes you say that?"

He looked uncomfortable and shuffled on his seat.

"Suppose I could tell you, seeing as you won't be staying here." He did that shuffling on his chair again. Drummed his fingers on the table, then pushed back on his seat. "I had a fallin' out with my dad six months back. Things came to a head after simmering for years. Sort of got into a tussle with him and I came off best. Sick of him treating me like a slave on the farm working for food and a roof over my head, not to mention the beatings I'd taken over the years. Not spoken to him since then, or worked a day for him on the farm. Only Mom stops him from throwing me out. I just hang around with the other losers in town to keep out of his way."

Jordan mentioning that his dad treated him as a slave reminded me of what my situation had been. For all his brash attitude, I was warming to him. But then thinking that, I was wondering if he was lying when he said he didn't talk to his dad.

"What about that day when you were in your dad's pickup? Surely you spoke to him."

"Oh, that, didn't talk to him then either. Just wanted to see all the fun when Mom told me what had happened after he'd phoned the sheriff."

"So what is it with Nat and Clarissa?"

"Well, I sort of have a little history with Clarissa, but that goes way back until she started seeing Nat behind my back. Last night was all about her using me to try and make Nat jealous. Everyone in town and their dogs knows he needs someone to look after his mom so he can work. Anyway, he proposed to her and she turned him down. Said she was too young and she wanted to go to college. He dumped her right away and she wasn't pleased about it, and well... I guess you know the rest from that split lip of yours. So go on, now you can tell me your story."

I turned and gazed through the window. Outside the snow was still falling heavy. I wasn't as much thinking about the past as I was about what to do about the future. If the snowstorm carried on, I'd be trapped there. It was as if the town had a mind of its own and it didn't want me to leave. A stupid thought entered my mind that I should seek out Nat and ask him to marry me if he was that desperate for someone to look after his mom. With the church only one hundred yards or so down Main Street and the priest saying he lived in the cottage behind the church, I wondered if we could get it over with before Pa returned.

A hand waved in front of my face.

"Hello, anyone in there?"

"Sorry, what were you saying?"

"I asked about your story."

"Oh, yeah. Same as you I guess. I've had enough of Pa's controlling ways."

"What, you mean he beat you?"

"Not for a while, just the odd slap. I'd learned to do as I was told. But I draw the line at him arranging my marriage."

"What! This day and age. Don't tell me you're Amish, or some other fringe religion."

"I don't know what we are really, except we follow the good book. I don't want to get married to who I think he's picked out for me. He's older that Pa."

Jordan rose from his chair.

"That's damned ridiculous. When was this supposed to take place?"

"He arrives Sunday. I guess the wedding is meant to be on Monday. That's the reason why I have to go today."

"But you can't go in this weather. You'll freeze to death."

"Well I can't stay here."

He paced around the table.

"Damn, there won't be any buses through here today in this weather. Where were you hoping to get to?"

I reached down and opened the pocket on my backpack. Pulled out the map of Colorado and opened it out on the table. Stabbing my finger on the map, I said, "That's where I'd planned to set up camp tonight."

He came up beside me and looked at the map.

"No chance. Not in this weather. Tomorrow, okay. The forecast says this'll blow over during the night and they'll have the plows out to clear the roads. Damn, I can't even take you there. Mom will be phoning soon. I might not be able to get back here if this blizzard continues."

His cell phone rang and he snatched it from his pocket to answer the call.

"Hi, Mom. Give me five minutes," he said, and then hung up. "When is it your dad will be back?"

"Prob'ly in the afternoon on Sunday."

"I could take you back there and pick you up early tomorrow. I have a better place that you could stay."

He leaned over the map.

"See here," he said, stabbing his finger on the map. "Dad has a log cabin in the woods next to the lake that he never uses around seven miles from here. There's a wood stove, two single beds and a few pots and pans. You could hide out there until the snow clears. Do you have money for food?"

"No, I don't have any money, but I have supplies and I know how to fish and snag small game. There's no way I'm going back to the house."

"No money! You won't get far without money. That's what stops me getting the hell out of town. I know, why don't you hide in the church today? I could borrow Mom's car again and meet you there tomorrow and take you to the cabin."

"I think the priest would have something to say about that. Besides, how would I get in there?"

"That's easy and it could solve two problems. For one, the door is never locked, and then there's a collection box inside next to the door. We've fixed it so we can take the bolts out of the hinges, so that would solve the money problem."

I could believe what he was suggesting.

"That's stealing from God."

"No it isn't. People give the money for the poor. It's just cutting out the middleman. Look I have to get going. I'll pick you up from outside here at around ten tomorrow." He took hold of my hand and gave it a squeeze. "Just tough it out tonight and we'll figure it all out tomorrow," he said, then turned and hurried out the door.

Folding up the map, I put it back in the pocket of my backpack. I had noticed the woman behind the counter listening in to our conversation which made me feel uncomfortable. She turned away when she saw me looking and wiped the back counter. Having drained the last of the coffee, it didn't feel right not having any money to buy another drink. I set down the cup, hauled my backpack straps onto my shoulders and set off out to the porch. As the door swung open, I caught sight of the woman in the reflection of the glass. She picked up a telephone handset from the fixture on the wall, and then looked my way.

Stepping outside, the wind had blown a carpet of snow out on the porch. Braving it, I set off walking toward the church. My mind was in turmoil. Much as his offer seemed genuine to take me to his dad's cabin, I didn't know Jordan. For all I knew, he could have been laying a trap to imprison me at the cabin. Then him and his friends could have their wicked way with me, I thought, as I recalled his friend doing that suggestive display with the beer bottle. When I arrived at the church door, I put my gloved hand on the handle, then stopped in my tracks at the whoop of a siren. I turned to see the sheriff's vehicle slide to a halt. The driver's side window slid down.

"I need a word," said the sheriff."

Chapter 22

Interrogation

The temperature was akin to a stifling hot summer's day in the sheriff's office. I took off my coat, scarf, and gloves and stacked them on top of my backpack. All she had asked me to do was to talk to her in her office, nothing else. Never said a word in her vehicle on the short drive over there with me sitting on the back seat behind a metal grill, which was kinda unnerving.

"Take a seat," she said, with the wave of her hand, and pointed to the chair facing her at the desk. "Just thought I'd better rescue you from the snowstorm, no need to worry. Do you want me to phone your dad to come and pick you up?"

Pa always said to say as little as possible to anyone in law enforcement. Said they'd twist you inside out and treat you like dirt to get you to confess to any crime they wanted clearing up at the time. It hadn't stopped him mouthing off his lies back at home with the deer incident, but I decided to be cautious.

"No thanks, I'll be fine. A little snow doesn't worry me. Besides, Pa's not at home just now."

"So you're from Alaska your dad said. I imagine that's why the snow doesn't bother you with the winters up there," she said, and took off her hat, then hung it on a peg next to the exit.

I nodded as she walked past me and took a seat opposite her at the desk.

"What do we call you? I'm Sheriff MacCaffrey, but everyone around here calls me Ann."

There was no need for her introduction. Her name was emblazoned in gold letters on a wooden sign in front of me.

"Clara."

"Nice name. How old are you?"

"Eighteen."

She picked up a buff file in front of her, opened it, then closed it again.

"So is that Clara Ackerman?"

I nodded, and glared at the buff file.

"I have coffee in the pot. Would you like some?"

I shook my head. My skin felt clammy under my jeans and heavy woolen sweatshirt. I just wanted to get out of there and back to the church.

"You don't say much. I won't bite. I like to get to know everyone that moves into town. What was it you were doing entering the church?"

"Sanctuary."

"Sanctuary! From what?"

"The snowstorm."

"Oh, yeah."

The sheriff picked up a pencil and chewed on it, staring into my eyes, then took it from her mouth and tapped it on her desk.

"So where in Alaska did you live?"

"Nearest town was McCarthy, but that was more than a hike away."

"Never heard of it. It's almost the same name as mine. Where is it?" Sheriff MacCaffrey asked, and pointed to a large map on the wall.

"Don't know exactly, but it's not far from the Canadian border down south."

She rose from her chair, walked over to the wall and ran her fingers over the map.

"Got it. That really is out in the wilds. Not far from the Yukon in Canada."

"Guess so."

"So what was all this scuffling about at the church hall last night?"

My shoulders sagged. Pa was right; she was a trickster trying to befriend me, then intending to slap me over the head. Prob'ly fixing to arrest me.

"It wasn't my fault. Some girl was jealous because I was with Nat. Said I'd kept looking at Jordan."

96

The sheriff grinned.

"Don't worry, no one is pressing charges. How come you hooked up with Jordan at the grocery store? I guess you know that Nat and Jordan have history after what took place last night. That's asking for trouble if you're thinking of playing them both."

I shrugged my shoulders. A vision of the woman behind the counter on the phone rolled through my mind.

"He gave me a ride into town, that's all. I didn't expect the snow to be so heavy when I set off."

"If you'll take my advice you'll steer well away from Jordan. I also wouldn't go near the church if I were you. If there's any money missing from the collection box, you'd be in trouble."

I let out a sigh. The woman at the grocery store had been listening in on our conversation.

"So where is it you were going with all that equipment?"

"Camping."

"Well, that's out of the question in this weather or you'll freeze to death during the night. C'mon, I'll take you home before it's not possible to get through. Otherwise, you'll have to sleep here for the night. We can talk some more on the way over there. I just need the bathroom first."

The sheriff had pointed to an open door when she'd said I could stay there the night. At the end of a corridor, I could see a barred cell door and inside the small room a single cot mattress and nothing else. A shiver ran from my head to my toes. It brought back a distant memory of being locked in a cellar at one of our houses, crying for days on end. The town was doing that thing again. It didn't want me to escape.

I couldn't be sure just how much the woman in the grocery store had heard. Last thing I wanted was that the sheriff would know I was running away. She could tell Pa the direction I was heading and he'd find me. Thinking that, I didn't want to return home, but neither did I want to sleep in a cell. I was all out of options. Letting her take me home seemed to be the lesser of the two evils. I prayed that Jordan was right and the storm would subside overnight, then they'd clear the roads so I could set off before Pa arrived.

With the sheriff out of the room, curiosity had been burning at me. I reached over and opened the buff file. The top sheet of paper was an incident report of Pa pulling his gun on Jordan. At least it explained how she knew my surname. Then I noticed there was another three sheets of paper under that. Flicking the top page, then the second page and on through to the last one, my eyes widened. I gasped at what I saw on the last page, before quickly closing the file. My soul leapt from my body when the sheriff came up beside me. I couldn't be sure if she'd seen me sneaking a look in the file.

"C'mon, get your coat and backpack. Best get you home."

Chapter 23

Outflanked

The sheriff dropped me off at home. I waved her off from the porch, sending her a false smile. Her questions on the drive over from town had left me mentally exhausted. I wasn't used to lengthy question and answer sessions from strangers. I'd had to feint coughing fits to give me time to think, so as not to fall into any trap she might have been setting. There were questions of my own I needed answers to after seeing what I did in the buff file, but dared not ask them. As soon as she was out of sight, head down, I walked at pace down to the barn, and not feeling comfortable at going back inside the house.

Once inside the barn, I opened the door to the small workshop next to the side door entrance. I unloaded my backpack from my shoulders and hauled it under the workbench, then covered it with sacks. The familiar sound of the wind blowing outside reminded me of my time in Alaska. All that was missing were the wolf howls calling one another. I often wondered what they were signaling, and envied their freedom to roam. They were beautiful beasts to watch from a distance, but real scary up close, especially if they were in a pack and hungry.

We had an old skinny wolf visit me that I called King. He'd started to come close to our cabin when Pa was away trapping at one time for a whole week after we'd just arrived at our home in Alaska. His eyes would look soulfully at me as if to gain my trust. I'd throw him scraps of food from the window of our log cabin, not realizing the danger. Then Pa returned home on his snowmobile with a deer. That was when I realized he was part of a pack. Pa barely managed to get inside the cabin before putting a bullet between King's eyes, as I watched the pack encircle his snowmobile and drag away the deer from the trailer sled. The sheriff reminded me of King, and the townsfolk were her pack of wolves. As Pa had said; demons in disguise, just like the wolf pack. I realized there and then that I couldn't trust anyone. Not the sheriff, not Nat, and the same with Jordan.

Hunger dug at my stomach. I glanced at my wet footprints on the dust covered concrete floor. Pa's ghostly boot prints led to the empty spaces on the wall where the chisels usually hung. They were the ones that he had used to barter with Nat for the tire chains. Other tracks led to a wall cabinet. I shivered at the thought of walking in his footsteps as I walked over and opened the cabinet doors. All that I could see were old oilcans. Shuffling them around, I couldn't think what use empty oilcans would be to him. Then I found Pa's moneybox hidden away and stepped back. I reached out and put the cans back in place and closed the cabinet door, then walked out into the barn.

Standing at the barn door, I opened it slightly and peered out. At a guess there was around six inches of snow on the ground. The last thing I wanted was to run down my food supplies from the backpack. The way the snowflakes were falling, if I hadn't gone to the house there and then, a snowdrift could have blocked me in the barn. Reluctantly, I hurried to the front door of the house. This hadn't been part of the plan. I felt defeated at returning. At least I had a good twenty-four hours to escape again. I took off my gloves, then screwed the lock catch back in place. My fingers were cold, so I stepped over to the wood stove, and using the tongs, I opened the door. A welcome blast of heat hit my face and I warmed my hands. I placed some more logs inside and closed the door. Over at the table, I dropped my backside on a chair. I was used to being locked up alone, and not easily scared, but the house had an eerie feeling to it that sent shivers running through me.

Tick tock, tick damned tock. The sound from the wall clock disturbed the quiet. My thoughts drifted to the sheriff's questions in an attempt to drown out the sound. She had wanted to know if Pa was divorced. Then how and where Ma had died. What she'd looked like. Where we'd lived before besides Alaska. "Don't remember," had been most of my replies. Truth was that I didn't know the names of most of the towns where we had lived, never mind the states. Told her Pa got all upset if I ever tried to talk about Ma, and that was the truth.

I began to wish I'd had the nerve to ask what she was doing with a likeness of Pa as a sketch in her file. It wasn't an exact likeness, but the trapper's hat he was wearing in the image told me she hadn't drawn it as a recollection of Pa after first setting eyes on him. It was colored in with the same red and black pattern as Pa's trapper hat that he'd discarded in Alaska when he'd bought his Stetson from a secondhand store before we left.

Then there was the hand written notes. The first one was headed "Clarissa MacCaffrey," and mentioned the church hall. The second note on the same page was headed "Susan MacCaffrey," the same name as on the signage for the grocery store. If only there had been time to read them. To make matters worse, the sign on the sheriff's desk said, "Ann MacCaffrey." I began to wonder at the time if all the townsfolk were called MacCaffrey and they'd been begat from the Devil himself.

My left eye involuntary twitched. It had been doing that ever since I arrived at the sheriff's office. With my elbows on the table, I leaned my head over, and grabbing my hair, I tugged at it until my scalp hurt as much as it had when Clarissa had a grip of it before they pulled her off of me. Hungry as I was, I didn't have any motivation to start cooking a meal. Pushing back on the chair, I rose to my feet and headed to my bedroom.

I removed my snow pants and jacket and draped them on the bottom of the bed. Sitting on the mattress next to the headboard, I wiped the moisture from the glass and gazed out of my window. It was something I felt that I had been doing all my life. The flakes of snow seemed to be smaller and less dense, but already my tracks from the barn had disappeared. At least it was a sign that the snowstorm would likely subside and I could be on my way again. One thing that I decided was that I wouldn't take Jordan up on his offer. If the storm blew over by midnight, or whatever time, I would set off again to my original plan.

Waiting around was tearing me inside out. The questions the sheriff asked got me to thinking. I'd tried many times to recall Ma, without success. I could vaguely remember Pa telling me that Mom had died in a car wreck, and the endless tears and grief that I suffered for weeks on end. Most of it was spent in a darkened room. He only let me out once I was all cried out. Beyond that, I sometimes grasped at images of me seeing a woman lying on a sofa, but try as I may to recall her, she didn't have a face. For all I knew it maybe wasn't an image of Ma. We no longer had a television, but the image included a television in the room. The picture I conjured up, she also had a child in her arms, or maybe it was a doll, because I didn't have a sister or a brother.

Last time we had a television, I must have been around seven, or eight years old. Pa would let me play endless cartoons on a playing machine up to that age. I knew most of the words they spoke off by heart. He once forgot to lock my bedroom door and I sneaked to the top of the stairway. I observed him stick a metal coat hanger somewhere in the back of the television, then he watched a grainy image. When his back was turned one day, I tried to do the same with the hanger and ended up thrown across the room. That was the last time I ever saw a television in any of our homes. A long drawn out breath escaped my lips at recalling the beating he gave me.

I wiped the moisture from the window again. There didn't seem to be any respite from the snow, though at least it wasn't heavy. I turned away from the window, then snatched a look outside again at the sound of a vehicle. It didn't belong to anyone I knew as it parked down by the barn. It was a cab with a flatbed at the back on the chassis. Some type of work vehicle. I stepped back at the sound of another vehicle approaching. This time I knew the vehicle, and gulped, then I fell backwards on the mattress. I had to act quickly, but my limbs failed to accept instructions from my brain. My eyes darted around the room. *Jacket, pants, red dress, purse, and shoes.* Then I looked down at my hiking boots and wanted to scream. Finally, I broke through the fog in my brain. Outside, I heard a vehicle door clunk. I scrambled to my feet and took a quick glance through my window. That's when I set eyes on him and felt sick inside.

Chapter 24

Resignation

Numb from the shock of Pa returning early with a visitor, I watched them walk over to each other, and then both of them stepped toward the house. A tear ran down my cheek. Pa always said that he's like an elephant that never forgets anything. Don't know where that saying came from, or what significance there was between Pa, elephants, and memory, but I hadn't forgot the stature and features of the sawmill owner. The sight of him made me want to throw up. My eyes darted around the room, but there was nowhere I could hide that they wouldn't find me. Like a caged animal, I paced around aimlessly, my thoughts fragmented.

The snow had stopped falling, but the trees were still swaying with the wind. I wondered if the snowstorm that prevented me from escaping was God's way of teaching me a lesson for abandoning him, by me not packing my Bible. My intended still had his tall spindly form, thin features, and a large hooked nose, framed by unusually narrow spaced eyes. Only his face was more wizened now, and his long bushy beard was completely gray. I was all fingers and thumbs as I perched my backside on the bed to unfasten the laces to my boots. Finally, I managed to pull them off, then I dumped them under the bed with my jacket, scarf, and the red dress. The sound of their laughter drifted from outside.

I scrambled to my door, opened it slightly, and listened. Pa's key scraped in the lock. The door creaked open on its hinges.

"You can give me the dowry now you're here," I heard Pa say.

"What, without seeing her? I'll give you it tomorrow after I've set eyes on her and we've said the words."

Pa was still insisting calling it a dowry. Maybe it was to ease his conscience. Then I thought that was stupid. He didn't have one.

"Stay here on the porch. I'll make sure she's out of sight."

"Clara, where are you?"

"In my bedroom, Pa." I said in a sweet voice, but with my entire body trembling.

"Don't come down, I'll see you up there." Then Pa said, "You can come in now and wait here. Clara's in her bedroom. I'll go and see to her."

Footsteps clomped up the stairway. My heart raced so fast, I thought it would explode in my chest. I'd stepped back, dropped my butt on the mattress and I had picked up my Bible by the time he walked into my room. A shiver ran through me at recalling the image of our visitor. Pa was laden with large shopping bags and he dropped them by the door.

"Good to see you're reading your Bible. Your intended has arrived." He looked down. "What's that on the floor?"

I put the Bible back on the table, rose to my feet, and walked to the bottom of the bed. A warm flush developed in my cheeks at seeing the red purse on the floor. I bent down and picked up the purse and threw it on the bed.

"Previous owners must have left it here. Found in in my closet." I turned to face him, trying to look composed, but inside I was shaking like a blob of Jell-O. "Anyway, I...I wasn't expecting you back until tomorrow."

"That was the idea. Thought it would save you getting nervous. Although it looks like it didn't work. Pull yourself together. Your wedding outfit is in the bags. You can try the clothes on, but stay in your room until tomorrow. I'll call you down when we're ready."

I was guessing them arriving early had nothing to do with my nerves, just Pa being his usual devious self.

"Why can't I see him today? If I don't like the look of him, can I say no?"

"It's custom for the bridegroom not to set eyes on the bride the night before, or you'll likely have bad luck. And as I said, you don't get to decide. You're doing this for the both of us. It's God's will."

I thought his words ironic. I had seen him, and to say I was having bad luck would have been an understatement. He dug his hand in his jacket pocket. Pulled something out and held out his hand.

"Here, put this under your pillow."

"What is it?"

"A vial of blood I managed to sneak from the medical center. After he's had his way with you, sneak it out and pour it between your legs and onto the bed sheet. Then pull down the bedcovers and make sure he sees the stain."

"Why?"

"Because he's expecting a virgin, that's why, idiot. Don't look so innocent. You know what's expected. He can't be knowing our family secrets. It's none of his business. You're never to mention it. It's between me, you, and God."

I wanted to throw up at the reminder. He wasn't the only one with a secret. I'd never told him about my intended's visit to our cabin when Pa was working, so I doubted the sight of blood would be much use.

"You still haven't told me his name."

"He likes to be called Tex, but his full name is Archibald Jeremiah Rhymer. So you'll be Mrs. Rhymer after the ceremony."

I tried to swallow and gulped. I couldn't be sure if he was lying to me about the custom of not seeing him before tomorrow, or if it was an excuse to make sure I didn't try to escape through the front door, by him insisting that I stayed in my room.

"What about something to eat?"

"I'll bring you a sandwich and coffee later," he said, then turned.

A surge of anger and defiance brimmed inside of me.

"Pa, I really don't want to do this," I said, and stamped on the floorboards.

He pivoted on his heels and faced me, his features contorted.

"Oh, you'll do it all right, because if you don't, do you know what the alternative is?"

107

"What alternative is that?"

He sent me his stinky-eyed look, and then stepped over into my space. I reared away.

"If I lose the dowry, I'll chain you to the damned bed and have men come here for them to pay to service you to make up for the loss. Don't think I don't mean it."

My jaw gaped open; I wanted God to strike him down there and then. I knew exactly what he meant. I'd always thought he was nasty, but I'd never heard him talk in that way. My legs gave way and I dropped back on the bed, covering my eyes with my hands. The door slammed to a close. Through a flood of tears, my mind searched for a way out. All I could think of was why I hadn't gotten away by now and the futility of my situation. If only this. If only that. But for this. But for that, kept circling, but nothing in the way of how to plan an escape. Then I experienced guilt at wanting to go to the dance with Nat out of devilish curiosity. There didn't seem to be anyone else to blame, not even God for my own stupidity that tomorrow I would be Mrs. Rhymer.

A sense of calm and resignation washed over me. I wiped my sleeve across my eyes. I'd survived eighteen years, and as I had proven, I didn't want to die. I'd been born on a path in life that fate had handed me a bad journey. I knew I wasn't on my own after reading those books, the magazine, learning about Nat's situation, and from talking to Jordan. I also knew that I wanted a different life to the one I had experienced. If it meant getting married to an old man for now, then so be it, I tried to convince myself. It changed nothing, only the time and the day of striking out on my own, especially if I wanted to be a survivor and not a victim of fate.

Rising from my bed, I walked over to the window. The porch roof was covered in snow. It was only maybe a foot from the window sill, then a slope, and from there an eight foot drop, unless I could somehow shimmy down the vine growing up the support. I imagined it would be just my luck to fall and break a leg. He'd nailed the sash window frame with two nails at the bottom. I could have kicked myself for leaving my backpack in the barn. Even if it had taken all night, I could have dug away at the wood with my hunting knife to release the nails. The if onlys surfaced again. If only I'd have gutted Pa with the boning knife in the barn when I had the chance, none of this would be happening. But then I thought that I would have been locked up by now with the key thrown away.

Looking out through the window into the distance, I hoped to see Jordan in the tree line. He'd know what to do. There wasn't anyone there. There never was when I needed someone. My resolve broke and I started to sob.

Through the tears, I watched a blackbird land on the drive. I gasped, when almost immediately a yard cat sprang from nowhere and trapped it with its paws, then grabbed it by the neck. It didn't hang around, skulking off with it in its jaws, leaving behind a few stray feathers. If it was the same bird, this time the blackbird didn't have his sparrow friends to watch over him and he'd suffered the consequences. I'd felt an affinity with the blackbird in life. His death had been a warning and maybe a life lesson. If only I could have made it into the church, Jordan could have helped me to get away. It was no use thinking, what if. All I could do was to wait and see what the morning would throw at me.

Chapter 25

Wedding Ceremony

Pa and Tex had been drinking all afternoon and into the night. All I'd done was to sniffle until I was all cried out, my mind ending up empty of emotion. I'd had the bolt on my door when Tex stumbled into the spare room opposite mine. Pa followed shortly after and I heard his bedroom door close. It wasn't long after that, what sounded like a rasping-bassoon orchestra of snoring filled the house, accompanied by the wind howling outside. Not that I would have slept much anyway. I'd wanted the darkness of the night to go on forever. But like all my wishes, I couldn't stop day following night.

At daylight, Tex's door opened, and then the bathroom door along the hallway. Shortly after I heard him gargling, then his footsteps creaked down the stairway to the kitchen. Pa's door soon opened. I didn't hear him walking along the corridor, but my body leapt when I saw the handle twitch.

"You awake?" he said.

"Yeah."

"Open the door."

Still fully clothed, I hauled myself out of bed, and unfastened the bolt, then opened the door ajar slightly. Pa was standing there in his long johns and with the hair on his head stood on end, looking the worse for the wear from his drinking session.

"We're not going to have a problem today are we?"

I couldn't see that there were any options other than to comply. Not without I'd get a beating.

"No."

"Good. Sorry about what I said yesterday. The Devil had gotten into my mind after all that driving with my back on fire. What I should have said was that it's what's expected in our religion under the eyes of God, so you weren't questioning me, but God's will. You'd do well to remember that Joseph was

111

thirty years older than Mary was when the priest arranged their marriage, and look at how God blessed them. Anyway, listen, it's gone eleven. We've all slept in. I'll get a quick wash and get dressed, then you can use the bathroom and change into your outfit. Call me when you're ready and I'll take a look at you."

I never heard him use the bathroom. All I heard was him rummaging around in his room. I didn't believe him for one minute that he was sorry for what he'd said. Neither did I doubt that what he'd said would be my fate if I refused him.

"All done," he shouted. "You can get ready now."

Pa only took a wash once a week. He obviously didn't think it was special enough to get washed for my wedding.

My shoulders sagged, along with the rest of my psyche as I shuffled over to the window and stared at the woods. I didn't know what I could have done to get away even if Jordan would have been out there waving at me to beckon me outside. Jordan would have realized by now that I wasn't going to take him up on his offer. That's if he had turned up. I doubted he would have come to see if I'd returned home, especially after Pa fired that round at him with his rifle. I wondered if maybe he thought I could have set off before he arrived and he'd gone looking for me along the highway. But then I thought, why should he have done? I was nothing to him and he was nothing to me. We didn't owe each other anything. It was the same with Nat. He'd not bothered to call around to see how I was after the fight. That just proved how much I must have meant to him. Pa had already proved just how much my own opinion counted. A big fat nothing. I was only valuable to him for the money he would get for me. Failing that, he'd sell the use of my body to anyone who would pay the price.

With a heavy heart, and dragging my feet, I went to the bathroom to get washed. As soon as I'd finished, I wrapped a large bath towel around me, picked up my clothes, then scurried back to my bedroom and bolted the door.

I hadn't even looked at the outfit he'd bought. By the size of the bags, at least I hoped for a fairytale wedding dress the likes of which I'd seen in the magazine. I guess it was too much to hope for when I saw the small packaging inside the shopping bags. Spreading them out on the bed, I opened them one at a time. All that the outfit amounted to was some white underwear, a thin white blouse, a very short red and black tartan skirt, and a cardigan with buttons at the front. None of them seemed practical for use after the wedding except for the cardigan and the blouse in summer. I hated bras and pants having gotten used to wearing all in one thermals in Alaska in winter.

Pa called out. "I'll be up there in fifteen minutes. Make sure you're ready."

I set about platting my hair, tied the ribbons, then dressed. I only had a hand mirror, and propped it against my Bible. I thought I looked stupid at showing far more of my legs than my ugly knees. To add to the insult, one of the socks kept slipping down my calf to my ankle.

"You ready," Pa called out.

Panic set in at the scuffs on the shoes. Spitting on them seemed to do the trick. I unfastened the bolt and let him in. He looked me up and down.

"Pull your sock up and wear this. I forgot to put it in the bags. I've tied the knot."

He handed me a tie that matched the colors and pattern of the skirt.

"A tie! I thought men wore those?"

"It's not my idea. It's what Tex wanted. Put it on and stop sulking. I want you down there in five minutes," he said, and walked out of the room.

As soon as I heard him pounding down the stairway, I lifted my pillow and picked up the vial. Stepping over to the closet, I took out a sanitary pad, unscrewed the vial and poured the blood on to it, then tossed it into the wastebasket.

"Clara, we're waiting," Pa shouted.

I placed the vial in the red purse, then left it on the bed in haste.

There was no wedding music playing like the magazine had said as I walked slowly down the stairway. I couldn't raise my eyes as I walked into the kitchen.

"Beautiful," I heard Tex's voice croak. "Do a twirl."

I felt a hand grab my butt and reared away. Pa stepped between us.

"Ya don't own it yet. Let's say the words over at the table. Then the dowry."

A glance out of the window told me it had started to snow again. I knew that I wouldn't have gotten far if I'd tried to cut and run in that weather with the clothes I was wearing. Besides, the key wasn't in the door, so Pa likely had it locked. Pa took my hand in a vise like grip and pulled me over to the table.

He forced my hand on his Bible and told me to keep it there. Tex put his hand next to mine. Pa picked up a sheet of paper and recited a monologue, but the words were indistinct and passed right through me right up to him saying, "Marriage brings a husband and wife together in the delight of sexual union and commitment to the end of their lives, according to God's holy law."

I could only hope that Tex's life was nearing the end. Pa coughed and spluttered through the rest, then he shook his script.

"I think we can skip this part. There's no one here going to object. You can remove your hands from the Bible. Have you got the ring?" he asked.

Tex took his hand away, dipped into his pocket and handed him a gold ring. It was quite chunky. The first thing that passed through my mind was that I could sell it. Pa was probably thinking the same as I could see him weighing it in his hand. Then he placed it on his open Bible. I knew the value of gold. Pa and me had panned the rivers in Alaska. Once collected a thimble full of it and Pa reckoned when he sold it that it would keep us in supplies for a month.

The rest of what was said was all a blur after Tex slipped it onto my finger. It was way too big. The sight of his gnarled hand holding mine repulsed me, but the weight of the ring had me snickering inside. Definitely more than a thimble full.

"I will," Tex said.

Pa repeated the words, emphasizing the word 'obey' then

waited for my reply. My mind went into meltdown. My cheeks flamed like a furnace.

"I... I." The words just wouldn't come out. I kept my head bowed, but glanced up at Pa. I could see the anger dancing in his eyes. A tear rolled down my cheek. I snatched my hand away from Tex to wipe away the tear and the ring fell to the floorboards.

For an old fart, Tex was nimble enough to bend down, then search for it on all fours. Pa glared at me, his lips so tight they looked like they were glued together. He wagged a finger at me, and then curled his hand to a taut fist until I could see the whites of his knuckles. Tex sprang to his feet.

"I've saved the day. I have it."

Any hope that it would have disappeared through a gap in the floorboards to halt the ceremony, made me think it was God's will that I should be wed as Pa had said, even if it wasn't my own. Goodness knows what would happen next, I thought, wishing that I could have slithered through the floorboards and be away from there.

Chapter 26

One too Many

Pa stroked his beard, scrunched up his wedding script and tossed it into the wastebasket, then said, "I now pronounce you man and wife. You may kiss the bride."

"Whoa, hold on a damned minute. I didn't hear her say I will," Tex said.

"Yeah, well, I heard her. You should turn up the volume on your hearing aid."

I glanced at Pa in disbelief.

"Okay, if you say so. I'll keep the ring safe and get it altered." Tex slipped the ring into his pocket and sidled up close to me.

My skin crawled. I reared away and turned my head, his lips swiping my cheek. Pa coughed.

"Ahem. C'mon, Tex, we have business to attend to in private. Time for you both to have some fun later. You go to your room. We'll be having drinks shortly. We're staying here tonight, and then going back to his home at the sawmill first thing. I'll call you down for the toast."

"Can I get changed? My legs are cold."

Tex took a tight hold of my arm and shook me.

"It's no good asking your dad. You'll do as I tell you now. And stop inspecting your feet. You'll look at me when we're talking. The answer is no, you can't get changed. If you're cold, put more logs in the stove."

Pa stepped into the fray as I raised my head and stared at Tex defiantly.

"She understands. It's just nerves. She'll be fine once you've bedded her. Now c'mon, let's get our business sorted."

"It's in my truck."

Tex let go of me and I rubbed my arm. Pa put his hand to Tex's back and ushered him to the door. He took the key from his pocket, opened the door and they exited. Leaving nothing to chance until they'd got their business over with, he locked the door from the outside. Any notion I'd had during the night that Tex would be a kind sweet old man, and I'd just have to suffer the sex, had just walked out of the room with him.

I burst into tears and ran up the stairway and into my bedroom. Standing back from the window, I watched them reach his truck. Tex opened his door and bent over as if retrieving something from under his seat. He turned to Pa, handed him a package and they shook hands. Tex set off back to the house, but Pa entered the barn. He wasn't in there long as he walked back out, a huge grin on his face, but no sign of the package, and he walked at pace back toward our house.

They entered our house and one of them walked up the stairway. My head pounded along with the footsteps drawing near. The door swung open. Tex walked in with a swagger.

"I don't know why you're acting all shy. You know what's expected. It's not as if we're strangers. Why are you sulking?"

"Because I can't... you know." I pointed to the wastebasket. "I've started my bleed."

He glanced in the basket.

"Oh, is that all," he said, and laughed. "Don't worry, there are other ways you can pleasure me tonight, just don't expect me putting my hand down there. Plenty of time for that when you've finished bleeding. Now get your ass downstairs for the toast. I've brought some good moonshine." He shook his head, turned and walked out of the room.

I dropped to my knees and covered my face with my hands, then clasped them together to thank God. Last thing I wanted was to be with child.

Using the mattress for purchase, I hauled myself to my feet and glanced out through the window.

It was only snowing light. But for fate closing the door in my face, I thought I could have been at my destination by now.

"Clara, get down here now. We're ready for the toast," Tex shouted.

I hurried outside my room and down the stairway. If nothing else, I wanted him to think I was living up to the vow to obey him. Then with a little luck, I could gain his confidence and escape his clutches.

Tex poured some of the moonshine from a jar into a mug.

"Drink this and it'll get you in the mood. Loosen you up some," he said, and slid it over to me on the table. I took a sniff. It didn't smell much different from antifreeze.

Pa raised his glass, then said, "To the bride and groom."

They both downed their drinks in one. I put the mug to my lips and pretended to drink.

"I'm hungry," said Tex, and poured more moonshine in to Pa's and his glasses. "Get something hot conjured up to eat."

"Come on into my den," Pa said to Tex. "I've gotten something to show you. It'll more that help you get into the mood for tonight."

Over the worktop while I prepared a stew, it ran through my mind that I'd gotten the wrong end of the bargain. Pa would have a free home and plenty of money. Tex had a slave, do his beck and calling. All I had was clothes that I hated, and not even a ring I could sell. I poured the moonshine down the sink drain.

Glancing over my shoulder, he'd left the door open to his den. Don't know what they were looking at on Pa's laptop screen, but they were drooling and laughing. If only he'd have closed the door to his den. The screwdriver was in the sink cabinet at the top of his toolbox. It wouldn't have taken a minute to get the screws out and I could have run to the woods. I let out a sigh. It was no use anyway with the clothes I was wearing.

There was also a claw hammer under the sink that I could make use of to take out the nails from the window frame. Pa's pickup blocked my view of the woods. I wondered if Jordan would be out there with his friends as I set the stew to simmer on the stove.

I opened the cabinet door under the sink, took out the screwdriver and claw hammer from his toolbox. Trying not to let them see, I slipped them under my cardigan, then shuffled away and up the stairway.

I didn't see anything of Jordan and his friends, but then it was too much to expect to be rescued. Pa and Tex's drinking session went on for what seemed like forever. I dug away at the hardwood frame surrounding the nail head. He'd struck the nails in so deep, I couldn't get the claw to gain purchase to lever them out of the frame.

"Clara, get down here now," Tex called out.

I closed the curtains, and then put the hammer and screwdriver under my bed.

"What is it?" I asked, as I walked into the kitchen, though really I didn't need to ask. I could hear the stew sizzling. "Sorry," I said, and turned off the gas to the stove.

"You'd better pay more attention when we get back to my house," Tex said. "You won't be using gas either. God only knows why you aren't using the wood stove."

He was obviously drunk and swaying about. I put the pan under the water tap and turned the faucet and the juices sizzled.

"No harm done. Caught it just in time."

I put the pan back on the stove, lit the gas, and waited for it to boil. Still not hungry, I ladled out two bowls of stew and set them on the table with some bread.

"You not joining us," Pa said.

"Not hungry."

Truth was that I was terrified of the approaching hour. It was already dark outside. He'd soon want me to pleasure him. That thought made me sick to the stomach as I watched him slurp his stew like a pig at a trough. As he gorged on the last of his bread, I stepped over to the table and poured them both some more moonshine, a little on the generous side.

"C'mon, time for another toast, Pa," I said.

Tex grabbed me and pulled me onto his knee. For all his years, he carried some strength in his arms. His hands were all over my breasts. I looked at Pa, pleading to be rescued. Pa rose from his chair, walked over to the cabinet, took out a glass and filled it with drink, then handed it to me.

"To a long life for all of us."

At last he let go of me. I rose to my feet, raised my glass and repeated the words, but with one arm behind my back and my fingers crossed. We all downed our drinks in one. I coughed and spluttered, the moonshine burning my throat on the way down.

"Lightweight," Tex said, and poured more drink for Pa and him. "Best you go to our room and leave the men to do the drinking. I'll be up there soon enough."

The last sentence he spoke filled me with dread. I couldn't believe that life could be so cruel, and wondered if I should have slit my throat when I had the chance. But then I wasn't finished yet. I still had one last trick up my sleeve.

Chapter 27

Trapped

I picked up the empty dishes from the table and took them to the sink. A shadowy figure darted between Pa's pickup and Tex's truck. In the reflection of the window, I could see Pa and Tex with their back to me. I thought maybe the wind was whipping up shadows from the trees and squinted. They were now swapping bawdy jokes behind me, and then burst into song. I near jumped out of my skin, when I saw a figure creep between the truck and the pickup, then to the base of the porch. He was late, twelve hours too late. Still, it wasn't his fault. I'd told him that the ceremony would be Monday. Jordan held up a sheet of paper on a spiral notebook.

"Can you get out?" It read, written with a felt tip.

The old farts weren't paying any attention when I glanced over my shoulder. I turned back and shook my head, and mouthed, "No," while making signs with my hands to signal that I couldn't unlock the door. He scribbled away on the notebook. I turned the faucet and ran some tap water and rinsed the dishes as he ducked under the balustrade and crept onto the porch. He held another message below the window.

"I heard the sheriff took you home."

I rolled my eyes. There wasn't any way to answer him. He scribbled some more.

"We've let down their tires."

I smiled to a rendition of *Ten Green Bottles* in the background.

He wrote some more.

"No vehicle. Transport here at ten sharp in the morning." He turned the page. "Can you get out then?"

I nodded, although I wasn't sure if I'd get the opportunity, or if we'd be gone by then. Hopefully the flat tires would stop us leaving. A chair scraped behind me, sending a shiver through my body. I waved in front of me for him to go away, drew the curtains, and turned.

"I've washed the dishes, I'll go up now."

"You do that," said Tex, slurring his words, and promptly fell with his backside onto the chair, almost tipping it over.

Wasting no time, I hurried up to my bedroom and closed the door behind me. I'd only managed to chip away enough of the frame to get at one nail, and hoped there would be enough time to free up the other one. Over in the tree line, I could just make out three figures running into the woods outlined against the snow covering. Working away feverishly with the screwdriver, I finally had enough of the head exposed. A couple of tugs with the claw hammer and out popped the nails. Constantly shaking and with my heart banging behind my rib cage, I cleared away the slivers of wood, closed the curtains, then stowed the tools in the closet.

The sound of laughter filled the hallway outside my room. Footsteps on the stairway were interspersed with stumbles and more snickers. I doused the oil lamp, dove onto the bed, and pulled the blanket over me. My door burst open. Tex's silhouette filled the doorframe. He was swaying, when he grabbed the doorframe for support. He kept reaching out with one foot, as if looking for steady ground. Finally, he made an attempt to enter, tripping over his own feet and fell onto the bed beside me. I inched over to put some space between us. Even though he was on top of the blanket, and I was under it, I couldn't stop the tremors. Rolling over on to his side, he threw his arm over me and trapped me.

That's how we lay all night, with him constantly snoring, the smell of alcohol on his breath polluting my every intake of soiled air. No words can explain fully the dread I felt that he might have woken from his stupor to have his way with me.

From sheer exhaustion, I finally drifted to sleep, but even in slumber I was tortured. In my nightmare, it wasn't as if I'd slept at all, but instead I'd been resting my eyes. My eyes popped open to a great weight on my chest and I couldn't breathe. I closed my eyes again. It was the same bedroom, with the same surroundings. My body couldn't respond to my brain telling me to move. I was pinned to the bed by some unseen force as if the Devil himself was paying me a visit, and was now pressing down on me. Finally, I broke free and sat upright and sucked in some air, sweat pouring from my brow. I was confused by the experience, not knowing if it had actually happened or if it was a dream. The first thing I did was to feel between my legs, but I still had my pants on and I was dry. I sighed with relief, but the torture wasn't over. I'd disturbed Tex. He rolled over, facing away from me, taking his arm with him and then groaned.

And so I sat, taking root to the mattress with my back against the headboard for an hour or two as night turned slowly to day.

Those last fifteen minutes as the big hand approached ten o'clock, added more tension until I thought my head would explode. At nine forty-five, I heard Pa's door open and him plodding down the stairway. Tex was still out of it when he suddenly turned and put his arm over me. I waited five minutes, with the hope he'd roll over again, but he wasn't for moving. Gently, I took a hold of his hand and moved it away, then after inching the bedcovers off of me, I slowly moved my legs off the mattress until my toes touched the floorboards. I rose to my feet to the creak from hell. Standing frozen to the spot, I prayed I'd not disturbed him.

A thought crossed my mind that Jordan wouldn't turn up. Regardless, spending the night in the same bed as Tex had told me I was going anyway, him turning up or not. I doubted that either Pa or Tex would be fit enough to keep up with the chase if I could make it to the woods. With the alarm clock ticking away, I knew I had to move fast.

My body leapt when Tex groaned, then said, "Wow, what a night. I think your dad drank me under the table. My head's still spinning. Watcha doing out of bed?"

"I was going to get dressed and fix you some breakfast. "

"No need, get back into bed. I need the bathroom, then we can have some fun," he said, and winked. Throwing his spindly legs over the side of the bed, he rose to his feet and I followed him to the door as he exited. As soon as I heard the bathroom

125

door open, I bolted the door.

Every muscle in my body ached as I rushed over to the bed, pulled out my clothes and boots, and changed. I heard the flush of water from the toilet as I threw the curtains open and grabbed at the window sash to lift it open. Damned thing wouldn't move. My eyes danced around looking through the window, but there was no sign of Jordan, or a vehicle. Whatever, I'd have rather have risked death than to have stayed there. I glanced over my shoulder to see the handle of the door turn.

"Clara, open the door."

"I can't, it sticks sometimes. Go get Pa, he knows how to open it." I said, trying to stall him, and with all my strength, I dragged the bed over to the door.

"Ya little bitch, watcha doing? Get this freaking door opened now."

I'd already grabbed the hammer from the closet, and took a swing at the glass, covering my eyes with my arm. I bashed out the remaining slivers. Draped the blanket over the frame. I glanced at the clock then at my Bible. It was one minute to ten. I stuffed the Bible under my jacket to the sound of pounding on the bedroom door. Then there was an almighty crash as the bolt snapped off of the frame and the bed legs scraped on the floor. The next thing I recalled was sliding down the snow covered shingles, desperation setting in and not being able to dig in with my boots to slow me down. It was over in the blink of an eye. My backside landed with a thud, sending a jolt through my spine. Luckily, I'd landed in a drift of snow piled up at the front of the porch. That was as far as my luck went, when I rose to my feet and stepped over to the drive. A pain from the small of my back ran through my left buttock and on down the back of my calf. I collapsed in pain as I put my weight on my left leg.

"You little shit. Don't you dare move," Pa called out. I glanced up at my bedroom window to see Pa and Tex shaking their fists, then they disappeared from the window. That was me done. There was no one there. No one waiting to rescue me.

126

Chapter 28

The Escape

My mind overloaded. Like someone demented, I picked up a handful of snow and threw it in the air, blobs of it landing on my face and I started to laugh. I couldn't see the point in crying. I'd just have to wait there and to take whatever punishment they decided. But then I did start to sob, when I noticed Nat's SUV pull off of the highway and drive at speed toward me. I was laughing and tearful at the same time, when he skidded to a halt beside me.

"Get in," he said.

I was in too much pain to move. Besides, it was too late as Pa and Tex appeared at the doorway.

"Stay right there, or I'll put one right between your eyes," Jordan called out.

I snatched my head to look in the direction of Tex's truck. Jordan was leaning on the hood behind the engine block. He had his rifle pointed at Pa and Tex who were now on the porch. Jordan had one eye closed and the other glued to the scope.

"You won't get away with this," Pa shouted through gritted teeth. Tex looked terrified.

"Hey, what the hell is this?" Tex said.

Nat reached over and opened the passenger door. No one answered Tex as footsteps crunched on the snow beside me. Arms scooped under my armpits, then they lifted me and launched me onto the passenger seat. Left speechless, Jordan's friends jumped in and clambered onto the back seat. Nat swung the steering wheel and turned his vehicle to face the highway. Jordan stalked across the drive, still shouldering his rifle, not taking his eye off Pa and Tex for one second. He jumped in the back with his friends, slamming the door behind him, and we sped away past Pa and Tex. That last image will stay with me forever as Pa took off his hat, threw it on the floorboards, then stamped on it and rushed inside the house.

"Damn, he's gotten a rifle, duck," someone in the back said.

We skidded past the gatepost and onto the road. Nat nearly lost control and he swung his steering wheel violently to bring it out of a skid. I couldn't stop laughing.

"What's there to laugh at?" Nat said.

"The rifle chamber's empty. I took the round out when he was away."

The guys started to whoop, though I doubted it was out of bravado, but relief at having gotten away unscathed.

"Where are we going?" I said.

There was some pushing and thrusting in the back. Jordan had moved between his friends and leaned between the seats.

"We'll hang out in town. I don't get Mom's car until two o' clock, then I can take you to you know where."

"What's that mean, 'you know where'?" Nat said.

"It's somewhere secret for her to hide away and it wouldn't be a secret if anyone else knew, dumbass."

"You never said. I've told my mom she can stay in our spare room."

"In your dreams, asshole."

Nat jammed on the brake pedal and slewed to a halt. I'd been wondering how they'd managed a truce.

"All right, that's enough. We'll see who's an asshole. Get out and we'll settle it right now. She comes with me."

Nat didn't look to be in any shape to fight with his wrist still bandaged and the cut under his eye, surrounded by a patch of purple, black, and yellow skin.

"Whoa there you two, settle down. For one, I'm not in any shape to go hiking to where we'd said, and I don't have my backpack. And secondly, I'm grateful to all of you for saving me, so I'm not going to come between you both and stay at Nat's house."

"What then?" Jordan said.

"I don't know," I said, and grimaced. The pain running through my butt was excruciating.

"What's wrong? Have you twisted your ankle?" Nat asked.

"No, I fell on my ass and I have a pain in my butt running down the back of my leg."

"That's sciatica," Jordan said. "I had it once when I fell off of a haystack. It'll take a few days of rest to go away."

Nat huffed and turned to Jordan, then said, "Are you sure you didn't fall on your head at the same time, 'cause you've still gotten shit for brains. Like I said, she'd be better off resting up at mine."

"F off, dipshit. All you want is a babysitter for your mom."

"Please, can we just get away from here?" I pleaded.

Nat gritted his teeth, not responding to Jordan's jibe, and put his foot on the gas pedal, and then we headed for town. The banter had taken away everyone's adrenalin rush, with no more words spoken as we hit the outskirts of town.

"What about the priest?" a voice said from the backseat.

"What about Father David?" Nat said, and pulled over to the sidewalk, then threw his arm over his chair and turned.

"I'm Drake, by the way," said one of them behind me, then he smiled as I turned, and he shook my hand.

"And I'm Rick," the other one said. He reached over, took my hand by the fingers and turning it over, he kissed the back of it, and then grinned. Jordan slapped him on the back of his head.

"Hey, less of that, moron," Jordan said.

"Go on then, what about Father David?" Nat asked.

Drake shrugged his shoulders. "Dunno, but maybe he can help. Isn't the church supposed to look after people in need? What's that word they use?"

"You mean like sanctuary?" I said.

"Yeah, that's the one."

Nat slapped the steering wheel. "Look, we're only five minutes from my home. I'll take her there."

"No, wait, Drake's right. Maybe the priest can help. How are you gonna work with two sick women to look after?" Jordan said. "At least we could ask him."

"Okay, but if he can't help, she comes with me. There's no other option."

Nat set off with the vehicle lurching. It was obvious that he was annoyed. We pulled up outside the cottage.

"Y'all stay here. I'll go and explain," said Jordan.

"What, you? You think he'll listen to you?"

"Okay, choirboy, we'll both go."

They both climbed out of the cab. Jordan opened the picket fence gate and beckoned Nat through with a sweep of his hand, then tripped him with his foot as he walked past and scurried to the door before him. Nat caught up with him and the door opened, then they disappeared inside.

"Is it true that Nat proposed to Clarissa?"

"Yeah."

"How come Jordan managed to get Nat to help him?"

"Beats me," said Drake. "It's obvious they've both gotten a soft spot for you. Maybe it's that."

"Listen, I can't thank you both enough. You've no idea what you've saved me from."

"Oh, I think we know. Jordan told us. Besides, it was fun."

"Fun!" Rick said. "I near shit my pants when he came running outside with the rifle."

They both roared with laughter, aiming imaginary rifles at each other. There I was thinking they were demons, and all the time they'd been my saviors. I jumped at a tap on the window.

"Help get her inside," Jordan said, and opened my door.

Drake and Rick climbed out of the cab, then helped me onto the sidewalk. Not sure which was more painful, the pain that ran through me when I tried to put weight on my foot, or them lifting me and carrying me down the pathway and on through to the living room.

"Set her down on the couch," Father David said. "You can stay here until you recover, then you'll have to decide what you want to do."

Nat looked to be pissed at his offer for me to stay there. Jordan nudged Drake and nodded in Nat's direction. I didn't have a clue what I'd do once I had recovered. All I did know; was that for now I was safe. I doubted it would be the end of it knowing Pa, especially if he had to give the so-called dowry back.

130

Chapter 29

Sanctuary

Nat looked on over Father David's shoulder as they all clambered around in the living room after settling me on the sofa. I sensed that Nat was uncomfortable from his expression, and the way he kept looking at his wristwatch. Then Drake's sleight of hand caught my attention. I glared tightlipped at him, when I'd noticed him pick up an amber paperweight behind Father David's back and he palmed it into his pocket. He must have gotten the message, and retrieving it from his pocket, he placed it back on the shelf in the display cabinet.

"C'mon all of ya, we should get going and leave her to settle in and rest," Nat said.

"Good idea," Father David said. "I'm sure it's all being very traumatic for everyone. You can call to see how she is later." Then as an afterthought, he added, "by telephone."

Drake and Rick headed for the front door, but Nat and Jordan stood their ground. Nat looked agitated and glanced at his watch again.

"After you," Jordan said.

"No, after you," Nat replied.

"Got somewhere you need to be?"

"Mom will need her medication and I'm late, that's all."

It was clear that neither of them wanted to be the first to leave.

"Oh for goodness sake, both of you come here and give me a hug, then the both of you can skedaddle."

I hugged each one in turn. Nat waited at the door and jostled Jordan into the hallway, then the front door closed.

"Well, young lady. Sounds like you've had quite a day."

"Guess so."

"Do you have any medical insurance?"

"No, nothing like that. If either of us ailed anything, either we caught salmon for the medics, or sometimes we gave pelts in exchange for treatment. Jordan says it'll pass if I rest."

"Ah, yes, the sheriff said you were both from Alaska. I hope Jordan is right about a quick recovery, but I wouldn't take all he says as the gospel truth. I have some over-the-counter painkillers, and muscle relaxants. You can try those. Don't worry, I won't expect you to go fishing to pay for them when you recover," he said, and laughed at his own pun.

I was grateful for the pills and swallowed them dry. It was looking as though everyone had Jordan down as the bad guy. Without his concern, I'd have been on my way to the Sierra Nevada Mountains by now. An urge to defend him surfaced.

"I know people don't like Jordan around here, but if it wasn't for him, I'd never have gotten away."

"Well, yes, I'll credit him with that."

It bugged me that he knew we were from Alaska. He'd likely talked to the sheriff about us. But then thinking about it, that was prob'ly from the sheriff making enquiries about the fight at the community hall. The note headed, "Clarissa MacCaffrey" in the sheriff's file was prob'ly her statement, though more likely it was her complaint pointing the guilt in my direction. Having the same surname as the sheriff, I wondered if they were related. Thinking about my encounter with the sheriff, I shuffled on the cushion. Panic rose inside of me that he'd tell the sheriff about what I'd done and she'd insist on taking me home again.

"Listen, you won't tell the sheriff about me leaving home, will you? Only, I don't want her taking me back there."

"No, don't worry. Jordan told me what happened. I can now understand why you asked those questions about arranged marriages. You're safe here. Looks as though they saved you in time."

How wrong he was. I was too embarrassed to tell him there and then that I was now Mrs. Rhymer. I hadn't even had the courage to tell Nat and Jordan that we'd had the ceremony. I slipped the Bible from under my jacket.

"Could you put this on the table for me, please?"

He took it from me, looked at the spine, then opened it and flicked the pages, stopping every now and then. Father David looked troubled.

"I see this Bible is well thumbed. Tell me, what are the passages underlined for in red on some of the Old Testament books?"

"Oh those. You'll find them all the way through. Pa used to mark some of them for me when we had study lessons."

"Really. I see there are some pages missing. The book of Leviticus has all the pages torn out."

"Yeah, Pa said that not all that was written in the Bible was to be followed. He said that the Devil had gotten into the heads of some of the scribes. He said there were many false Bibles out there with the different religions all claiming the truth. Pa said that God came to him and gave him the truth."

Father David lifted his eyes over his half-rimmed spectacles.

"Did he now? So I take it you've not been brought up in the Catholic faith?"

I hoped this wasn't a prelude to him preaching at me. I'd had enough preaching from Pa to last a lifetime.

"No. Pa says we're nearer to Protestant."

"Tell me, have you ever been baptized?"

Recollection of the event as if it were branded on my brain had me shuddering. Pa had filled an old tin bathtub with water after we returned home from a long car journey. It was one of my earliest memories as a child, and one of the first things he did before telling me about Ma dying after her accident. I could still recall standing there naked with my feet in the tub of freezing cold water, then him forcibly immersing me.

"Yeah. Pa did it. Ducked me under the water in an old tin bath we had and said the words. Why?"

"I won't trouble you with it now, how are you?"

"Just a dull pain here," I said, and pointed to my butt. "I think the rest and the tablets have helped. Can't feel the pain in my calf, but I daren't stand."

He closed the Bible and placed it on the table. Next to it on a small sloping desk was a large embossed leather book, the likes of which I'd never seen, and it was covered with a glass case.

"Is that your Bible?"

"Well, I'd say that I was more of a custodian. It was brought here from Ireland by the original settlers of the town, and gifted to the church.

"Would that be the MacCaffreys?"

"Ah, so you know of our history? I suppose that as Nat's a MacCaffrey, he's told you about the town's past."

"No, he never said. But now you say that, it seems as though everyone I've met is called MacCaffrey. Is that an Irish, or a Scottish name?

"Tis Irish," he said, in a funny accent. "But no, the townsfolk aren't all called MacCaffrey. We have our fair share of O'Neils and a whole host of others. The town was first established near to where the Hunters had staked out some territory."

"You mean trappers?"

"Well yes, they were trappers, but their family name was Hunter. That's where the town's name came from when they bequeathed the land to us. Then there was a falling out with the Hunters during a harsh winter when food supplies dwindled, and the town ended up in a feud over trapping rights. It was quite a bloody affair. There's been an undercurrent of bad blood ever since, but it's kept behind closed doors."

My mind drifted to the sign for Hunter's Farm where Jordan lived.

"So is Jordan a Hunter?"

"Yes. I'm surprised you didn't know that already."

I wondered if maybe that's where the rivalry came from between Nat and Jordan.

"So is Clarissa related to Nat?"

"No, she comes from a different far removed line of MacCaffreys who arrived later. Listen, I'll let you put your feet up on the sofa and rest. I'll be in my study if you need anything. You can sleep on there until you can make it to the spare bedroom. I'll get you a blanket later."

There was a knock on the front door. Father David left the room. Hearing the voice of the caller, my chest tightened.

Chapter 30

Somehow, I didn't feel right to be under the roof of someone that was the custodian of a so-called house of God. Maybe it was because Pa had berated other religions than his own as false and not worthy. Pa ramming down my throat that Mary married an older Joseph at the behest of a priest played heavily on my mind. It was there in my Bible in black and white. The words of God. If arranged marriages were the will of God, then I knew that I had sinned and could expect to be struck down at any time for disobedience. All my life, Pa had used that fallback of God's retribution to add to the fear of his own wrath, and that had kept me passive to his abusive nature and to obey him. It was only recollection of Father David saying it wasn't the done thing for arranged marriages in this day and age that gave me hope of redemption. There was that, and the fact that I hadn't been turned to a pillar of salt like Lot's wife for her disobedience.

Straining my ears, I attempted to listen into the conversation at the door. I prayed that he wouldn't ask the visitor inside, or should I say visitors. It was too much to expect for my prayer to be answered, when the visitors appeared at the living room door. Clarissa appeared first, then two of her friends, followed by Father David.

"I'll go to my office and leave you to it," Father David said.

Totally unexpected, I was mystified why'd they'd want to see me. I hoped they'd not come to gloat. They all shuffled inside the living room, with Clarissa to the fore. The gauze that Jordan mentioned was gone from her nose, but there was a small gash on the bridge.

"We've come to say sorry... you know... for the other night at the dance."

I sighed with relief.

"Likewise," I said, though I thought she deserved the punch I gave her.

"Here, we've brought you these," she said, and held out a large shopping bag.

I half-expected it to be some kinda joke, and took the bag from her and peaked inside.

"It's just a few items of clothing we've rustled up. We hope they fit. Nat phoned me. He explained the situation and said you didn't have any changes of clothes."

Emotion gushed inside me. My eyes moistened.

"Hey, keep yourself together," Clarissa said, then took a seat beside me. She placed her arm around my shoulder and gave me a hug.

"I... I don't know what to say."

"Then don't say anything. Father David said not to stay long. Said you injured your back and needed rest, so we'll be going. Maybe if you're feeling better tomorrow night, we can call around and have a girly evening."

I didn't have a clue what she meant, but I was overwhelmed at the change in attitude and kindness.

"That would be great," I said. "Thanks for the clothes."

"Don't mention it," she said, and rose from the sofa, then they all shuffled back out of the room.

"We'll see our own way out, Father David," Clarissa called out, then the front door closed.

The whole episode left me floundering and wondering if there was some ulterior motive that would manifest at this so-called girly evening. Father David walked into the room.

"They're good girls really. It's as I said when I took you home; jealousy tends to rear its ugly head in town from time to time. I think the clothes they gave you will count as penance for their sins."

"Penance! What's that?"

"Atonement for sins."

"Atonement?"

"It's a means of amending for one's own sins, to make things right in the eyes of God for forgiveness."

"Oh, yeah, Pa never preached that. So if you do a good deed,

God forgives your sins?"

"Well, yes, that's the idea, but I was thinking more in terms of our confession rites where you confess your sins and I ask you to do penance, which can be say to recite three Hail Mary's for God's forgiveness for your sins, or maybe an Our Father. It could even be to go away and do a good deed."

I gulped and pushed back on the sofa. My eyes popped.

"You mean Clarissa was tortured into giving a confession, and then forced into giving me the clothes for her picking that fight with me, like in the inquisition?"

He clasped his hands together as if about to pray and looked up at the ceiling.

"Dear Mary, mother of Jesus, no, not that type of confession," he said, and laughed, then took a seat on the chair opposite.

"What's a Hail Mary?"

"It's a prayer. I have a copy somewhere." He reached over to his bookcase, retrieved a small Bible and pulled out a piece of paper.

It sounded a better way of getting forgiveness than having Pa standing over me and making me gargle with soap and water.

"Here," he said. "This has both the Hail Mary and the Our Father prayer."

I knew The Lord's Prayer off by heart, but the Hail Mary one was a new one on me.

"So have I got this right? I confess my sins to you voluntary, then you ask me to recite prayers and after that I'm forgiven?"

"Yes, that's how it works for all in the Catholic faith. Maybe tomorrow if you feel better I can give you a tour around the church. We have a confession box I can show you. I sit in one side of a screen, and the person sits in the other side." He placed his Bible on the table next to mine. "Listen, I'd love to keep you company, but I have a sermon to write. Put your feet up on the sofa and try to rest. Sorry I don't have a television. Can I get you a sandwich and coffee?"

"I couldn't eat or drink anything just now. I didn't sleep last night, so I'll just try and relax. Then hopefully I'll get some shut-eye."

"Good, good. Mrs. O'Ahern brings me a meal in the evenings. I'll phone her and ask her to make some extra."

Father David rose from his chair and stepped out of the room. Not having a television didn't bother me in the slightest. As much as I was pleased with everyone's help, I was still befuddled with doubts. The questions I had weren't all about where I went from there. I was a married woman on the run. I couldn't imagine how any man would want a woman who ran out on their husband. Those thoughts didn't bode well for any sort of the future I'd dreamed about recently. My brain must have overloaded with all the unanswered questions and my eyelids became heavy. Finally, I succumbed, yielding to the inevitable, and drifted into oblivion.

I awoke to find a cover over me, surrounded by darkness, and I was sweating. The front door closed, and throwing my legs over the side of the sofa, I sat upright. With all the hubbub, I'd not really noticed the heat in the room. Now I was mystified as there wasn't a stove in sight. My subconscious must have known that the heat troubled me before I'd dozed off. I'd imagined it was hell's fires burning in a nightmare I'd had. The townsfolk had been surrounding me, threatening torture if I didn't confess my sins. Father David entered the living room and flicked the light switch.

"Ah, I see you're awake. Good, good. I have your meal here," he said, then set the plate down on the low table in front of me.

"Thanks."

I tucked in and devoured the meal, hardly coming up for air.

"How do you feel?"

"Fine, the pain has gone, but it's hot in here," I said, and fanned my face with the prayer paper. "Where does the heat come from?"

"We have oil-fired heating. There's an oil burner out back. It heats water in a boiler and pumps it through pipes to radiators in all the rooms. I'll turn down the thermostat."

Relief washed through me. It wasn't worth asking what he meant by a thermostat, because I sensed awkwardness in Father David's demeanor. I hoped it wasn't at my ignorance.

"Not wishing to pry, but when were you due to be wed?"

I hesitated to tell him the truth that I was already wed. Pa had told me about Chinese whispers on the outside, and that was one reason for us not to have contact with them. The few hours I'd spent in town had so far proved him right. Jordan had told his friends and Nat about my plight. In turn Nat had told Clarissa, and she had told her friends. The sheriff had obviously spoken to Father David about us coming from Alaska. I guessed that the entire town would know by now.

"W... we. I mean—"

The words stuck in my craw again, just as they did at the ceremony. It was a fight with my conscience as I looked around, wishing I had a magic spell to make me disappear. Father David's landline rang, giving me more time to think on how to answer him. He picked up the handset and answered the phone call.

"Yes. Yes. Oh dear." He looked at me over his half-rimmed spectacles, and then glanced away. "Okay, if you hear anything else let me know," he said, then placed the handset on the cradle. A troubled expression appeared on his face. He hummed and ahhed a few times. It looked as though it was his turn to have the words stuck in his throat.

"Is everything okay?"

"I... I have some news about your dad and his friend that could mean trouble."

Chapter 31

The Revelation

Not wanting to miss a word of what Father David had to say, I leaned forward. My brain was still mashed with all that had happened. I guessed it would have been too much to expect for Pa to have gone with Tex to his sawmill and forgotten all about me. It wasn't Pa's way. An eye for an eye and all that. Still, it was no good guessing what news Father David had of them. He had his handkerchief to his mouth, coughing and spluttering. I didn't know if he was coming down with a cold, or if it was nerves, with him now regretting having told me that the call was about Pa and Tex.

"Well, what have you heard?"

"Excuse me, sorry about that. Maybe I shouldn't have said, but forewarned is forearmed. That was Tiff MacCaffrey from the garage. He was called out to your homestead, something about flat tires."

I stifled a snicker, and attempted to keep a straight face.

"Apparently, your dad was asking if he'd seen you, and they gave him a description. Same thing with Jordan and his friends. Oh and Nat too. He actually named Nat. Your dad was asking where they lived."

He did that coughing thing again.

"And?"

"Sorry. Of course, Tiff told him he didn't know anything. The strange thing was he described you as the other person's wife." He glanced directly over his half-rimmed glasses again, but this time with an arched eyebrow. "They said they'd come looking for you and the others first light tomorrow. Is there something I'm missing in your story?"

It was those Chinese whispers again. I imagined that Jordan had told Tiff to expect a phone call. Now I definitely knew all the town would know that I'd ran away from my husband.

Especially when Pa and Tex came to town asking questions and getting into conversation with some made-up trickery. Pushing back on the sofa, it was my turn to cough and splutter, then the floodgates opened. I was thankful he didn't come to me to offer comfort. The last thing I wanted was the sympathy of a man. Pulling myself together, I took a deep breath, then wiped my sleeve across my eyes.

"You might as well know. I... I'm... married." I'd sucked in faltering breaths between the words and tried to hold it together. "Pa pronounced us man and wife on Sunday. I'm Mrs. Rhymer now."

He curled his fingers into a fist under his chin, leaving one free to tap his lips.

"Go on."

"I didn't say 'I will.' I only managed to say the 'I', but Pa insisted he'd heard me say the words."

"I take it your dad holds a license to perform ceremonies in Colorado and you both signed the certificate?"

"Didn't sign nothing. I wouldn't know anything about him being licensed."

"Really!"

"We haven't had... you know, if that's what you're thinking. He was too drunk."

"Well, that's a relief. So you haven't consummated the marriage. In that case from all you have said, I can tell you with certainty that in the eyes of the law, and in the eyes of God, you're not married. So you can rest easy."

"But how can I not be married just because we haven't, you know?" I said, and blushed. "Wasn't Joseph married to Mary and she remained a virgin even with the birth of Jesus after they were wed?"

Father David let out a childish snicker.

"Well yes, but you have to consider the circumstances and to factor in that it was important for Jesus to have a legal father and mother, given the customs and laws of the day for the Jewish Nation. Bear in mind that this was pre-Christianity. We now live in the United States of America in the twenty-first century and there are laws of the land, which are in this sense no different from those in ancient Israel. Marriages have to be entered into with both parties in agreement. That's why by law in the US, both have to be present in person at the register office to show them the certificate, and to have it recorded for it to be legal. And that has to happen within twenty-one days of a ceremony."

"So are you saying I'm definitely not married?" I said, followed by my mouth gaping, and fixing a wide-eyed gaze at him, desperately hoping this wasn't some sort of trickery that Pa would use.

"That's what I am saying. I'm also saying that other than what you said about Mary and Joseph, which was at the priest's behest, the Bible doesn't mention anything as to His stance on arranged marriages. That's not to say there weren't any in those days that are mentioned as historical stories. You should also note that the contract Mary and Joseph entered into was consensual. Your arrangement certainly wasn't that."

The weight pressing on my shoulders and the dark cast behind my eyes lifted.

The landline rang again and he answered the call. Covering the mouthpiece, he whispered, "It's Jordan. Are you up to talking to him?"

"Sure."

He passed me the handset.

"Hi," he said. "How do you feel?"

"On top of the world."

"That's a difference. Listen, I don't like to tell you this, but stay inside tomorrow. I've had word that your dad and that old creep are coming looking for you in town. Don't worry, I've spoken to Nat and we'll get word around. Well, Nat will. No one will listen to a Hunter. None of them will give you away."

"I already know. Father David was tipped off. Listen, you, your friends, and Nat, be careful. He'll not only be looking for me. Pa will be looking to settle a score for what you all did."

"In his dreams. Don't worry. I can look after myself."

"Jordan?"

"What?"

"Be really careful."

143

"You too. I have to go. Dad doesn't let me use the home phone and my cell phone is out of credit. I can hear him in the hallway."

"Damned freeloader," I heard a male voice call out, and the line went dead.

I handed back the handset to Father David.

"Does everybody around here always find out everyone's business?"

Father David smiled.

"Well, we are a small tight knit community, so word does get around. I think I get to know more than most because of the confessional, but as I said before, what I hear in the confession booth is between me, the individual, and God."

He was obviously a kind and warmhearted person of the cloth. For the first time in my life—no make that a second after Nat, Jordan, and his friends—I felt he was someone I could trust. I began to wish I was of his faith so I could confess my sins.

"Do you feel well enough to make it to the spare bedroom?"

"I'll try." Using both my hands on the cushion, I pushed up to my feet. "So far, so good."

I glanced at my Bible, then at Father David's Bible. He must have seen be looking between the two of them.

"You can take mine with you if you like. No pressure. I'm wondering if you would consider reading Leviticus, then maybe we could discuss what you find in there tomorrow. It's up to you. I'm not insisting."

He didn't have to insist, curiosity had been getting the better of me ever since I'd awoken.

"Thanks, I will."

I scooped up his Bible and followed him out into the hall, then up the stairway. He pointed to the end of the upstairs hallway.

"That's your room." He looked at his watch. "The heating cuts off in one hour, so you'll be snug as a bug in a rug by then. Mrs. O'Ahern has made the bed with fresh linen. You'll find the key inside the door. I have a few more things to attend to in my office, then I'll turn in myself. I'll see you in the morning."

"Thank you," I said, then turned and walked on into the bedroom. Closing the door behind me, I locked the door.

He was right about it being hot. It was such a difference to the musty smell back at the homestead, with the freezing air that you could cut through with a knife. I pressed the switch on the bedside lamp. There were some fresh flowers in a vase on the nightstand. I picked up the pillow and held it to my nose. It was so soft, with the smell of freshly laundered linen.

Glancing out of the window, despite the darkness of the night, the town looked as picturesque as the first time I had seen it. I could still see the houses set against the blanket of snow and from the streetlights, together with the glow from the windows and a full moon. Pa had been lying to me. These weren't the disciples of Satan taking warmth inside their homes, they were God-fearing people. I wondered just what other lies he had indoctrinated me with over the years, and leaping onto the bed, I flicked open the Bible to Leviticus. If nothing else, I hoped to find out why Father David had led me to reading the book, without him insisting I did so.

Chapter 32

Confession

I'd been awake since dawn broke, and I pulled the bedside chair in front of the window. With my feet pulled up onto the seat and my arms cradled around my legs, I swayed back and forth. Gazing out through the window, there hadn't been any movement on Main Street, except for the odd stray cat or dog. Although, saying that, there could have been people around I'd missed, as I'd kept drifting in and out of a trance like state when counting my bobbing on the chair. The rhythm of the movement emptied my head, but not for long as I kept losing count.

I glanced at Father David's Bible on the nightstand open at Leviticus, chapter eighteen, verse six, and reached across, then picked it up to read it one more time. I pulled it to my chest. Tears welled and ran down my cheeks. I looked up at the ceiling and closed my eyes. I prayed that God would put a gun in my hand so that I could kill Pa, if, or should I say, when he turned up in town. I opened my eyes and placed the Bible back on the nightstand.

I felt dirty as though my very soul was soiled. Rising from my chair, I stripped and wrapped a blanket around me, then unlocked the door and hurried to the bathroom. Stepping under the shower, I scrubbed my body with a soaped nailbrush until my skin was raw to the touch, in the hope God would understand my pain, and that He would forgive my ignorance. After drying myself, I trudged back to the bedroom and then dressed.

A rap on my bedroom door snapped me out of my thoughts.

"Father David?"

"No, it's Mrs. O'Ahern. Breakfast is set, dear."

"Okay, I'll be down soon."

I didn't want to go down for breakfast. If only I hadn't left

147

my backpack at the barn, I could have sneaked away through the back door, hopefully to leave the embarrassment of what I'd discovered behind me. No wonder Pa had torn Leviticus out of my Bible. Rummaging through the bag of clothes from Clarissa, I dressed, and then one last time I glanced through the window. The sheriff pulled up outside her office in her SUV. She climbed out of her cab, unlocked the door to her office, then entered. She wasn't in there more than a minute as she rushed out to her vehicle, and then drove off in the opposite direction of our homestead. So much for wishing that she had something on Pa in that file of hers that would lead to his arrest before he showed up in town.

The street was busy now. People going about their business. Opening stores. Clearing away the snow from the sidewalk. A truck passed by with a snowplow to the fore, pushing all before it, and spreading rock salt on the road. It was time to face Father David and to hope that I could avoid questions about what I'd found in Leviticus.

At first, I labored down the stairway, but then I breathed in the aroma of bacon and coffee vying for my sense of smell and I hurried along the hallway to the dining room.

"Slept well, I hope?" Father David said.

I nodded, not wanting to tell him the truth.

"I've made you bacon and egg, dear," said Mrs. O'Ahern, as she poured coffee in to a mug next to my plate, then beckoned me to sit at the table.

"Thanks for all this. Least I can do is to clear up the breakfast dishes and wash them when we've finished."

"I won't hear of it," said Mrs. O'Ahern. She turned to Father David, "After you've finished and I've cleared up here, I have shopping to do. I'll collect your vestments and the choir's garments around eleven and take them for cleaning."

Father David nodded in the middle of taking a bite of toast.

Avoiding his gaze, I concentrated on eating my breakfast. Father David drained the last of his coffee, then pushed back on his chair. He picked up a napkin and wiped his lips.

"Well, young lady, what are we to do with you today?"

I shrugged my shoulders, still chewing on the last sliver of bacon that had long since wanted to slide down my gullet.

"Ah, yes, I'd said that I'd show you the church. We can go now if you're finished. I have the vestments to gather, and I'm expecting someone visiting to discuss repairs that I need to be done on the spire. Better that you stay by my side in case your dad turns up in town."

I could hardly tell him that I just wanted to hide away in my bedroom. Especially after the kindness he had shown me.

"Incidentally, I've spoken with our Bishop this morning. We have a home in Denver that we sponsor, and he says there is a place for you there. It's completely free and they have councilors to help you to adjust to a new self-reliant lifestyle. Most of the women there are taking shelter from violent and abusive families. What do you think?"

I didn't think anything. He did that looking up again at me over his half-rimmed spectacles, with his head bowed, waiting for an answer. It wasn't company that I was seeking, or counseling, but solitude.

"I'm a bit mixed up at the moment. Can we talk about it later?"

"Oh, yes, sorry. You're welcome to stay here a few days. So there's plenty of time for you to get your head together."

Reality set in. A few days could mean two or three at most. What then? I thought. Pa had talked about freeloaders. That's what I imagined I'd be while ever I stayed there. He rose from his chair and shuffled to the side of me.

"Shall we?" he said, and beckoned me with a sweep of his hand to go with him. "There's no heating in the church I'm afraid, so grab your jacket from the stand in the hallway."

We made our way to a side door to the church through the backyard. For all that the town was supposed to be dying; the wooden fascia boards had the appearance that they were freshly painted. My eyes widened as we walked inside. A sense of serenity washed over me as I gazed around. All the walls were painted white, but the ceiling was painted light blue as if it were open to the sky. Representations of clouds were evenly spaced with the edges painted gold, and with the images of angels in the center. Father David walked to the center of an aisle between two rows of oak pews and knelt in prayer on a carpeted step facing an altar area. I felt like a spare part standing there, taking it all in. In the center of the altar was a brass crucifix, framed with candlesticks and statues either side, with Jesus holding out a hand, and the other of Mary holding her child. All the windows in the altar area had beautiful stained glass depictions of Saints, bathing the altar area with rainbows of colors. The rest of the windows where ordinary glass letting the natural light stream through. What seemed out of place was a large gnarled and twisted wooden cross, maybe ten feet high, to the left and front of the altar, and draped with a white soiled cloth. Father David made the sign of the cross to his chest, then rose and turned to me.

"The wooden cross looks out of place with that dirty rag draped over it."

"Ah, yes, the cross. It was brought here by the first settlers all the way from Ireland. The cloth is the cover from MacCaffrey's station wagon that brought it here. That cross is very dear to all our hearts. We carry it together with a crucifix in our Good Friday procession." He stroked his chin. "You look troubled. Is there anything you wish to talk to me about that is troubling you? I was thinking last night. As you said you're a Protestant and you've been baptized, I could take your confession. Seeing as how you are starting a new life, this could be an opportunity for you to absolve yourself of all sin for what lies ahead."

Father David went on to explain what he meant and how the confession ritual unfolded. He pointed to the confession booth. I looked down at my boots. It didn't sound as though I'd have to explain the sins of my Pa, only my own.

"Okay," I said, and looked directly at him, raising a faint smile, but inside I was trembling as I stepped over to the booth and took a seat.

I drew in a deep breath, soaking up the smell of lavender wood polish, not really knowing how to start off my confession. I knew what was troubling me and blurted it out. "I... I have one sin that is with me daily that I can't get out of my head. I wish my Pa dead. Not only that, I have visions and thoughts of me killing him by my own hands in any number of ways."

"Do you wish to tell me why?"

I sucked in faltering breaths, overcome by emotion.

"N... No... not really."

"Hmm. Well, what I can tell you is that Satan manifests in many ways to get into your mind to do evil deeds. You must fight to push him away. Turn your cheek the other way to those who sin against you. I'm going to ask that you find forgiveness, and to walk out of here with love in your heart, and to recite an Our Father and three Hail Mary's from the prayer paper that I gave you, for you to ask for God's forgiveness, and then you can walk out of here renewed in the faith of God."

It seemed to be such a small price to pay, except I'd left the prayer paper in his Bible at the side of my bed.

"Thanks, I'll do that."

"Good, good. I'll leave you here to contemplate while I collect the vestments."

In the darkness of the booth, I descended into depression and closed my eyes. All I'd heard were his words. The words didn't make sense. How could he expect me to have forgiveness and love in my heart for someone who had defiled me? I still wanted Pa to burn in hell, even if I had to send him there. My eyes flicked open when I heard a voice that I recognized call out Father David by name.

Chapter 33

Two Offers

The sound of his voice bounced of all the walls in the church. It had never occurred to me Nat would be the one that Father David wanted to discuss repairs that he needed to be done to the spire. I stepped out of the booth.

"Hi, Clara, is Father David here?"

"Yeah, he's in the back collecting clothes for cleaning."

"Okay, I'll wait here," he said, and took a seat on a pew. He slapped the wooden seat. "Come and join me."

Instead of sitting next to him, I took a seat on the pew behind him. He was wearing dark blue overalls with a waist belt adorned with the tools of his handyman trade.

He turned sideways.

"Listen. I have an offer to make you. All I'm asking is that you listen. You don't have to answer right away."

As flattered as I was, I hoped he wouldn't dare propose to me in church. There was no doubt that I liked him, but I hardly knew him. Thinking that, I also knew enough from Jordan to be wary of him and his intentions.

"I was thinking. You can't stay with Father David forever. My offer still stands for you to stay with Ma and me, but before you say anything hear me out. I'd like to make it a formal arrangement."

I could feel the heat rising in my cheeks and decided to slap his face if he proposed. There was a sense that the slap would come sooner rather than later if I had him figured as to what he meant by a formal arrangement.

"Look, I need someone to look after Ma while I'm working and to do the cooking and cleaning. I can't pay anything, but I can give you a roof over your head and all your meals. You'll have your own room, but I'm hoping we can sort of start seeing each other and see where it goes."

I let out a long sigh of relief, and looked up at the angels on the ceiling, hoping for inspiration as to how I would answer him without hurting his feelings. Last thing I wanted was to be at someone's every beck and call. I'd had a lifetime of that.

"Nat, you're really sweet, and I do like you, not to mention that you rescued me, but that wouldn't work. I need away from here while ever Pa is at the homestead. Sorry. Besides, Clarissa wouldn't take kindly to me living under the same roof as you."

His little boy lost look was replaced with a questioning glare.

"What's she got to do with it?"

"You know the answer to that. It's obvious she's still in love with you. That's why she turned on me at the dance. It had nothing to do with Jordan. She was trying to make you jealous by flirting with him. It must have been driving her mad that I was with you. You must know that. You really should try and sort things out with her."

He huffed a few times, then his cheeks flamed.

"That aside, if your Pa wasn't on the scene and Clarissa was at college, would you consider the offer, even if it was just to try it out?"

I sucked on my bottom lip. It felt like I'd been walked into a trap. There was no doubt it would have been tempting, given that I didn't want to move into the women's shelter in Denver.

"It's a maybe. It's the wrong time to be asking me just now, I'm so messed up."

"Well, the offer is there," he said, then rose to his feet.

"Ah, there you are, Nat. Come this way. I can show you what I need doing," Father David said, rescuing both our embarrassments.

Sitting there, I stared at the crucifix on the altar. I wasn't for clasping my hands in prayer, but I did hope that I would be forgiven, even if I still harbored evil thoughts about wishing Pa dead.

"Boo," someone said, at the same time that their hands clasped over my eyes from behind. "Guess who?"

I leapt to my feet and snatched the remaining hand away.

154

"Jordan, did you have to do that? I near jumped outta my skin."

"Sorry, don't be so jumpy. You're safe in here. There's no sign of your dad. Nat's spread the word, and my friends are watching the street. You can't stay here in town though. You know he'll turn up like a bad penny."

"Yeah, I know."

"That's why I'm here. Hear me out and tell me what you think."

I couldn't believe I was going to get a second proposal of sorts in such a short space of time. I bowed my head and rubbed my forehead.

"Go on then, what hair-brained schemes have you come up with this time? I hope it doesn't involve robbing the collection box."

"No, listen. I've had a serious talk with Mom. Mom's leaving Dad to go and live with her sister in Denver. She's had it with his drinking and abuse. Long and short is, before she does, I'm going with her this afternoon and she's buying me an SUV. She's also going to give me some money so I can leave here and strike out on my own."

"Well, good luck with that," I said, then dropped my butt back on the seat.

"Yeah, well, that's the thing see. What I was thinking is, we could go to Dad's cabin. Stay there a while. You could teach me to live off of the land, then we could move on in spring. What do you think?"

I rose to my feet and put my hands on my hips.

"We! There isn't any we. So get that right out of your head."

"Hey, keep your shirt on. Jesus, what the hell are you going to do then?"

"Have you no respect for the church. Go wash your mouth out."

Jordan mocked me by placing his hands on his hips and put his face close to mine.

"For your information I have zero respect. Never set eyes on a Bible, so it don't mean diddly to me. It's not like I'm offering to jump into the sack with you. Just friends getting together on a crazy jaunt, that's all. God damn it. Where's your sense of adventure?"

It wasn't adventure that I was after. Part of me wanted to jump at the offer, but I had my head to sort out first, and that would mean going solo.

"I thought your dad was a God fearing man. Didn't he take you to church?"

"Who said he was God fearing?"

"The sheriff did after Pa came out with his Bible that day."

"Oh, her. I wouldn't believe anything she says about our family. She's a MacCaffrey. She probably meant that he was fearful of anyone with religion that wielded a Bible, especially after what the townsfolk did to our ancestors."

"Yeah, Father David told me about the history. Listen, I appreciate the offer, I really do, and it's tempting, but I need some time on my own, then maybe we can catch up with each other."

Jordan punched the air.

"Whehey, at least it's not a no."

The door at the front of the church burst open. Drake stumbled inside out of breath. He doubled over sucking in air, then straightened up.

"They... they're here," he said, still blowing hard.

Rick joined him and slapped him on the back of the head.

"Close the door, moron. They'll see us."

"You were last in, you close it."

"Oh for goodness sake, I'll close it," I said, and stepped forward.

We all gathered around the side window. Pa's pickup was parked outside Mrs. MacCaffrey's store where I'd had coffee with Jordan. Pa walked out onto the porch and taking off his hat he slapped his thigh with it.

"He looks pissed," said Rick. "He won't have gotten any change outta Susan MacCaffrey."

"Hey, less of the foul mouth in church," I said.

Mrs. O'Ahern was walking along the sidewalk toward Pa. He stopped her and they had words. I ducked, after I saw her point at the church. It was looking as though everyone had overlooked telling her to keep where I was a secret.

"Damn it, he's jumped in his pickup and he's heading this way," Jordan said.

I gave up trying to tell them to watch their cussing. Jordan took hold of my hand and pulled me to my feet.

"Stand tall. What's he gonna do? He can't just walk in here and take you home," Jordan said.

I didn't know about standing tall, my whole demeanor shrank along with my shoulders. The rock salt had melted the snow. I wished it could have done the same for me and I could have melted away.

"What's all the fuss," Father David said, with Nat following in his wake as he swept down the aisle. Both were carrying large garbage bags. Prob'ly it was the vestments he'd collected for cleaning.

"Mrs. O'Ahern has given her away. Her dad and his friend are outside and getting out of his pickup. Oh crap, he has his rifle with him," Jordan said.

"Oh, dear, I never thought to tell her why she was here," said Father David, and he dropped the bag of clothing. Nat did the same and pushed past him. Father David caught hold of his belt stopping him in his tracks.

"Leave this to me," said Father David. "All of you go further back down the aisle."

Much as I applauded his bravado as I backed off down the aisle with the others, I didn't think that he knew what he was letting himself in for, and I held my hands together in prayer, while shaking from head to toe.

Chapter 34

Final Conflict

The door to the church swung wide open. Pa was standing there, holding his rifle across his waist. Tex hovered around behind him.

"She's there," said Tex.

Father David faced up to them and showed them his palms.

"You can't come in here if it's Clara that you're after. Especially not with a rifle. She has the sanctuary of the church."

Pa hawked some phlegm and spat it on the floor at Father David's feet.

"If ya knows what's good for ya, you'll step out of the way and let me collect what's mine," said Pa. "Clara, get your ass out here now."

I glanced around looking for somewhere to run and hide, but I couldn't have moved if I wanted to. Fear rooted me to the spot. Rick and Drake had no such problem, scrambling left and right along the pews.

Pa swung his rifle at his waist and pointed the business end at Father David.

"Whoa there," said Tex. "I want none of this. I'll wait in the pickup. Just return the dowry and forget the whole thing."

"No way, she'll come with us."

"You'd do well to join him, or face the wrath of God," Father David said.

"God, what do you know about God? This is the house of the Devil filled to the brim with idolatry. Now this is your last warning, step aside."

Father David stood his ground. Peering around Nat and Jordan, I saw that familiar cobra look in Pa's eyes and screamed out, "No, Pa, no."

In the blink of an eye, Pa swung the rifle butt, sinking it into

159

Father David's gut, then followed through as he stooped over, crashing the stock onto the back of his head. Father David keeled over and crumpled to the floor. Pa stepped over him, pointing the rifle down the aisle at us and stalked forward as we all backed away toward the altar.

"That's as far as you go, old man," Jordan called out from the front of the three of us, and he stopped backing away.

Nat stopped too and reached to his tool belt and grabbed his claw hammer.

Pa shook his head, then spat on the stone floor of the aisle.

"Oh, you're that sassy one. Jordan isn't it. If you aim a rifle at someone, you should be prepared to pull the trigger. You didn't have the balls back at the homestead, but I have. Now walk away and let Clara come home with me and no one will get hurt. We'll settle our scores later."

"You can't shoot all three of us. Not with a single-round, hunting rifle," Jordan said.

I rolled my eyes, knowing differently. I'd seen one of his rounds rip through two bears and end up embedded in a tree trunk. Rick and Drake ran out the door behind Pa.

"Best you put the rifle down, old timer. They've gone to get the sheriff," Nat called out.

"Don't matter none. I ain't got nothing to lose, but ten thousand reasons to gain," Pa said, and shouldering his rifle, he racked the slide with the bolt.

Pa closed one eye and aimed at Jordan through the crosshairs of his scope. I knew exactly what he meant by 'ten thousand reasons' and it sent me into a rage. I'd seen and heard enough. A red mist descended, freeing me from all fear. I pushed past Nat and Jordan.

"Clara, get back," said Jordan, and grabbed at my shoulder. I pushed his hand away.

"This is between Pa and me," I said, and glared at Pa, "What you gonna do, shoot me?"

Pa lowered his aim, then held his rifle across his waist.

"I'll deal with them later. Get in the pickup with your husband."

Pa backed off to the door as I marched at him. He stumbled

over Father David, losing his footing. I rushed at him, planting both my palms on his chest with as much force as I could muster. Pa staggered backwards through the door, then hit the step and fell outside onto his backside, losing his grip of his rifle. In the heat of the moment, I think it was Drake who grabbed his rifle and emptied the round from the chamber, then he threw it back at him. I stamped my feet, and shook my fists at Pa.

"How dare you think that you own me? You sold me for ten thousand dollars to marry that old creep in the pickup," I screamed, while standing over him. "You chained me and defiled me, beat me, and treated me as your sex slave, but no more. My whole life has been a lie. I'll see that you rot in hell fire."

Someone grabbed me from behind and pulled me away. I kicked out in Pa's direction but missed, while spitting and screaming at him. Turned out it was Jordan that had dragged me away as I was told later.

"Leave him. Let Nat and me deal with the pervert," Jordan said.

Next thing I saw was Nat charge at Pa with his claw hammer held aloft, and then he stopped in his tracks. Pa had thrown his jacket to one side and he'd pulled out his pistol. He scrambled to his feet and picked up his rifle. Then he clambered into the pickup and sped away.

That's when I saw Nat's hammer twisting through the air and smashing through the rear window of the pickup.

"You're dead if I see you again," Nat called out, top note.

"Yeah, that goes for me too," said Jordan, dancing on his toes. "Freakin' pervert. You're dead all right."

I dropped to my knees and clasped my hands over my eyes, then I shook my head.

"Grrrrr," I roared, and looked up at the sky, then out onto Main Street.

It was as if I was deaf and time had stood still. Nat was over at the butchers, standing on the sidewalk with Clarissa, both of them looking at me with horrified expressions frozen on their faces. A crowd had gathered, all of them drilling me with their own horrified expressions. Then as if released from the time warp, I heard the grumbling of the townsfolk all around me as they shuffled away, some turning to give me sideways glances. I turned to see Mrs. O'Ahern with Father David's arm over her shoulder and her helping him to the cottage. Drake and Rick averted their gaze when I glanced their way, and then inspected their boots. Jordan had his head in his hands, then turned and lashed out with his fist, destroying the plywood sign for the opening times of the services.

There was no need for Chinese whispers. Now everyone knew I'd been defiled from the words of my own mouth. I imagined they'd all think I was soiled. Like having crap on your shoes and turning your nose up at the stench. Nothing but dirt. No one came to offer solace. I didn't give them time, and scrambled to my feet, then ran to the cottage.

There were no tears as I slammed the bedroom door and turned the key in the lock, then dove on the bed. The rage that had consumed me left me drained of emotion. Calmness washed over me. I knew what I had to do. I reached out for the Bible and took the prayer paper from between the pages and slipped it into my pocket. It was time to leave the town behind. A sense of resignation and determination took over. I rolled over and stared at the ceiling. As soon as darkness fell, I determined that all I would need to do would be to sneak into the barn for my backpack, then for me to disappear. All I had to worry about was for Pa not to see me.

Chapter 35

Return Journey

There was a tap on my door. I'd not moved from my bed all afternoon, constantly staring at the ceiling. I'd run through my life many times over, grasping at the sordid memories of captivity and doing Pa's bidding. That's not what I had tried to do. I desperately wanted to conjure up pictures of my Ma, but all I had seen in my mind's eye was that faceless image of the woman laid on the sofa and holding a doll to her chest. I'd heard the phone ring many times, but none of them could have been enquiring about me, because no one had come to me to answer a phone call. I came to the conclusion that I was no one to anyone. No one cared. Why should they? I'd never wanted Pa dead as much as I did there and then.

"Who is it?"

"It's Mrs. O'Ahern, dear. Father David said not to disturb you earlier, but I'm preparing an evening meal."

The thought of sitting opposite Father David at the table and having to explain myself had my stomach churning.

"I'm not hungry. How is he?"

"A sore head, but he'll live. He's resting on the sofa with his feet up and a pack of frozen broccoli on his bump. Listen, sorry about what happened. No one had told me about you. I thought you were just visiting. Pity the sheriff was out of town, but no doubt she'll catch up with him."

"It doesn't matter," I said, and scoffed at the idea of the sheriff ever finding him. Likely he would be long gone, together with that creep of an excuse of a man that he called a friend. More like a partner in crime.

"I'll leave your meal plated. You can heat it up in the microwave when you've a mind to eat."

"Thanks."

Microwave! A week earlier and I wouldn't have had a clue

what she meant. There was much I would have to learn. Maybe not. At least I thought that I had the skills to live in the wilds without all the modern gadgets.

My mind wouldn't take any more in the solitude of my bedroom. I didn't care to read Father David's Bible. I'd had it with religion. I couldn't see how God could have put me through what I'd experienced. Time was dragging, though day had turned to night outside. Rolling off of the bed, I walked over to a chest of drawers and rummaged through the contents. All I found was a book called *David Copperfield* by Charles Dickens. I dove onto my bed and read it anyway, even though the content wasn't what I expected. The more I read, the more I was sure that I wanted no part of society. It was gone eleven according to the alarm clock on the nightstand. I'd only reached the halfway point in the story and closed the book, then turned off the bedside lamp.

Footsteps creaked along the hallway. Dark moving shadows appeared at the bottom of the door, then stopped, blocking some of the light penetrating from the hallway through the gap. I held my breath. Thankfully there was no knock on the door. I pulled the pillow to my lips and breathed out as the footsteps continued along the hallway. Prob'ly Father David turning in for the night, I thought, as the hallway light extinguished. A door opened then closed. Despite my heart thumping in my chest, I could hear his every movement, then the springs squeak as he climbed into bed.

I had hoped to wait for thirty minutes for him to fall into a deep sleep, but with fifteen minutes gone, I couldn't contain myself. It had started to snow lightly outside. I slipped on my snow pants over my jeans and donned my jacket. As quietly as I could, wearing my boots, I tiptoed to the door and turned the key in the lock. Every action I made amplified the sound in the dead of night, from the key scraping in the lock, to the door hinges creaking, not to mention my heart pounding. I gave up trying to move stealthily, thinking it best to get it over with as quickly as possible. I was down the stairway in no time. The living room door was open. Not wanting to leave any trace of me behind, I stepped inside and picked up my Bible from the table. If Pa was still there, then if nothing else, I thought that I could leave it in the barn with a note to tell him that I knew the truth as to how sick he was.

I arrived at the front door. It was only a Yale lock. I turned the knob and then I was outside, the cold biting at my face. I pulled up my scarf over my nose, and then lifted my hood. Head down, I set off toward an alley to take the back street. Getting my bearings, I walked through a gap in a hedgerow, and set a route across the field as the crow flies to get to the barn.

Along the journey, I could see Hunter's Farm off to my right silhouetted against the sky. I imagined Jordan would be tucked up in bed, contemplating his friends telling him what a lucky escape he'd had. I guessed Nat wouldn't need telling, though I imagined that Clarissa would have something to say. Regardless, I was now free, with the moon and stars guiding me to my target, and with only the critters for company who wouldn't care about my past.

The woods screening our homestead grew ever nearer, yet at times it felt like I would never get there, because I kept getting bogged down in the slush under the fresh covering of snow. The trek took its toll, with the pain in my butt returning and on down through my calf. Luckily it wasn't as bad as when I first had the pain. The wind picked up and the snowfall became heavier as I limped that last one hundred yards to the tree line. Once there, I rested my back against a pine tree trunk, the branches breaking the snowflakes swirling around. I took the painkillers from my pocket Father David had given me and swallowed two of them dry. It was now snowing really heavy, but not so heavy I couldn't see my tracks that had sunk to the dirt for the last twenty yards or so, which was as much visibility as I had.

Recollection of the blackbird swooping down for a meal, leaving his tracks behind, then flying away, only for his tracks to be covered as if he'd never been there, gave me hope that the same would happen when I'd finished my business back at the homestead. Dread followed me through the woods that I'd encounter Pa. All I hoped for was that in that event, I could get to my hunting knife in my backpack first, and then I could slit his throat.

At the edge of the woods, I stopped for a breather. The house was barely visible, save for the glow of light from the kitchen window fighting its way through the sheets of falling flakes, but I could see the outline of his pickup. Tex's truck had gone from the entrance to the barn, which was something of a relief. I worked my way around to the side entrance of the barn, opened the door and stepped inside. In the pitch-blackness, I took off my gloves and slipped them into my pocket. Using my fingers to feel my way, I edged along the workshop framework until I found the doorway and stepped inside. Working my way to the right with my arms outstretched, I felt the workbench, and bending, I dragged out my backpack. The tablets had thankfully worked their magic.

It would have been easier to get out there and then, but then I recalled his moneybox. He owed me more than money, but if it was still there, I decided to take it and felt for the side pocket and pulled out my flashlight. Craning my neck, I listened, but all I could hear was the wind howling. Knowing visibility outside was bad and that there were no windows in the barn, I flicked the switch to my flashlight with my thumb. Over at the cabinet, I opened the door and moved the oilcans to one side. That's when I saw a package that hadn't been there before. My immediate thoughts turned to the dowry. Eagerly, I ripped away at the packaging to reveal stacks of bills. It felt like divine retribution as I stuffed the package and the moneybox into my backpack, but I had to pull out some clothing to accommodate it.

Sapped of strength, I struggled to dead lift my pack, but finally managed to get both straps on my shoulders. A sudden sound had me stopping in my tracks. I turned off the flashlight and slipped in into my jacket pocket, then felt for my hunting knife in a side pocket on my pack. The noise had appeared to come from inside the barn. My breaths picked up speed with my heart leaping. Holding my knife out front, I used my other hand to find the doorframe with my fingers and moved in slow motion. I stepped out and strained my eyes to look out into the barn, but it was too dark. My body was on fire, despite the freezing cold and I listened intently, but heard nothing. It could have been my mind playing tricks, or clumps of snow falling from the roof. My body relaxed and I stepped into the barn.

I snatched my head to that sound again, stepped forward and bumped into something. To a flashing light in my vision, and a searing pain in my head, a mist of anger descended.

That was the last I remembered until I opened my eyes to yet another bright light blinding my vision. My hands were covered in something sticky as if I was sitting in an oil spill. I felt the handle of my knife, picked it up and held it out front.

"Put the weapon down. Don't move. You're under arrest for the murder of your dad," a voice had said from the direction of the blinding beam of light. I knew the voice. It was Sheriff MacCaffrey.

I dropped the knife, and the beam shone briefly to the center of the barn as she began to spew out more words, something about remaining silent. I couldn't remain silent at what I saw, and started to laugh aloud, rocking back and forth as she tethered my wrists with handcuffs behind me.

Pa was strung up by his ankles from the beam with the rope pulley. His gut was slit open, with his innards spewing out and his head lodged in a bear trap. There was a God after all, I thought, while still laughing aloud, and shaking my head.

Chapter 36

Detective Bossé

Detective Alana Bossé stared at her case files on the desk. Overworked, underpaid, and feeling under recognized for her contribution, she sighed. It wasn't the workload that had her reaching for the headache pills, but the headline in the local paper.

"NOT GUILTY" it read, followed by a picture of Jeremiah Coulter and a picture of her alongside of him. She read on for the second time that morning.

"Mr. Coulter has had his sentence commuted and a judge has ordered his immediate release after serving twenty-one years incarcerated for a murder that he didn't commit."

Bossé chewed on her bottom lip and carried on reading.

"New methods of producing DNA have proven beyond a doubt that he was not the murderer. Now questions are being asked as to the evidence presented at the time by the prosecutor, following the results of an investigation provided by the lead investigator, Homicide Detective Alana Bossé, pictured above."

Bossé pursed her lips and let out a rasping sort of whistle at the fact that they'd photoshopped her skin tone to a lighter shade, making her look white.

"Having claimed his innocence all along, he is reported to be bitter that the original trial was held in his home town that he feels was against him, just because he was African American, and claims that his public defender was negligent in presenting his defense. To add to his complaints, we understand that he lays the blame firmly at Detective Bossé's feet for not following up other lines of inquiry that could have led to the apprehension of the real killer. We have been unable to obtain a statement from Detective Alana Bossé or the prosecutor's office at the time of publication."

Bossé rolled up the newspaper and tossed it into her wastebasket, thinking it was rich with the racist overtones, seeing as how she was mixed race, and three of the jury had been black, presenting the judge with a unanimous decision. All she had been was the messenger, she thought, and scoffed at the fact there had been no other suspects. At the same time her stomach knotted with pangs of guilt, wondering if she had missed any other line of inquiry.

"Throwing it away won't make the press go away, Alana," said Brennan, the division's head detective.

"Yeah, I know. Switchboard says the press is phoning every third call."

He tossed a file onto the desk.

"I can make you disappear though for a few days until it all dies down," he said. "I have a new case here for you. It's cut and dried, we have more than probable cause, but we need forensics to make it tighter than a duck's ass. The perp is locked up in the county jail. I need you to visit a small town sixty miles south of here. Hunter's End. The freak weather has held up a forensic team visiting, but now it's cleared up I want you to meet them there at the scene. They're holding the body at the funeral parlor to prevent decomposition. Coroner's personnel are collecting the body later today."

"How did he die?"

"There's a photo in the file, but the report is thin on details." He looked at his watch. "I'd go now if I were you and take the back door. The press is camped outside."

Bossé opened the file as he went about his business.

"Victim, Joseph Ackerman. Suspect, Clara Ackerman (daughter). Age eighteen. Local sheriff found her at the scene with the weapon and she was covered in blood, but she's not talking. Bail refused. Prosecutor successfully argued flight risk, due to her background of living off the grid. Her public defender was successful with a motion to have her mental competence evaluated. Pre-trial conference scheduled in three weeks to discuss mental competence."

Tucked inside the file was the search warrant for Hunter's Lodge. It also covered any vehicles or data extracted from computers and cell phones found at the site, or on the victim and the suspect's person. She flicked the file to the crime scene photo and winced. Whoever this Clara was, she was one sick puppy to have murdered her dad in that fashion, she thought. It looked more like a torture scene.

She closed the file, picked up her purse, then headed for the back stairway. It wasn't another crime case she needed, but time off work and a case of wine. Preferably a quality merlot. Her mind wasn't on the new case, but on Jeremiah Coulter being released. It had been her first case, short on forensics, stuffed with circumstantial, but the motive had been strong. All she'd done was to compile her investigation report and passed it on to the prosecutor's office. The jury did the rest from what was presented to them, but she knew the press would tar and feather her for the error of justice. She didn't need the press to torment her. Bossé's mind did that all the way to Hunter's End.

On the drive over, she wondered if she wouldn't be better resigning. Bossé knew that she would always be remembered as the detective who got it wrong and took someone's life away for twenty-one years. She sighed at thinking it was something that she would have to carry for the rest of her life with the sentence reversed. Only it would be her mind that would imprison her and not a six-by-eight cell.

The town looked ramshackle as she approached Main Street. Dilapidated pickup trucks parked up along the street. Most looked as though they were rusting out and ready for the scrap heap. Her tires threw up slush on to the mounds of plowed snow at the sidewalk, already blackened by spray of the vehicles that had gone before her. She passed a boarded up store with a faded vintage mural painted on the brickwork.

The sign advertised Lee Riders Cowboy Pants, and with the image of a rodeo cowboy on a bucking bronco. Set against the gray sky, the buildings and church looked desolate, with few people on the street, which for lunchtime seemed odd to her. The ones that she did see weren't exactly dressed for a trip to the mall. She felt overdressed and underdressed at the same time in her thin polyester trouser suit, but thankful she had a heavy bomber jacket hung over the back of her seat to guard against the cold.

A quick check of the crime statistics before she'd set off showed this was a low crime area, and with no murders as far back as records went, but she had noted that there had been an increase of break-ins lately.

The internet was a different story. Apparently, the original settlers had a feud with the Hunter family who originally settled in the area. Left six MacCaffreys massacred and scalped, with four of the Hunter family dead in a shootout. Carried on for two more years with four more deaths until the Marshals stepped in and put an end to it and they called a truce. Knowing the internet, she wondered if it was folklore.

The Coroner's van was parked outside the sheriff's office with the forensic team's van behind that. She parked and opened her door against a mound of snow. Bossé cursed and scrambled over to the passenger side and climbed out onto the road. The sheriff appeared at the office door.

"No good wearing stilettos this weather," she said, and leaned over the mound of packed snow to pass her a pair of rubber boots. Bossé wobbled as she stepped out of her shoes and put on the rubber boots, using the hood for balance.

"Thanks," she said.

"Good thing I had spare boots, or it would be a waste of time you visiting Hunter's Lodge. Come on in, I have coffee percolating. Then we can all head out to the funeral parlor. The Coroner's guys say they'll set off back with the victim after forensics have done with the body and we can go to Hunter's Lodge. County has sent a deputy over there to guard the scene."

"Good. Let's get inside before I freeze to death."

The forensic and Coroner's body snatchers were deep in conversation about the technicalities of finding the time of death. Not that the Coroner's guys would have a clue. Turns out that the roads were snowbound and the body had to stay in the barn overnight in-situ during freezing temperatures, which would make estimating the time of death difficult. From what she heard, apparently his body had been stiff as a board by the time they removed it to the funeral parlor.

"So you found the body and his daughter at the scene?" Bossé asked the sheriff.

"Yeah,"

"Did you actually see her gut him?"

"No, but she was sitting in a pool of blood with a hunting knife and her clothing covered in blood. Made a mess of my vehicle when I brought her back here."

"Have forensics taken swabs inside your vehicle."

"No point. Washed my uniform and had my SUV valeted yesterday the day after the murder. Couldn't pick up felons in the state it was in at the time, or drive it. Clara vomited in the back and it stank to high heaven. I took photos though. Besides, it's cut and dried. The girl's demented. All she could do was laugh when I arrested her. Now the cat's gotten her tongue. Refused to say anything after I read Clara her rights. She just kept on laughing, then went into a sort of trance and looked right through me."

Bossé rolled her eyes. She hoped that the scene of the crime had been better preserved than the sheriff's vehicle and clothes. She'd heard the term 'cut and dried' too many times. It's what she'd said to the District Attorney when she'd handed him her file on Jeremiah Coulter. She determined that she couldn't leave any stone unturned on this case for her own peace of mind. Cut and dried had to mean just that, no doubt whatsoever, however long she had to stay there.

Chapter 37

Not Wanted

They were all drinking coffee in the sheriff's office. Bossé was taking her time, not looking forward to scratching around in the barn with the freezing temperature outside. The sheriff didn't appear to be over friendly as if her mind was somewhere else. Not surprising really, Bossé thought, seeing as she found the victim of the first murder in town. Her own mind was wandering in all directions, still feeling embarrassed at the situation with Jeremiah Coulter. It was frying her brain and she knew that she needed to get into detective mode as a distraction.

"Where are they holding her?" Bossé asked Sheriff MacCaffrey.

"County Women's Correctional Facility."

"What have you done in the way of processing?"

MacCaffrey bit on her bottom lip, then sucked air through a gap in her top front teeth, finishing with a smack of her lips. Finally, she pushed back on her chair.

"That was tricky. She had no ID, and I couldn't even get her social security number from her, or her date of birth. I took her fingerprints and a DNA swab. Forensics here has them, together with the clothing she was wearing and the weapon. Oh, and I have her backpack here, together with a few dollars short of ten thousand that she had stowed away. There's also a small locked box. I haven't opened it, but there is something inside."

The locked box intrigued Bossé. She wondered if it was where Clara kept her personal papers and IDs.

"Really, ten thousand. If it's not her money, then that could be the motive if she stole it from him."

"Maybe. There was nothing else of interest, just a tent, a sleeping bag, some provisions, and sundry survival items. It's

175

waterproof, so no blood seeped inside. John over there has taken a swab of the blood stain on the outer surface."

"So she'd planned a getaway by the sound of things. Leave her backpack here. I'll take a look at the contents later when we get back from the search, and then John can take it to the lab. We're bound to find her ID at the homestead. Did she have any injuries?"

MacCaffrey clasped both hands behind her head, then raised one foot on her desktop, followed by the other foot. She blew air between her closed lips, making a rasping sound. Bossé got the sense that the sheriff resented the questions and saw her as an interfering city slicker. Her reply cemented that notion.

"You'll be asking me for a recipe to make blueberry pie next. Hell, I caught her at the scene with the weapon. What more do you want?"

MacCaffrey repositioned her hands to her forehead and moved them up and down. She looked odd with her eyebrows doing a dance.

"It's routine. I have to ask. Well, did you?"

"Never thought to check. I had someone from the county come over and take her to the courthouse jail. They'll have had her checked over. She had a cut on her lip that I noticed, and a swelling on her forehead, but that was from a fight she had at the local church dance a few days earlier."

"So she's been in trouble before?"

MacCaffrey pulled her feet off of the desk. Bossé could see the agitation written all over her face. It was as if Bossé was someone encroaching on her territory where the sheriff was used to being top dog. MacCaffrey unclasped her hands, reached out for a pencil and tapped her lips with it a few times.

"Only that one time. Had a few run-ins with her dad though. I've made some notes in my file. They'd only moved here from Alaska two weeks ago. Neither has prior history on record. She'd run away from home the day before and she'd been staying at Father David's cottage next to the church. Had an altercation with her dad on the church steps around lunchtime, and he left in a hurry with a visitor of his. There was obviously bad blood between them, never mind the money as a motive. Father David says as far as he knows, she was in her room until eleven when he went to bed. Fifteen minutes later he heard his front door close. When he went to investigate, her bedroom was empty."

"How long would it take her to get to the homestead?"

MacCaffrey sighed, and set down the pencil.

"That's like asking how long a piece of string is without a tape measure," she said, and did that sucking the air through the gap in her teeth again. "Depends on the route. It was snowing heavy at that time. There were footprints from the woods to the side entrance at the barn. If she walked across the fields from town, she'd have found it hard going. Maybe fifteen minutes to half an hour."

"Is there just the one photo of the scene?"

"No, I took a few more from different angles once I had her locked in my vehicle. John has the copies. Then I switched off the light and taped the two entrances. There was no light on in the barn when I found her and her dad's body. The Lodge was broken into and the light was on. Door locking mechanism was on the floor inside. The screws were busted out of the lock and the place looked to have been ransacked. I had a look around but the place was deserted. I taped up the door and called the county to have a deputy keep guard. Then he got snowed in after we removed the body. Hell, the whole town was snowed in."

"Yeah, I know, and you said before about the deputy."

She was about to ask the sheriff what she had been doing there late at night, but one of the coroner's guys rose to his feet and ambled over. He glanced at his wristwatch.

"Sorry to interrupt, but if you don't mind, we need to go and collect the body. Can't sit around here all day drinking coffee and chewing the fat. It's forecast to snow again, and it's quite a drive back to the morgue."

"Sure," said the sheriff, looking relieved the question and answer session was over, and rising to her feet, she pulled her jacket from the back of her chair. "We can walk. It's only a short distance along Main Street. Can't miss it." She turned to the coroner's guys. "You can drive over there to collect the body. I'll guide the rest of you out to the farm after, but I'll have to leave you there, I have other work to do."

Bossé pulled out her notebook from her purse and scribbled a few notes. One of the forensic guys grabbed his aluminum case and they all departed. MacCaffrey strode ahead and not waiting for anyone, she crossed the road, then she entered the funeral parlor.

"MacCaffrey's Funeral Parlor and Fine Furniture," the sign read. Bossé stepped inside.

"This is my cousin, Shamus, our mayor," the sheriff said, and pointed to a small statured guy wearing an apron and carrying a chisel. Then she stepped back outside.

Bossé shook the man's hand. She'd been expecting someone wearing a suit and tie, and a dour expression. This guy was all smiles.

"This way," he said.

Bossé hung back and glanced around. She'd seen enough corpses at the morgue and scenes of crime to last a lifetime. All there was that gave a clue that the store was connected to funerals beside the signage were three full size coffins, and three mini-coffins leant against the wall. The rest of the store was loaded with artisan rustic furniture that looked as distressed as the town.

She caught up with them along the hallway and they entered a workshop with a rocking chair on the bench. At one time it must have been a chapel of rest seeing as how it had a narrow altar at one end with an ornate crucifix and candlesticks, overlooked by a faded mural on the wall. Jesus looked to be releasing a dove from his hand, with the bird in flight heading toward some cherubs.

"Through there," he said, and pointed to an open door.

"Not what I was expecting for a funeral parlor," Bossé said.

"It's only ever been a part time business, now it's a dying business with people leaving the town, forgive the pun. Hell, I make more coffins for pets than dead people now. I was union rep and worked full time at the furniture factory until it closed. Now I mainly repurpose old furniture. The mayor's hat is only ceremonial."

"Damn, it's warm in here," John the forensic guy called out.

"Oh dear, maybe I should have kept the door closed," Shamus said, and walked into the room where the body was held.

"I thought the sheriff said you kept an even low temperature in the embalming room when we agreed to her moving the body to here?" John said.

"Well, yes, we do normally. But what with the snowstorm knocking out the town's power overnight, it wasn't possible. Then when it came back on, it fried the AC circuit. Not been able to get anyone to fix it."

John put his thermometer back in his case.

"No point checking the body temperature then. What with the freezing temperatures when he was found, we'll never be able to estimate time of death from his body temperature. We'll have to leave that for the medical officer when they carry out the autopsy."

The Coroner's guys hustled in with their gurney. John unzipped the body bag to the instant smell of death wafting around the room. Bossé took a handkerchief from her pocket, covered her nose and avoided looking at the corpse.

"At least we have keys, but nothing by way of identification I'm afraid," John said.

"I'll take those," Bossé said, and caught site of the corpse. "Holy crap, what a mess."

The bear trap had left deep incisions in his neck, but it wasn't that which upset Bossé; it was the cut from just below his rib cage to his crotch and exposing his organs that had her stumbling out for the exit.

"How do you think I felt," MacCaffrey said, as Bossé stumbled outside and retched. "I had to stuff his innards back inside before we bagged him."

She composed herself and shook the bunch of keys at the sheriff.

"There's more here than a vehicle and a front door key. Let's hope we can find what they open when we get to Hunter's Lodge."

Chapter 38

The Search

Bossé arrived at Hunter's Lodge, having passed a patrol car just before the turning at the open gate to the drive. Buried in the snow, the vehicle was only recognizable by the rack of reds and blues on the roof. Following on at the back of the convoy, she parked in an area that had been cleared of snow. A young man shoveled at a drift from in front of the barn door. He glanced their way, and then threw his shovel into the back of his SUV pickup which had a plow attached. It looked as though he'd cleared the area out front of the lodge, but there was an ancient pickup buried in snow that was parked outside the front door. The young man ambled over to the sheriff's vehicle. MacCaffrey climbed out of her cab and Bossé joined them.

"This is my nephew Nathaniel. Nat, this is Detective Bossé."

"Pleased to make your acquaintance," Nat said.

"Likewise," said Bossé, and shook his hand.

John the forensic guy clomped over.

"Who said to clear the snow?"

"I did," the sheriff said. "Otherwise we wouldn't have had access. What's the problem?"

"Problem! I'll tell you what the problem is. You've had the area around the crime scene destroyed. No footprints, no tire prints, nothing."

Sheriff MacCaffrey rolled her eyes.

"Calm down, I've told Detective Bossé here what tracks there were. It was only ankle deep when I arrived and found the body, but it was knee deep this morning so there were no tracks to see."

John huffed, then lifted his shoulders, seeming to accept the situation. No option really, seeing as he had the same view as Bossé, and she couldn't see any tracks to the side entrance of the barn from the woods, not with the terrain covered in a thick blanket of snow. Nat huddled with Sheriff MacCaffrey and they had words. The sheriff nodded and Nat sidled over to John.

"I found this cell phone," Nat said. "It was next to the pickup at the driver's side. Either the battery is dead, or it's waterlogged." He handed the phone to John, and then turned to his aunt. "What do you want me to do now?"

"You could shovel the snow at the pickup so we can open the door. Then you'd better dig out the deputy's vehicle. That's if it's okay with you, John? After all, you'd have missed the cell phone if he hadn't cleared the area," the sheriff said in a sarcastic tone.

John's cheeks were already red with the freezing cold air, and they flushed a little brighter.

"Fine, we'll start inside the lodge," John said.

The young man's cheeks that were pale pink had turned bright red when the sheriff introduced him, and he'd mostly avoided looking directly at Bossé, which she thought was charming.

Bossé waited outside on the porch as the two forensic guys suited up in their white overalls, and then they disappeared inside. Bossé pulled out some gloves and plastic covers for her boots, put them on and stepped over the threshold.

"Have you moved or touched anything?" John asked the deputy who'd been guarding the property.

"Yeah, what do you expect? Been here twenty-four hours. I made coffee and a sandwich and I've used the john. Oh, yeah, I've stoked the fire with logs, and slept on the sofa."

John tutted.

"You can go now," said the sheriff. "Give Nat a hand to dig out your patrol car. He has a winch if it's stuck."

Bossé overheard Greg talking to his colleague John.

"No signs of blood or a fight anywhere down here, but all the drawers and cabinets have been ransacked. I'll take a look up the stairway at the bedrooms," Greg said.

Bossé scanned around the room. She didn't think that any forensic evidence or anyone else needed to tell her what had happened. Clara had run away, that much she knew. She'd probably decided to return to get the money after her argument with her dad. The empty whisky bottle on the table and only one glass said that he'd been drinking alone. He could have been out cold with the drinking after retiring to his bedroom when she had kicked in the front door. Maybe she disturbed him when she was looking for the stash of money and he chased her to the barn, then... She paused in thought, recalling the horrific image of the corpse and shook her head.

An open door at the far end of the room caught her attention. She wandered across and entered. All that was in there was a desk with a laptop computer on the top and a chair. The drawers to the desk were on the floor with the contents tipped out. This wasn't a professional job as far as she was concerned. Professionals would have started at the bottom drawer to save time and rummaged inside, leaving it open, then they'd move onto the next drawer above. This was a mess.

She fished about in the paperwork and found the documents for the pickup with a receipt, but he hadn't changed the name. No driver's license or insurance card. At last she found his birth certificate and some correspondence from disability entitlement with his social security number listed.

"Found anything?" Sheriff MacCaffrey asked.

"Yeah, I have something to identify him, but no photograph."

"Once Nat's cleared the drift from his pickup door, there's his gun carry certificate behind the sun visor. It has his photo. And like I said, I can identify him from when I've encountered him."

"Can't find anything to identify Clara. No birth certificate. No family photos, nothing. Strange."

"Yeah, well, strange family."

Bossé's mind was distracted when Greg called out.

"You need to see this."

She pushed past the sheriff and trotted up the stairway. Greg was at a bedroom door when they all arrived. He squeezed through the halfway open door and they all followed him. The bed was skewed as if it had been dragged to block the door, and then pushed back as someone had entered. The bolt was in the closed position with the clasp on the floor. The glass in the window had been smashed out, leaving a few shards still in the frame. A blanket was laid over the bottom of the windowsill and frame.

"Someone tried to barricade themselves inside and escaped through the window," said Greg, stating the obvious.

John picked a claw hammer up off of the floor and bagged it. He removed the blanket hung over the bottom of the frame and tried to open the window, but the frame was stuck.

"The frame's warped with the damp. It looks as though it had been nailed closed at one time," John said.

Bossé ambled over to the closet and opened the door. "Looks as though this was Clara's room with some of the clothing she's left behind."

"How old was she?" said John.

Bossé turned to see him holding a skirt that was more like a scarf.

"Eighteen," said the sheriff as she entered. She walked over to the window and leaned out. "Nat, did you bring the plywood I asked for. You'll need to secure the window when they've finished here."

Bossé walked over to the window as the sheriff stepped aside and she peered out through the window frame. The pickup door was open and Nat was leaning inside."

"Hey, don't touch anything inside," Bossé called out.

Bossé stepped over to the clothing on the floor. She tapped her finger on her lips. For an eighteen year old, she thought it odd that Clara had a young-schoolgirl's outfit. She picked up a red dress from the floor and held it out. If it was Clara's, Bossé thought that she must have been smaller in stature than she imagined. Skinny even. Not the sort of size for someone who could haul a person the weight of the corpse on a rope pulley. Still, Bossé thought that she'd seen stranger things happen when people garnered strength to punch above their weight.

Nat squeezed through the opening at the door, carrying a

sheet of plywood. He leant it against the wall and took his claw hammer from his tool belt. Sheriff MacCaffrey tapped Bossé on the shoulder.

"There's an attic room. I only gave it a glance to make sure no one was hiding. Nothing to see in the other bedrooms."

MacCaffrey lifted the glass on an oil lamp, lit it and dropped the glass, then shuffled out of the bedroom. Bossé followed her along the hallway and through the attic door.

"Take a look in that chest over there. We might find some ID for Clara in there," Bossé said.

MacCaffrey hung the lamp on a nail, opened the chest and rummaged inside.

"It doesn't belong to them. The O'Leary's must have left it behind. Nothing but old clothing and family photos of them and their daughter Kate, and some bric-a-brac."

"What's that over there?" MacCaffrey said.

"Just some tarp."

"It looks like it's covering something." Sheriff MacCaffrey lifted the corner, and then threw it to one side. "Well, well, what do we have here?" MacCaffrey said, and then answered her own question. "A case locked with a padlock. Do you have those keys with you?"

Chapter 39

The Contents

Bossé and the sheriff waited patiently while John dusted the small suitcase for prints. She took the opportunity to ask MacCaffrey what business she had there on the night that she discovered the body.

"Official business," she said. "I'd been away from town all day helping the county sheriff's office with a search for a missing tourist. Arrived back late at night. Had a report that Clara's dad had assaulted Father David, so I came out to arrest him. Found the house ransacked. When I stepped out onto the porch, I saw a light flashing through a gap in the wooden planks at the barn, and well, you know the rest."

"Who reported the assault?"

"My sister-in-law. She saw most of it. Phoned Father David and he explained what happened. Said he hadn't heard what was said between Clara and her dad. He was out cold after her dad knocked him out inside the church with the butt of his rifle. He was there trying to bring Clara back home."

John interrupted them.

"You can move the suitcase now. I have a good print," said John. "Luckily the tarp had prevented it getting damp."

Bossé was beginning to think Clara's dad was trouble with a capital T, and that he could have made quite a few enemies in the town to say he hadn't lived there that long. Regardless, as she made her way to the kitchen with the suitcase, she thought that it was looking as though Clara was the guilty party. Over at the kitchen table, she placed the case on the surface. Fishing the keys from her pocket, she offered a few of them to the lock until one slipped inside.

"Bingo," she said as she unfastened the lock, then flicked the clasps and opened the case just as her cellphone rang. Her office number showed on the display when she slipped it from her jacket pocket. She signaled MacCaffrey not to touch the contents, when her eyes caught something that unnerved her in the suitcase. MacCaffrey ignored her, lifting each of the contents by the corner until she'd seen them all, then sighed. She looked to the ceiling and made the sign of the cross on her chest. Bossé glared at MacCaffrey, not knowing what to make of her and her actions and closed the lid on the case.

"Hello," she said, after pulling her cellphone to her cheek.

"You wrapped it up there?" said her boss.

"Not yet."

"What have you found so far?"

"There was a package in her backpack with around ten thousand dollars in small bills." She described what she had found at the house and about the argument at the church.

"There's your motive and the trail of events right there," said her boss. "Sounds like he caught her stealing his money and he chased her to the barn, then she got the jump on him."

"Maybe."

"Well, don't waste too much time over there."

"Why's that?"

"DA says all he'll need is the DNA from the blood on her clothing and on Clara's knife blade, and for it to match the victim's DNA. Oh, and the sheriff's statement. If the DNA is a match, he says it's a done deal unless she's found mentally incompetent to stand trial. Last thing he said he wants is red herrings thrown into the mix at full discovery with her public defender."

"Who is the DA?"

"Gilbert Rhodes."

Bossé held the phone away from her ear. Gilbert Rhodes was the same DA who won the case against Jeremiah Coulter. She put the phone to her lips to answer.

"I'll not make it back tonight. Still need a few more statements to sketch the full picture. Probably get finished tomorrow."

"Whatever, just don't go off at a tangent. You still have all those cases on your desk, remember?"

"Yeah, got it." The call closed at his end. "John, I need you down here," Bossé called out and lifted the lid on the case.

The sheriff took a seat at the table. Elbows resting on the surface, she masked her face with her hands.

"What is it?" said John.

"If I'm not mistaken, that's duct tape, a knife, and handcuffs tucked in at the side of the clothing," Bossé said.

"No, you're not mistaken. I'll take a look." John removed the top garment, a child's dress. It would probably have fit a five year old. "I think I'd better do a presumptive test on that stain. Better I take the case into the office and close the curtains."

The sheriff stayed put, but Bossé followed him.

He opened his aluminum case and took out a fluorescent lamp.

"Tell me it's not what I think it is?" Bossé said.

"Well, it's only a presumptive test so it isn't conclusive, but seeing as it appears yellowish under the light, I'd say it could be semen. A lab test will confirm or dispel that conclusion one way or another."

He took out a second garment and ran his flashlight over it. Glances exchanged between them. This dress had a slit in it, surrounded by a dark stain.

"I hope that isn't blood," Bossé said.

"We'll soon find out."

John took a spray canister from his case.

"Luminol?"

"No, Fluoresceine. Just as effective and it doesn't degrade later DNA tests."

Bossé's worst fears were confirmed when he ran the fluorescent lamp over the garment.

"So it is blood!"

"Looking that way, but like I said, these are presumptive tests. I need to get the clothing to the lab for confirmation."

"How many items are there?"

John worked his way through the garments, careful not to move them too much.

"Twelve."

"Those first two dresses are different sizes. Are you thinking what I'm thinking?"

"I'm not paid to make conjectures. But from a personal point of view, I'm hoping these aren't trophies and we have a serial killer on our hands."

Bossé turned to a gasp coming from the direction of the closed door.

"I heard that. Damned pervert. Son of a bitch, I knew it. Damn and blast."

The sheriff must have been listening at the door. Bossé pulled the door open. MacCaffrey was pacing around, still cussing, then she dropped her backside on the chair and started to wail. Bossé exchanged glances with John. She thought it was an over-the-top reaction.

"You okay?"

"Do I look like I'm freakin' okay? Clara said that he'd defiled her when they had their fight at the church. I didn't know what to believe when I was told, now I do."

"Whoa, what's all this about defiling. Are you saying she accused him of incest?"

"I don't know. I only heard it as hearsay."

"Who said?"

"Hunter."

"Who is that?"

"Jordan Hunter. He's a young bum that she's been seeing. He phoned me after I spoke to my sister-in-law. Can't believe anything he says, so I ignored what he said."

"Where do I find him?"

"Hunter's Farm. The drive to the property is the next one along on the road toward town."

Bossé sighed and took a seat next to MacCaffrey. The sheriff's features had a look of thunder written all over her face. She took a handkerchief from her pocket and dried her eyes.

"Is there something I'm missing?" Bossé asked.

"No, I'll be fine. It's not as though we get a murder every day here. And if he is the pervert we think he could be... well, it's all too much. If you don't mind I'll head for my office. I'll tell Nat to board up all the windows and ask headquarters to get another deputy over here to guard the property."

"Good idea. I doubt I'll finish the search today. We'll take a look in the barn when you've gone. Nothing in there you haven't already seen. Any hotels in town?"

"No, but we have cots in the cells. You could bunk down in a cell for the night and it'll cost nothing. Just don't expect service," she said, and half-heartedly smiled as if to signify she was joking about the service. Her expression quickly reverted to looking pained. The sheriff's moist eyes were a clear signal that she was still emotional.

"Go on. You go. I'll see you down there."

Bossé walked on over to the office door as she exited. Now she wasn't so sure what they had found in the suitcase was anything to do with a serial killer. For all she knew it could be Clara's clothing from when she was a child. John was sitting at the desk, tapping on the mouse. His face was contorted into a pained expression.

"I hoped not to see this," he said. "It gets worse. Better come here and take a look."

Chapter 40

The Barn

John showed Bossé the palm of his hand as she stepped over to the computer, then he switched off the power.

"What's wrong?"

"I can't look at it anymore. It's too sick." With his elbows on the desk, he sank his head into his hand. "Damn it, I have grandchildren that age."

"Are you saying Ackerman has child pornography on there?"

He was stuck for words to reply and simply nodded his head. Greg walked into the office.

"I'm all finished upstairs. Do you need help down here?"

"No, I have all I need." John said. "We should all take a look in the barn. Then we can load everything up in our van and get the hell outta here. This place gives me the creeps."

Nat was standing outside the office door when Bossé exited.

"Aunty says to board up all the windows. Is that what you want? Only I'll have to go and get the plywood and a ladder."

"How long will it take?" Bossé asked.

"Maybe an hour."

"Okay. Could you secure the lock back on the door first?" John asked. "Then we can lock up if we're finished before you arrive. Listen, before you go, could you give me your prints. Only you're not wearing gloves and we'll need to eliminate any of your prints we might have dusted."

Nat pulled a face at first, and then smiled.

"Sure."

"I'll leave you to do his prints, Greg."

John picked up his case from the kitchen table and Bossé followed him outside. John yanked on the door handle to the pickup. Bossé reached past him and removed Ackerman's carry license from behind the visor.

"Not much we can do with this," he said. "It's been open to the elements. The back window is smashed and the snow's piled inside. Can't see any blood specks. Still, I'll arrange to have it transported to get it checked out."

He closed the door and they walked down to the barn. The door was partly open and they stepped inside. John flicked on the light switch, and then swept his arm across Bossé's waist.

"What is it?" Bossé asked.

"Shoe prints everywhere in the dust. Stay there while I take photos."

Bossé scanned the barn. In the center was the pulley hanging from a beam. She imagined the shoe prints would take some sorting out seeing as how the scene would have been trampled over to remove the body. The bear trap was to one side of a dark patch under the pulley where he'd bled out.

"Someone has just been in here. There are wet boot prints." He took his cell phone out and stabbed at the dial pad. "Greg, ask Nat if he's been in the barn."

It didn't take long for him to get his answer and he hung up. "Was it Nat?"

"Yeah, he said he was looking to see if there was any plywood for the windows."

He looked pissed as he hunkered down and took samples of the blood, and then still kneeling, he glanced around.

"The bear trap likely killed him before he was gutted."

"How do you work that out?"

"The wound from one of the spikes to his carotid artery that I saw at the funeral parlor. And see there." He pointed. "Whoever did this will have been covered in blood. The initial pressure would have caused the blood trajectory to spurt with his heart still pumping. Looking at that stain, it has hit someone stood right there. If he'd have been gutted first, it's unlikely there would have been any blood pressure left to spurt that distance."

"What about taking prints?"

"Waste of time. It's too damp in here to get prints."

"What's that over there by the water barrel?"

John rose to his feet and walked over to the barrel.

"It's an apron made from an animal skin. Blood stained by the look of it. I'll take it with me to the lab."

Bossé scratched at her head and she stared at the pulley. Her mind tried to picture events. She'd worked out that it was possible Clara had forced entry to the house, then disturbed him and he'd chased her into the bedroom where she smashed the window to escape. But then why not run for the woods? Maybe she thought that Clara had panicked and ran into the barn to hide, especially as she was carrying a heavy backpack. She couldn't grasp at any logic for the way he'd been dispatched. If he'd been drunk and say tripped and banged his head which rendered him unconscious, that would have been her opportunity to escape. She doubted someone of his size and weight wouldn't have put up a fight unless he was out of it.

"Penny for your thoughts?" John said as Greg joined them.

Bossé shook her head. "Just trying to make sense of what happened here. Why string him up? Why not just slit his throat if you wanted him dead? It all seems so elaborate, intentional even, especially to go to the lengths of setting a bear trap under him."

"Torture," said Greg. "Maybe they wanted to extract something from him and kept lowering him with the ratchet on the pulley."

Bossé stroked her chin. She wondered if Clara had tortured him to discover where he kept his stash of money, then killed him anyway.

"How could a young girl have managed to pull his weight on the pulley?"

"The ratchet," John said. "She could have lifted him in short bursts and lowered him gradually the same way."

"I don't buy that. I doubt that I could have tugged his weight," Bossé said.

"Well let's test it," said Greg.

"What, you want me to hog tie your ankles and try it out?"

"No nothing so dramatic. There's a sack over there. We could load it up to the approximate weight of the deceased and you could give it a try. I have a weight scale in my case."

Rolling her eyes, she stood back and left them to it to load the sack. John used a two by four length of wood to move the pulley along the beam, and then attached the sack.

"There you go, give it a try," John said.

Until it took the weight, it was relatively easy. The rest of the way not so much, but eventually Bossé lifted the sack some height until her arms wouldn't move it anymore.

"Now let it down. Pull and release, and to stop it, work the ratchet with the rope like this."

After his demonstration, Bossé took the rope. The sack gradually lowered, then all of a sudden Bossé let go of the rope as it slipped through her hands to a burning sensation, then the sack came to a halt half an inch from the concrete floor.

"Ouch, that freakin' hurt," she said, blowing on her hand.

John and Greg exchanged glances.

"What?" Bossé said.

"Maybe it wasn't intentional. I'd say whoever did it possibly wanted answers, not to kill him."

"Then why gut him?"

"Anger of a crazed mind obviously, and not getting what they wanted is one possibility," Greg said. "Whatever, we'll have to wait for Nat to get back with the ladder and to remove it for testing back at the lab. Then we can see if it's possible to replicate what just happened."

Bossé walked over to the bear trap.

"Can I try this?"

"Yeah, I've taken swabs."

She tried with all her strength to open the trap, but try as she did, she couldn't set it.

"If I can't do it, how could Clara have set the trap?"

"There'll be a knack to it," Greg said. "Didn't I hear someone say back at the sheriff's office that they both lived out in the wilds of Alaska before moving here?"

"Guess so." Bossé didn't think there was any more she could do. She'd need to get to the sheriff's office and to write up a report, but first Bossé thought she'd pay Jordan Hunter a visit to see if he could throw any light on Clara's background and state of mind.

"I'll leave you to finish up here. Phone me when you get the results of your tests." She handed him the keys. "Drop these off at the sheriff's office for me on your way home."

"Will do."

She headed out to her car and set off for Hunter's Farm. The journey was something of a blur until she saw the sign for the entrance to the farm. The demonstration with the pulley and her aching arms had her mind working in overdrive. There was nothing cut and dried about events in her mind, other than whoever did this had serious mental issues. All she could hope for was that Jordan could shed some light on the Ackerman family.

Chapter 41

Clara's Journey

I had a good idea why they were taking me for a journey, but not where, other than I'd heard them say it was to a mental institute. The only other thing I overheard was that the county would be less than pleased at paying for my visit, but there was no psychiatrist available at the jail in time to prepare a report the judge had ordered. I was the only passenger in the mini-bus, shackled with the chains secured to the floor. It was as if my life had come full circle from my earliest childhood memories.

The scenery flashed by. The sky and clouds were a mixture of dark gray hues, set against the white pristine landscape and towering pine trees. The hideous yellow prison suit they'd given me was uncomfortable against my skin, but shackled, I couldn't do anything to scratch the itch that tormented me. No one had spoken to me during my time in my cell, only to bark orders when I first arrived and to direct me from my cell to the mini-bus. But then I hadn't spoken to anyone either, not since the sheriff handcuffed me at the barn. Not even the judge and my so-called public defender could give me a reason to answer them, without I thought they were trying to trick me.

"Name, date of birth, blah, blah, blah." Their words had ripped through me with their tone of delivery, although the public defender had tried his best to be polite and to pretend he was on my side. I didn't trust any of them. Their questions repeated over and over again, with all of my inquisitors glaring at me as if I was dog dirt. Whatever trickery they were trying to use in asking those questions had only made me more determined not to answer them.

We turned off of the highway and drove along a winding country road flanked by dense woods. As the road narrowed the branches of the trees reached out and touched each other, bathing the inside of the bus in darkness. I closed my eyes, desperately trying to remember what had happened at the barn. All I could grasp at was a fleeting image as the beam from the sheriff's flashlight passed over Pa's lifeless body, tethered upside down, his neck fastened in the bear trap, and his eyes bulging. It was as if he had seen his fate when Satan's reaper had claimed his soul, and he'd witnessed the fires of hell burning.

They said I did it, murdered him that is. At least that's what the sheriff said and some guy with a suit and tie in the courthouse. If I did, then he deserved to die. God had listened to me finally, and now He was protecting me by erasing the deed from my mind. There was no need to answer to anyone else.

A sudden jolt and I opened my eyes. The driver had missed her turning and reversed, then she turned left through a gate and stopped at a barrier. A security guard ambled over to her and they exchanged words. The barrier lifted and she drove on.

We pulled up outside a large gray stone building. My escort helped me out of the bus and guided me up the fifteen steps to the entrance. Each shuffle up the stairs took the itch on the back of my legs to a new level. She pressed a button on the wall and spoke into a small square box. And there I was thinking that I was the crazy one. My body leapt when a voice came back from the box as if by magic.

"I'll release the door."

The door lock buzzed. We entered to be met by two men wearing white pants and jackets. They exchanged words with my escort, signed a paper on her clipboard and she handed them a copy, then she exited. It seemed to take forever to shuffle down the corridor. One of them swiped a card across a glass square on the wall to the sound of yet another door lock buzzing open. They still flanked me as they pushed the swing doors open. As soon as I stepped through, I sensed evil surrounding me. We stopped at an open steel door.

"This is your room. Clara isn't it?" The skinnier of the two said, and then signaled for me to enter. It was no different from the cell I'd just left. "I hope you're going to cooperate while we remove your shackles. Take a seat on the edge of your cot. You'll be interviewed soon. We'll come back for you."

The guards looked to be on edge as if I'd pounce on them. They removed the shackles, and then spoke as if I wasn't there.

"She's on special watch. Inform the CCTV room we have a new guest."

They backed out of the door and it closed with a clunk as the metal handle turned. I knew exactly what they had meant. Pa had pointed out cameras once when we walked through a town and we played a game of spotting and avoiding them. There was one in the top corner of the cell at the ceiling. The red LED glowed like the Devil's eye, just as Pa had said, signaling they were watching me. I shuddered at the thought that I'd swapped one life of been incarcerated and watched, for another situation equally as distressing. The only consolation was that they'd not beaten me yet. I fixed my vision on the camera and rocked back and forth.

My mind was in a better place as I rocked on my cot and imagined running free through a meadow. But I kept hearing the odd pained wails of women in distress and shuddered each time. The tortured cries of the women made me think some evil fate awaited me. Time had slipped by. The door handle clunked, and then the door opened.

"We're ready for your interview, come this way."

This was the first trust I'd been shown since I was arrested as I walked along the corridor unshackled. But then I wouldn't have stood a chance to do anything against two burly guards either side of me. Just because they wore white, I wasn't taken in by them. Not after hearing those eerie cries for help. One of them tapped on a door.

"Enter."

I matched the voice to the middle-aged woman who sat behind a desk and wearing a white cotton coat.

"Clara, isn't it? Do take a seat."

Glancing around, there wasn't a window, but I could feel a cold draft coming from a machine high on the wall. Then there was another of those Devil's eyes in the corner at the ceiling.

The camera pointed right at the only empty seat. The woman's pen was poised over a sheet of paper on an open file. As soon as I sat, she made a note.

"Good, so you understand me. How was your journey?"

The door was ajar, and out of the corner of my eye, I could see the guards outside. I glared at the camera and started to recite. "The Lord is my shepherd; I shall not want. He maketh me to lie down in green pastures. He restoreth my soul: He leadeth me in the paths of righteousness for his name's sake. Yea, though I walk through the valley of the shadow of death, I will fear no evil..." Once finished, I felt comforted that I would be protected from evil.

"The Psalm of David. You have a good recollection. At least we know you can speak. I have your name as Clara Ackerman, but I don't seem to have your date of birth. What is it?"

"Our Father, Who art in heaven. Hallowed be Thy name..."

The woman waited patiently until I'd finished.

"Is this a game you're playing, young lady? Or are you going to speak to me? I'm here to help you."

"Hail, Mary, full of grace..."

I ignored her sighs and continued to the end. She closed her file, rose from her seat and stepped outside. I could hear her whispering, but not what was said, then she returned.

"We'll leave it at that for now. Perhaps you need more time to settle in. David and Antonio will take you to the lounge. They'll arrange for the nurse to give you some medicine, and then you can mix with the other patients."

There was no one in there when we arrived. Antonio lifted a handset from the cradle on the wall and spoke to someone.

"Take a seat, some of the patients will be along shortly after you've taken your medication," he said, and joined David.

A woman entered pushing a cart, the wheels squeaking across the polished tiled floor.

"I have some medicine for you, deary," the nurse said. "It's only a mild sedative to relieve the stress."

She passed me a small plastic cup with what looked like a tiny amount of milk. I took a sniff, but it didn't smell of anything. Lifting my eyes, Antonio and David were glaring at me. The woman smiled.

"Go on, it won't hurt."

I put it to my lips, gave a silent prayer, then tipped the cup and swallowed the content.

"Good, girl."

A rage overpowered my calm at her words.

"I'm not a girl, I'm a woman. My name is Clara," I said and stamped my foot.

"Whoa there, calm down," David said, and stood between the nurse and me. "Take a seat. I can hear some of the patients arriving." They stepped back and both leaned against the wall as the woman with the squeaking cart walked away.

"Why are you wearing a bright yellow jumpsuit? It looks horrible," said a woman around my age as I took a seat at a table. "My name is Janine," she said, and she joined me, taking a seat opposite. Janine was wearing a T-shirt and jeans, thankfully not white.

"Not my choice."

"Why are you here?"

"Don't know."

She leaned over and whispered. "I know. They asked me to talk to you to see if I could get you to open up. They're watching you. They watch us all."

I looked over to the corridor. The woman who had tried to interview me was standing there, watching.

Chapter 42

Hunter's Farm

A light rap on the Hunter's farmhouse door did nothing to stir anyone inside that she could hear. Bossé sighed and used the side of her balled fist to give the door a few of her best detective knocks.

"All right, all right, I'm coming."

The door opened to a man in his fifties. He must have had a black mop at one time, but now his hair was mingled with gray streaks and receding. He was wearing suspenders to hold up his jeans that were doing their best to defy gravity, with his waist hidden under his potbelly.

"Detective Alana Bossé. I'm here to talk with Jordan Hunter."

"I'm his dad, Jake Hunter. What's he done now?" he said; the smell of alcohol wafting under Bossé's nose. It wasn't that which bothered her, but the way he looked her up and down as if he were giving her a mind screw.

"Nothing. Just making enquiries."

"Well he ain't here."

"When will he be back?"

"Never, if he knows what's good for him."

"Why's that?"

"Bitch of a wife left me a note. She wants a divorce. Sacked our joint account, and from what I hear she's gone and bought the little runt an SUV and given him some money to move on. She's at her sister's house in Denver, but Jordan isn't with her, unless she's lying."

He obviously didn't hold his son or his wife in high esteem, she thought.

"Do you know the address?"

"No." he said, and made to close the door.

"Hey, hold on a minute. I'm investigating a murder. I haven't

205

finished."

"Murder!" he said. "Is that the Bible thumper over at Hunter's lodge?"

"Joseph Ackerman, if that's who you mean. I understand Jordan had been seeing his daughter, Clara."

"You'll have to ask him. I wouldn't know. We don't talk to each other," he said, holding onto the door handle and swaying.

"Well he isn't here for me to ask, is he? Perhaps I can come inside and you can tell me what you know about Ackerman and who else Jordan hangs around with?"

He huffed and snorted a few times. With the look on his face, she half-expected the door to be closed in her face.

"Better come in. But if you find him, you'd better tell me where he is."

Bossé smiled behind his back as she followed him staggering down the hallway and into the living room. Nothing like alcohol to loosen someone's tongue, she thought.

"Take a seat."

She didn't have to prompt him; he rattled off his encounter with Ackerman and calling in the sheriff after he caught him setting traps, and that he suspected him of shooting a deer on his property.

"So why do you think the sheriff decided not to press charges?"

"Because she's a MacCaffrey. As soon as he brought out his Bible I knew it would be a waste of time. I told her to forget it. They all piss in the same pot in this town where the Bible is concerned. Don't know why I bothered. I should've sorted it out myself."

Bossé glanced at a painting on the wall above the fireplace. It was a portrait of a woodsman from the settler days judging by the clothing and long rifle he cradled. He was standing next to an enormous bear hanging upside down by a rope from the bough of a tree, and there was a bear trap to one side.

"Is that one of your ancestors?"

"Yeah, Jesse Hunter. The MacCaffreys done shot him. Some gratitude after he gave them the land for their settlement for nothing, only a bag of seed corn. They still run the freakin' town."

"Ah, yes, I heard about the history. Why would they hang the bear like that?"

She pointed to the painting.

"So it can bleed out before they skin it for the pelt. Grizzly bears were a valuable source of meat and fat for the pioneers in those days, until they were hunted to extinction in Colorado."

The style of hanging the animal to bleed out compared with how Ackerman died didn't go amiss, which gave her cause to pause.

"Getting back to Jordan. Can you tell me who Jordan hangs around with?"

He reeled off two names and Bossé took a note. What she wasn't expecting was Jake going into a rant about the bad blood between his son and Nat MacCaffrey. He reckoned that's where Jordan got his violent streak from when he was expelled for assaulting the school's principal, after he'd been taken to task for missing lessons. He said it was because Jordan couldn't face Nat bullying him that he missed school, and he called him all the wimps under the sun for not beating Nat's ass.

But it wasn't that information that she found interesting. It was how he thought the MacCaffrey's had killed one of their own, after Nat's dad died in a car wreck when he ran off a mountain road. That was just after rumors in town that he'd abused Nat as a child and his wife was about to report him. Said that his brakes had failed according to the newspaper reports, yet he saw his car in for service up on the ramp at Tiff MacCaffrey's Garage on the morning of the day he died. Bossé put it down to the drink talking and the animosity he had for the MacCaffreys. She glanced at her watch.

"Thanks for your help. If he contacts you here's my card."

"If he contacts me face to face, he won't be talking to anyone," he said, trying to stand, but fell back on his seat.

"I'll see myself out, thanks, but before I go, when was the last time you saw Jordan?"

"Didn't see him, but he sneaked into the house Tuesday night for his clothes around midnight. He was gone by the time I came down."

Bossé closed her notebook and saw herself out to her car.

She wasn't one for conspiracy theories, but her mind dwelt on what she had heard on the drive to the sheriff's office. It was the fact that the sheriff said Jordan and Clara had something going between them that troubled her. There was that, and her doubt that Clara would have had the strength to pull on the rope pulley on her own. From the sheriff's description, she reckoned she can't have been more than one hundred and ten pounds, half the weight of her dad. Tuesday when Jordan left home was the night the sheriff found Ackerman's corpse and arrested Clara. She let that thought simmer as she parked and climbed out of her vehicle.

"You took your time. Find anything else?" Sheriff MacCaffrey asked.

"Yeah, I tried to interview Jordan, but he's left home." She opened her notebook and relayed his friends' names. "Any idea where they live? I want to interview them tomorrow to see if they know where he is?"

"You'll be lucky to find them at home. Most mornings they hang around outside my sister-in-law's grocery store." She opened her desk drawer, took out a file and slid it over to Bossé. "You'll find their details in here."

"Thanks."

"Here's the office key. The cells are back there. There's coffee in the pot. I have to be going to get to a council meeting at the church hall."

"Where does Father David live?"

"The cottage next to the church."

"Good, I'll pay him a visit. Incidentally, Nat seems like a decent young man, how old is he?"

"Twenty-one, why?"

"Nothing really. How old was he when his dad died?"

The sheriff rose from her chair, walked over to the coat stand and lifted her Jacket from the peg. "Best part of seven years now, he'd be fourteen. Did Nat tell you?" she asked, not turning to face Bossé.

"No, Jake Hunter."

"Oh, him. What else did he have to say?" she asked, and turned to face Bossé.

"Not much really, apart from his wife has left him and she wants a divorce."

"That doesn't surprise me. She's well shut of him. I've been out there a few times when he's battered her, but she'd never press charges. Look, I have to be going to get changed for the meeting. The key for the evidence locker is the small one on the key ring. Number one. You'll find Clara's backpack in there."

MacCaffrey walked out of the office and closed the door. Bossé wandered through to the cells, switched on the light on to one of them and stepped inside, closing the barred door behind her. She took a seat on the corner of the cot and glanced around the confined space. The cot was all that was in there, with a barred window providing light.

Bossé scrunched her nose at the foul smell of stale vomit and urine. She opened her purse, took out her perfume and dabbed some under her nose. The headline and newspaper report on Jeremiah Coulter being proven not guilty passed through her mind. The cell walls seemed to close in on her. Her breathing and heart rate increased. Despite the perfume, the stench in the cell overwhelmed her. She rose, quickly opening the door and she stepped outside. Bossé's stomach knotted and her legs weakened. She staggered into the office with her surroundings spinning and took a seat at the desk. Bossé took some slow even breaths until some semblance of calm was restored. She knew full well that her report had put Coulter through hell for twenty-one years, and sitting in that cell had brought it home to her just what that meant.

She picked up the key for the evidence locker. A sense of determination cemented in her mind that this would be her last homicide case and she'd work it to death, starting with Clara's backpack.

Chapter 43

Secrets Within

L ooking out through the window at the sheriff's office, Bossé
knew that she only needed to write up a report and to let
forensics and the DA deal with the rest. All she had to do then
was to get into her car and to have driven away. Her
conscience was driving her in a different direction, unable to
get a picture of Jeremiah Coulter out of her head.

It was dark now and the streetlights were on. She could see
the sign illuminated for the grocery store. A few doors down
was where she had visited the mayor's funeral parlor. At the
corner, a little further on Main Street, she noticed a swing sign
for the local garage. "Tiff MacCaffrey's Garage" it read. An SUV
pulled up outside the grocery store and Nat climbed out of the
cab, and then he entered the store. She turned to see the
sheriff's name gold leafed on a sign on her desk. It was looking
as though Jake Hunter was right and the MacCaffreys did run
the town.

The Ackermans had been outsiders. Maybe, she thought,
that's why the sheriff seemed indifferent, and not exactly
forthcoming about events at the church, which she must have
known in more detail. Then there was her reaction when they
found the case with the clothing, which she thought was odd.

Bossé sighed as she ambled through to the locker room and
unlocked the door to get at the backpack, when she heard
someone open the office door.

"Anyone at home?" She heard John's voice call out.

"I'm through here."

John appeared and gave Bossé the keys to Hunter's Lodge.

"I'll give you a hand with the backpack," he said, as she
struggled to drag it out of the locker.

"Jesus, that's some weight," said Bossé, as she watched him

struggle with it into the office and set it down on the floor.

John put on a pair of gloves and set about emptying the backpack and placed the contents on the desk.

"Don't touch anything, I'll go and get my case."

Bossé stared at the locked security box, itching to try one of the keys he'd given her, when he returned with his own box of tricks.

"I'll try to open the security box," Bossé said.

She offered the smallest key to the lock and opened the lid.

"More money," John said.

The bills were fastened with a rubber band. John opened his case and dusted the top and bottom bills.

"I have one print I can get at least five points on," said John, and used his lifting tape to secure the latent print, then stuck it to a card. "You can count it now. There's nothing I can get from the box."

As she counted the contents, it struck her that Clara hadn't had a key in her possession when she was arrested. That in itself was damning evidence that she had stolen the money from her dad as the key was found on his person. She knew this wouldn't look good for Clara and would strengthen the case against her.

"Fifty-five hundred. Add that to the bundle over there, and that's quite an amount for motive, and solid evidence for a first-degree murder charge," Bossé said.

"Only if that print isn't hers. I've taken prints from the victim. If it's his, I guess you could be right."

He turned his attention to the bundle of money wrapped up in a newspaper that was ripped open.

"We're in luck. The bills are in plastic bags still with the bank's wrapper and date stamped. Where we're out of luck is that the sheriff emptied it to count it and one of the packages has been opened," John said.

John set about dusting for prints. Bossé noticed the date and name of the newspaper.

"It's too late to call the bank. Besides we might need a warrant to get them to talk. I'll phone the office later and see what they can do," Bossé said.

The bank's stamp date and the newspaper date matched. It was the Friday before Ackerman was murdered. Bossé knew the newspaper. It was local to the towns at the foot of the Sierra Nevada Range.

"I've got a few more prints. I can't see anything else that would be of interest to check. I'll take photographs and leave the backpack and contents with you to take for evidence storage and I'll be on my way."

Bossé scanned the items on the desk and was drawn to a foil-covered bundle. She teased it open.

"What's that?"

"Venison, still curing by the looks of it. There was lots of it hung in the pantry back at the lodge. I'd say it was from a full deer carcass recently processed."

That seemed to back up what Jake Hunter had said. She imagined it would mean they must have processed it at the lodge. Clara must have taken the venison for provisions, but the only other thing she could see in the way of something to sustain her was a bag of beans and a container of water. The rest was just clothing a sleeping bag and sundry items to use for survival.

"Make sure that you take a close-up photo of the newspaper and the bank stamp on the bills," she said, and picked up the Bible. She flicked through the pages. "What comes after Exodus in the Old Testament?"

"You're asking the wrong person. Why?"

"There are quite a few pages torn out."

"Maybe that's all she had at onetime to light a fire when she was camping, who knows?" John said.

"I don't know about that. There's a dictionary over there she could have used."

John picked up the dictionary and flicked through the pages.

"Maybe she used both. There are pages missing from this as well. One of the letter I pages is missing, and others."

She closed the Bible and picked up a well-thumbed map. When she opened it, Bossé noticed a route marked out in black felt tip pen. The mark ran from the town to fifteen miles to the outskirts.

"Looks like that's where she was going," she said, and walked over to a large map on the wall. "Looking at the topography, she was heading for that forest area."

"Maybe."

Bossé picked up the second map and laid it on a table next to the wall.

"Any idea what these notations are on the map in the different states?"

John peered over her shoulder.

"They're just a series of numbers next to a dot. Not got a clue what they mean."

"Better take a photo. They could mean something."

John took a photo, then stowed away his camera and closed his case.

"Unless there's anything else that's me done here? I'll get back to you on the prints as soon as I get to the lab and put them through the database. The DNA results will take a little longer. I have everything I need from the backpack. I leave it with you."

"No problem," she said, and walked with him to the door. As soon as the door closed, she busied herself, putting everything back in the backpack. She tugged on the straps. At a guess, including the snowshoes and tent, she thought it probably weighed more than half of Clara's body weight. That took her full circle to the power needed to haul Ackerman's body on the rope pulley as she dragged the backpack and hauled it with some difficulty into the locker.

Bossé took one last look around, then ambled out of the office and onto the sidewalk. She locked the door and shivered. The light was burning in Father David's cottage. She lifted the collar on her jacket, and head down to avoid the biting cold, she walked quickly over to his front door. Stamping her feet at his doorstep, and with her teeth chattering, she gave the door a knock.

"Yes?" he said, as the door opened.

"I'm Detective Bossé."

"Oh, yes, I heard you were in town. A most unfortunate occurrence indeed. I only wish I could have done more for

Clara, then perhaps it wouldn't have happened. You'd better come in out of the cold."

She followed him into the living area and he signaled with the sway of his arm for her to take seat.

"I have coffee in the pot. Would you like some?"

"Please."

When he left the room, she picked up a small Bible from the coffee table and turned the pages to the third book of The Old Testament. She closed it again and set it down as Father David returned and handed her a cup of coffee.

"Find anything in there of interest?" he asked.

As a matter of fact, yes. I'd just been looking through Clara's Bible from her backpack and noticed some of the pages were torn out."

"Ah, so you noticed too. And did it indicate to you the same as it warned me when you discovered what was missing?"

"No."

"Then I suggest you read it," he said, and picked up the Bible to offer it to Bossé. "Turn to Leviticus, chapter eighteen, verse six. I think that you will find possible mitigating circumstances for her actions in the text."

Bossé read the words, then looked over at Father David and pushed back in her chair.

"These are God's laws about forbidden sexual relationships and families. Are you suggesting she was in an incestuous relationship with her dad?"

Chapter 44

Bible Lesson

Father David leaned forward on his chair, picked up his coffee and took a sip, and then set the cup down. Bossé waited for the answer as to what he was suggesting by asking her to read Leviticus.

"You're the detective," he said. "All I can say is that she had her Bible here with Leviticus missing. I pointed that out to her and offered her my Bible. She told me her dad tore out the pages. After she left, I noticed my Bible open at Leviticus on her nightstand. Something triggered her to leave suddenly. I'm just saying that there is the possibility that Clara realized her dad had forced an incestuous relationship on her, and that could have been the trigger for her to leave."

"But did she actually say that?"

"Well, no, but if you look at some of the passages underlined in red in her Bible, her dad could have used them to reinforce the notion that it was acceptable behavior."

Bossé took a sip of coffee. As plausible as his theory was, it was supposition and changed nothing, except that the sheriff had said something about Clara saying that she had been defiled during the fight at the church. She thought back to John saying that one of the pages in Clara's dictionary was missing the letter I. That could have prevented Clara looking up the word incest. Again it wasn't proof, but Bossé didn't hold with coincidences.

"Did she have her backpack here with her?"

"No."

Bossé paused for reflection, and wondered if Clara had left her backpack at Hunter's Lodge when she ran away from home.

"Did she mention anything about money?"

"Only that she had none. The only other thing I heard mentioned was her marriage dowry, but I was groggy at the time after her dad struck me."

"So she's married?"

"No, but that's the problem Clara was facing and the main reason she ran away and why she was here."

"Sorry, I don't understand, could you explain?"

He glanced at her over his half-rimmed spectacles and hesitated. His look gave the impression he was churning over how to reply. Finally, he relaxed and pushed back on his chair.

"Her dad had arranged a marriage for her, and they went through a sham service which took place on the Sunday. She arrived here on that Monday with Nat and Jordan and his friends. Jordan said they'd helped her to escape after she climbed through her bedroom window. She'd hurt her back with the fall and couldn't walk. They had to carry her inside. She was clearly troubled and it took some time for her to open up about the ceremony her dad performed. I had to convince her that she wasn't legally married. That's what all the fuss was about at the church. I never expected her dad and her supposed husband to break the sanctuary we had given her. They'd come to take her back home. Her dad threatened us with his rifle inside the church."

"When was this?"

"Tuesday around midday."

"How were they stopped?"

"I can't help you there I'm afraid. Her dad struck me with the butt of his rifle and I was unconscious for a time. But before that, her supposed husband said that he wanted no part of it and said her dad would be better leaving it and to give him the dowry back. You'd need to ask the others what happened. "

"Others?"

"Nat was there with Jordan and his two friends."

Bossé took a long swig of her coffee. This mysterious friend of Clara's dad piqued her interest. Especially as he was with Ackerman on the day of the murder. Not only that, her notion of the order of events was looking doubtful. If Clara had escaped in a hurry, that would have given her a reason to go back for her backpack and not with premeditation to kill him. A knock on the door interrupted her stream of thoughts.

"I'll go and see who's here."

As he left the room, she rose from her seat and stepped over to the window. The front door opened, followed by muffled

GIRL AT THE WINDOW

conversation, and then it closed. She watched the mayor close the gate and then he walked over to the church community center. A crowd of around twenty people were milling around the door. She recognized Nat standing and holding the handles of a wheelchair. Sheriff MacCaffrey was there, but there was no one else that she recognized as the mayor opened the door and they trouped inside."

"Council meeting?" Bossé said, as Father David returned.

"No, or I'd be there. The MacCaffreys are holding a family meeting."

She wondered why the sheriff would lie to her. But then she thought, maybe it was a local term when she'd said it was a council meeting, and she'd meant a family council meeting to discuss family business. Her mind picked up on when Father David said Clara had no money when Clara arrived at his cottage, but let it ride.

"Where are you staying?"

She stepped back to the sofa and took a seat.

"In a cell at the sheriff's office. Sheriff said that there are no hotels."

"Yes, that's right. The last one closed six months back. Well, I have to say that I find that most commendable of you, but I won't hear of it. You're welcome to stay here."

"That's kind of you. It shouldn't be more than for a few days. I have some work to do over at the sheriff's office and I'll need my overnight bag. If I'm back around ten, would that be okay?"

"Not a problem."

Bossé rose from her seat and he followed her to the door.

It was troubling her that having met Nat, no mention had been made of him helping Clara to escape, never mind knowing her. With her mind loaded with what she had heard, Bossé found herself at the sheriff's office and unlocked the door. She felt for the light switch, then stepped inside. Her cell phone rang and she retrieved it from her purse. Her office number appeared on the screen.

"Hello."

Brennan, her boss answered.

"When will your report be ready on the Ackerman case? I need you back here. Don't worry about the press. The DA is taking the heat with you not being here. I've just spoken with him, and from what he hears on the grape vine; the preliminary findings are that the psychiatrist report will clear her for trial. He wants your report so he's ready for when the forensic findings are finished."

"What's the hurry? Sorry, but you'll both have to wait. There are a few doubts surfacing about how things transpired."

The line went quiet.

"Did you hear me?"

"Yeah, I heard. What doubts?"

"Her capability of being able to lift him with the pulley for a start. She was half the victim's weight and she'd taken a fall the day before and hurt her back. I'll need you to get a hold of her processing report to see if she had any injuries reported, or any medical treatment required at the time. I can't be sure, but I'm going to make inquiries to see if she had an accomplice. I also have a few other lines of inquiry to make."

Bossé waited for his response, then waited some more.

"Do what you have to do. Report back when you have news," he said, and hung up.

He'd sounded pissed, save for the silence, with a few occasional sighs when she'd stood her ground. She'd seen the statistics reported in the press and it wasn't looking good on the year's solved cases. That aside, she was determined not to be bullied into getting a result. Not after Coulter had been proven innocent.

Bossé dropped her backside on the chair at the sheriff's desk and dragged the file on Jordan and his friends toward her, knowing that forewarned would be forearmed before she sought them out to interview them in the morning. More than anything, her mind drifted to her conversation with Jake Hunter. Jordan arriving home at midnight on the day of the murder hung there in her mind's eye.

Chapter 45

Tossing and Turning

If Bossé had realized that the room where she'd be sleeping was where Clara had slept, it would have been better to politely decline Father David's invitation. The night spent in the same bed that Clara had slept in was fraught with nothing but tossing and turning. Bossé felt bad enough that she had followed in Clara's footsteps from the lodge to the barn, and on to the sheriff's office.

In her nightmare, Bossé had experienced Clara's fear as she smashed at the window to escape. To make things worse, Bossé thought that she had probably sat on the same cot as Clara in the cell. She imagined that was what brought on her nightmares in which she was Clara, or at least that she was inside her head and not looking on.

Bossé had felt the anger that had probably tortured Clara, and how horrified she would have been at discovering the truth in Father David's Bible. That alone would have caused imaginable distress, with no doubt a few short circuits in her brain, making her not think straight. The sham marriage was as close to sex trafficking as she could imagine, and with the dowry Father David mentioned—well! She imagined that was a polite word for receiving payment for her as you would have done with a slave.

Bossé was thankful that she awoke just as she was about to strike him with the knife. It made her wonder what she would have done in the same circumstances. She imagined her fury might have given Clara the strength to pull twice her weight on that rope pulley.

Bossé shook her head and wondered what the hell she was thinking. This wasn't the time for sympathy and excuses, but to find cold hard facts. That was her job. It was the way it was meant to be. Clara had been found at the scene with a weapon.

221

That was damning in itself and within spitting distance of the scales of justice, tipping toward guilty. It wasn't her job to be judge and jury, and to sift through her mitigating circumstances offered by the defense attorney, and to set a sentence if found guilty. She rose from her bed and dressed. There was a knock on her door.

"Yes?"

"It's Mrs. O'Ahern, detective. I'm Father David's housekeeper. Breakfast is ready."

"I'll be right down."

Bossé stuck to polite conversation at the breakfast table, not wishing to outstay her welcome by asking more questions. She drained the last of her coffee.

"I can't thank you enough."

"It's not a problem, detective," Father David said.

"Please, call me Alana."

"Beautiful name."

"Thanks," she said, and blushed. She hadn't expected that line from a priest, but she'd heard it a few times when she'd been propping up bars back home. "Sorry, but I have to get to work." She rose from her chair, collected her purse, then walked to the front door.

The Main Street was busier than yesterday, with overnight rain clearing all but the most persistent mounds of snow. At least it wasn't freezing cold, but there was still a chill in the air, and a gray sky with dark clouds that cast a gloomy ambience over the town. She was used to seeing people scurrying around in her hometown, where no one gave her a second glance. Here, she was acutely aware that she was the outsider as people glanced at her then looked away. The sheriff's office was still locked up when she arrived. Bossé let herself in, opened the blinds, and then flicked the light switch. The sheriff pulled up in her SUV. Bossé was sure MacCaffrey had seen her, but the sheriff turned away and drove on. Through the slats, she could see two young men on a bench outside the grocery store and hoped they were her targets.

"Time to get started," she said aloud, and locking the door behind her, she strode across to the store.

'Rodger Drake and Rick Hunter," she said, as if she already knew them.

"Who wants to know?" the thinner of the two of them said, and stubbed out a cigarette.

She already had her ID palmed and showed it to them.

"I'm Detective Bossé, robbery and homicide if you can read? I need a word across at the sheriff's office, now."

They exchanged glances.

"I'm Rick Hunter. We don't know shit, honest."

"All the same, let's go. You don't even know what I have to ask yet."

"We don't have to say nothing about nothing," said Drake.

Bossé unfastened the single button on her coat, revealing her shoulder holster and the cuffs on her belt.

"No problem. I'll lock you both up for smoking cannabis then. I could smell it a mile away," she said, and not taking her eyes off of them, she reached down and picked up the cigarette stub.

They both laughed.

"What's so funny?"

"It's legal, or haven't you heard?"

"How old are you both?" Bossé asked, already knowing the answer from the file.

"I'm twenty and he's nineteen, so we're adults."

"More fool you then. The legal age is twenty-one, or haven't you heard?"

"Damn it, we were only joshing. Listen, we'll talk to you. Just forget about the joint," Drake said.

"Depends. Get walking."

She followed them across to the sheriff's office and let them inside. Bossé had them where she wanted them.

"You take a seat at the desk," she said to Drake. She pointed to Rick Hunter. "You can wait in the cell and I'll talk to you later. Both tell me what I want to know and you can both go about your business."

Bossé walked him through to a cell and locked him inside.

"What is it you want?" Drake asked as she returned and took a seat at the desk. She opened the top draw and took out the sheriff's file.

"What relation is Rick to Jordan?"

"Cousins, why?"

"I'll come to that." She opened the file. "I see you were at the community hall the night Jordan had a fight with Nat. What was all that about?"

"Nat attacked him."

"And?"

"And what?"

"What caused the fight?"

"Two girls were fighting. We stepped in to break it up. Nat got the wrong idea 'cause one of them was with him."

"Who was with Nat?"

"Clara. Don't know her surname. She was new in town."

"Why were the girls fighting?"

"Clarissa started it. She was jealous that Nat was with someone."

Bossé closed the file. What he'd said was no different than the sheriff's summary, but her notes didn't mention Clara by name. It bothered her that the sheriff had said Clara was hooked up with Jordan and not Nat. She wasn't interested in the other things that the sheriff thought they were involved in on file, as that was a local matter.

"To say you didn't know this Clara, you thought enough about her to help her run away."

"Oh that. Man that was cool. She jumped right out of her window and slid on her ass on the shingles down to the drive. Didn't think anything of her, but, man, she's cute. It was Jordan that was sweet on her. Hell, he even called a truce with Nat to help us."

"But I thought you said she was with Nat at this dance?"

"Yeah, Jordan was sweet on her too, that's why he knew Nat would help with the escape."

"And where is Jordan now?"

He fidgeted on his chair. She had a good idea what the answer would be.

"Dunno."

"Okay, let's leave that for now. What happened that day at

the church?"

He recited what she already knew from Father David. The rest stunned her as to Clara standing up to her dad and calling him out for abusing her. She picked up a pencil from the desk and chewed on it.

It was looking as though Clara's motives were cemented, both as revenge, and needing the money for when she'd left home. The defense attorney would have his work cut out to convince the judge and jury to have leniency, especially taking the circumstances into account of the abuse, in view of the manner in which she had exacted revenge.

Even though she knew Colorado was considered a de facto non-capital punishment state, having only put to death one inmate since 1997, it was still on the books. She tapped her lips with her finger. All the DA had to provide was proof of premeditation of an especially heinous, cruel, or depraved conduct in carrying out the crime, and that was there for all to see in the way Ackerman had been dispatched. The other was for pecuniary gain, if it could be proven she had tortured him to find the money that she had in the backpack. If anything, the mitigating circumstances could be turned on its head to prove premeditation. Still, she came back to the idea that Clara couldn't have done it on her own.

Bossé placed the pencil on the desk and leaned forward.

"So getting back to Jordan. I guess he ran away from town after you all helped Clara to kill her dad, following her revelation outside the church that he'd abused her?"

Chapter 46

Closing Ranks

Drake slouched up to the point of Bossé accusing him of being a party to Ackerman's murder. There was no need to wait for a reaction, it was immediate. He pushed back hard on his chair, the wooden legs scraping on the floor. His eyes popped and his jaw slackened. Then his eyes darted around the room.

"Don't even think about it. The door's locked."

"I—wasn't... Look, I—I didn't have anything to do with his murder. I don't have a gun. None of us did. We were all driving around in Jordan's new SUV until he decided his dad would be asleep so he could get his clothes."

"What time was this?"

"He picked us up around seven, then dropped us off at my house around eleven. Rick stayed at mine. I swear. Ask Mom."

"Don't worry, I will. This SUV, what make and color was it?"

"Two-tone, maroon and silver. Chrysler I think. It has a winch at the front."

Bossé made a note.

"So you're still saying that you don't know where he is?"

Bossé snatched her vision to the door when the handle twitched, then someone gave the door a pounding. A pair of eyes looked at her through a gap in the blind slats.

"Open up. This is Rick Hunter's dad. Drake, don't you dare say anything," he hollered.

Bossé was at a loss to know how he knew they were there. She rose to her feet and walked over to the door, unlocked it, and stepped outside.

"What is it you want?"

He thrust a card at her. "That's my attorney, he's on his way. I've told Rick not to say anything."

"How did you know he was here?"

"He used his phone to call me from the cell. He overheard what you're accusing them off."

Bossé rolled her eyes, both at her own stupidity and that her voice had carried. The sheriff's office and layout wasn't exactly geared toward private interviews.

"For your information, I caught them smoking dope. I have every right to hold them."

A car pulled up outside. Some guy climbed out and Rick's dad greeted him.

"I'm here to see my clients," he said. "Have you charged them?" He looked to be a retiree, and hardly dressed as an attorney, wearing a white Stetson, a plaid patterned shirt, jeans, and cowboy boots.

"No, they're helping with my inquiries into a murder investigation. But before that I caught them smoking dope."

"So charge them. Misdemeanor first offence. Slap on the wrist. They still aren't saying anything. Now step aside, I want to talk to them."

"Look, I'm not interested in the dope offence. All I'm trying to find out is where Rick's cousin is so I can eliminate him from my investigation. It's a simple enough request. If they cooperate, I can forget about the marijuana charges."

"I'll ask them," he said, and brushed her aside. She followed them inside and unlocked the cell door.

"Your attorney is here."

Rick smirked. He strutted through to the office as though he owed it.

"I need to talk to them in private," said their attorney.

"Not much chance of that in here or in the cells from what Rick's dad said." She looked around. "I'll wait outside."

She didn't have to wait long on the sidewalk when the door opened and their attorney called her back inside. Drake had answered her by instinct and out of fear. She doubted he was involved after mentioning a gun.

"Okay, ask your questions," he said.

She turned to Drake and said, "All I want to know is where I can find Jordan?"

The attorney nodded.

"He didn't want us to know. Said he didn't trust that Rick would be able to keep a secret and not tell his dad where he'd gone."

"What about a cell phone number? Both of you must have that."

"We have," said Rick, "but it's a waste of time giving it to you. He threw the SIM card away on the night he left. Said he didn't want his dad calling him."

"You can give me the number anyway."

They both looked at their attorney. He nodded. Bossé wrote down the number. If nothing else, she knew she could get a warrant for the provider to give her a list of calls and cell tower movements. They'd have been better using a current practicing attorney, more up to date with modern technology, she thought. Still she wasn't about to point out his mistake.

"You finished?" The attorney said. "A deal is a deal."

She couldn't think what else she could do to keep them, only to charge them for the misdemeanor. But as he had said, a deal was a deal. Besides, Bossé felt as though she had enough details to be going on with to investigate further. A two-tone SUV wouldn't be hard to find if he wasn't out of the area.

"Yeah, it's a deal for now."

"You have my card. I've instructed them not to say anything in future without me there."

Bossé cursed at herself under her breath. She realized that she should have cautioned them first for the dope offense and searched them before doing anything else. It made her realize just how little sleep she'd had.

A pickup truck screeched to a halt outside. Next thing she knew, Jake Hunter stepped inside the office. His cheeks looked as though they were on fire, with his face contorted in anger.

"What the hell is all this about you accusing my son of murder? You have your murderer."

His brother stepped between Bossé and Jake, and then grabbed his shoulders. For all he had bad-mouthed his son when she'd interviewed him, he was now firmly in parent mode.

"Calm down, Jake. Everything is cool," his brother pleaded.

"Calm down! I bet this is that bitch Sheriff MacCaffrey's doing. Where is she?"

"It has nothing to do with her. Listen, Mr. Hunter, I asked a question of Drake here. He denied they had anything to do with the murder. Now I just need to talk to Jordan to hear his version of what he did that night before he arrived home. If he wasn't there at the scene of the murder, he's nothing to worry about."

"Worry about! Serves that son of a bitch right that he's dead. You know he took a pot shot in the woods next to the lodge at Jordan and these two here last week when they were in the woods?"

"Whoa there. That's enough talk," said the attorney. "Get him outta here."

His brother pushed Jake out of the office and the rest followed.

Bossé closed the door and shook her head. She glanced at the name on the attorney's card. 'Gordon Hunter' it read. It was looking as though the battle lines were clearly manned between the MacCaffreys and the Hunters in town.

To say the interview hadn't gone according to plan, she'd learned more than she had expected. Jordan was definitely a person of interest, especially if she added the sheriff's report of Ackerman pulling a gun on Jordan and his friends outside the grocery store. Now she'd found out he'd taken a pot shot at them. Add that to him hearing about Ackerman abusing Clara outside the church, and there was enough there to be motive for Jordan to exact revenge and to help Clara. It wasn't just that supposition. If Jake Hunter knew he'd taken a shot at his son, together with his beef about the deer and traps, he could have stepped in at the barn before Clara arrived to exact his own revenge.

She picked up her laptop and took a seat back at the desk, then started to type. With the report almost finished, her cell phone rang and she answered.

"Hi, it's John. I have news."

"Go on, what have you found?"

"Trivial things first. The fingerprint from the bills inside the security box matches the prints I took from the corpse. His prints were also on the newspaper that formed the outside of the package, but not on anything else. Where it gets interesting is that a print from one of the plastic bags inside the package belongs to one Archibald Jeremiah Rhymer. And guess what? He's got a rap sheet."

"What sort of a rap sheet?"

"Molesting children. Young girls. He's a registered sex offender. The address we have is in the Sierra Nevada Mountain Range, a saw mill."

"That would be an area where the newspaper came from. What about the bank?"

"That's the Gardnerville branch of the bank in the nearest town to where he lives. We also have a match to him on some prints from the kitchen and in one of the bedrooms."

It sounded to Bossé that the money was likely the dowry, and Rhymer was Ackerman's friend and intended husband of Clara.

"That's hardly trivial."

"Oh it is, when you consider what we found when we charged up that cell phone that the young man found by the barn."

Now he really had her attention.

"Go on then, enlighten me."

"There's a last text message. 'Better get that dowry to me or your dead' it says. It's dated at eight thirty on the night of the murder."

Bossé shook her head. Her list of persons' of interest was growing by the minute. The cell phone message was about as incriminating as it gets, she thought.

Chapter 47

The Text Message

A phone call from John at forensics, confirmed that the cell phone Nat had found with the death-threat text message belonged to Ackerman. From earlier messages, it was clear that Rhymer had sent the text. Bossé had made arrangements for a search warrant and for the local sheriff to bring Rhymer in for questioning. It was on to other business as she waited for a result. She opened the file on the desk and ran her finger down the sheriff's notes. Finding Drake's home phone number, she picked up the handset and dialed the digits. Fingers crossed, she hoped his mom hadn't had word of what had happened.

"Hello, who is it?"

"Is that, Mrs. Drake?"

"Yes. Who wants to know?"

"Detective Bossé. Nothing to worry about, Mrs. Drake. I've just spoken to your son Rodger. We're trying to locate his friend, Jordan Hunter. Apparently, he's moved out of town. He was saying that the last he saw of him was when he dropped him off at your house with Rick on Tuesday evening. I'm just trying to get a handle on the exact time, because he was a little vague."

"Jordan! I hope he's gone for good. Rodger hasn't said anything. Nothing but trouble that one leading my son astray. Tuesday you said? Oh yes, I remember now. It had just turned eleven when they arrived. I made them supper right away."

"Did they get changed out of their clothes when they arrived?"

"Well, no they didn't, but why ask? Rodger's not in trouble is he?"

"Not that I know of," she said, and laughed to hopefully put her at ease. "It's Jordan we're looking for. Anyway thanks for your help that's all I needed. If you hear anything about where Jordan is staying, you can leave a message at the sheriff's office if I'm not there."

Bossé ended the call, not wanting to get into a question and answer session. She'd heard all that she needed to know. Without a time of death, Jordan and his friends were still in the frame. Drake mentioning a gun could have been deliberate to throw her off the scent. She wondered if Jordan, Drake, and Rick Hunter could have been involved in the break-in at the lodge, and the murder was a separate incident. Sheriff MacCaffrey had them as suspects for the break-ins that were plaguing the area, so it could have been a possibility. The whole case was looking more complex by the minute.

Sheriff MacCaffrey breezed into the office.

"What the hell rattled Jake Hunter's cage? I've just had an earful over the phone. Couldn't make out half of what he was saying."

"I've printed a copy of my report. I think you'll have your answer if you read it."

"I will if I can have my desk back."

Bossé rose from her chair and took a seat at the small desk holding the printer. MacCaffrey leaned back on her chair and rested her legs on the desk.

Finally, she finished reading, removed her legs from the desk and leant forward.

"None of this gets away from the fact that I found her with the knife covered in blood at the scene."

"Yeah, I'll give you that. Talking about the scene. Where did you find her backpack?"

"She was wearing it. Had to remove it to cuff her. It looked as though she'd slipped on the pool of blood and she was struggling to get to her feet when I first saw her."

"Did she touch her head or her back on the way to your vehicle?"

"No, why?"

"I'm just wondering if she walked in on the murderer and someone whacked her."

"Clutching at straws there aren't you. Surely she'd have said, but she said nothing, only laughed as I said in my statement. Besides, I already told you. The lump on her head was from the fight she had at the church hall. Rhymer, I can't tell you about, but from what I've just read, I'd say he's the sort of scum that might have tortured him to get his money back. I'd speak to my sister-in-law over at the grocery store if I were you. She overhears half the goings on of Jordan and his friends."

"Wouldn't she have said something at your family meeting last night?"

MacCaffrey blushed.

"Why should she? She's not a mind reader. You wouldn't expect her to find out what you only found out today."

Her tone of voice was defensive. Bossé got the impression that she resented the intrusion.

"Yeah, never thought. I'll have a word with her later. Then I'll need to speak to Nat."

"What for?"

"Well, he must have known Clara to take her to the dance. Then he helped to get her away from the lodge. He was also at the church when Ackerman turned up, so he'd know what was said. So far, I only have what little Father David knows and what Drake said, which wasn't much. It'll help me find out what her state of mind was."

"I suppose there is that. Listen, I have to be going. How long will you be in the office?"

"I'm not going anywhere until I hear if they've picked up Rhymer."

"Good, phone me when you hear something. I'll keep a look out for Jordan's SUV."

MacCaffrey left in as big a hurry as when she'd entered.

Over at the window, she watched MacCaffrey drive off. She didn't go far and stopped outside the grocery store. Bossé thought that she wouldn't like to get on the wrong side of a traffic stop with her. She had given nothing of herself away, apart from showing anger when she'd listened in on the conversation with John at the lodge. But then thinking about it, Bossé hadn't given anything of herself. She decided that she'd have to rectify that if she wanted her full cooperation and to try a little socializing away from the office. The phone rang and she answered.

"Detective Bossé, please."

"That's me."

"Carson City Sheriff's Office. Deputy Morris. We have your man in custody."

"That was quick. Custody!"

"Yeah, we turned up some child porn, both on his computer and his cell phone, so he isn't going anywhere. You're welcome to interview him here today, but tomorrow he'll be in the county jail awaiting arraignment. Doubt he'll get bail though, he's a parolee. We've not mentioned your interest in him."

"Good, I'm on my way from Hunter's End. I'll arrange a flight."

Bossé hung up, and then dialed Sheriff MacCaffrey's number.

"Hi, Bossé here. Thought I'd let you know I'm on my way to Carson City. They have Rhymer in custody. I won't be back until tomorrow."

"No problem, take your time. I'll be around when you get back."

She picked up her laptop and purse, locked the office, and then walked over to Father David's cottage. She didn't have to knock, he was just leaving.

"Hold on there, I need my overnight bag. I have business in Carson City and I won't be back until tomorrow."

"Not a problem, I'll wait here."

Bossé hurried inside and collected her bag.

"Good luck with your business," Father David said.

"Thanks, I'll see you tomorrow."

She was beside herself with anticipation, already planning her interrogation as she climbed into her car, and then drove along Main Street. She glanced at the grocery store. Sheriff MacCaffrey was standing at the door remonstrating with Nat. They both glanced her way then averted their gazes, and then Sheriff MacCaffrey continued to chew his ear as if it was none of Bossé's business.

Her cell phone rang. She reached over, slipped it out of her purse, placed it in the hands-free cradle and noticed Gilbert Rhodes' name from the DAs office on the screen. Bossé reached over and stabbed the off symbol. She wasn't ready to have to explain herself to him just yet. At least not until she'd finished interviewing Rhymer.

Chapter 48

Hot Suspect

Over at the Carson City Sheriff's Office, Bossé read through the transcript of messages and phone calls taken from Rhymer's cell phone and exchanged between Ackerman and the suspect. Conversations had started with telephone calls between them in the week before the murder. The first text message was from Ackerman saying he had to go for a medical in Denver, and they should meet up to go to Hunter's Lodge together on the Saturday; and for him to be sure to bring the money. Rhymer had replied that he'd go to the bank on the Friday, followed by a list of clothing he wanted Ackerman to buy for Clara to wear on the wedding day. That explained the short skirt and the other clothing they had found in her bedroom. It also said a lot about his intentions and perverted mind.

The search hadn't turned up any bloodstained clothing, and his truck was clean, so Bossé knew that she didn't have any concrete evidence to tie him to the murder. She hoped that with his vehicle impounded, and his dirty clothing confiscated, that forensics would find some of the victim's blood traces. There was no way to know if he'd ditched the clothing that he wore on the day, and if he'd cleaned out his cab. All she had was that he was at the scene at some time before the murder and the threatening text he'd sent. As damning as the text message was, she wasn't expecting an easy interview.

"Do you want me to go into the interview room with you?" Deputy Morris asked.

"No, I'll be fine. The uniform might make him nervous. He'll be on edge enough knowing he's being shipped back to prison as it is. I'm just relieved no one has told him why I want to talk to him. Just make sure the camera is recording."

"Sure, I'll watch on the monitor from the viewing room."

She'd gone over how to start the interview hundreds of times in her head on the journey over to Carson City. None of the outcomes seemed to work in her favor. All it would take would be for him to demand his rights and to say nothing, and it would have been a wasted journey. Bossé arrived at the interview room. She smoothed down her skirt with the palm of her hands, took a deep breath, and then she entered wearing a false smile.

"Mr. Rhymer. I'm Detective Bossé. Looks as though you've gotten yourself in a heap of trouble, but I'm not here about that," she said, and took a seat, laying her file on the table.

He looked to be a pathetic excuse of a man, but then knowing he had downloaded child porn, and that he had a history of sexually assaulting children, she knew that she was biased. Whatever, seeing how old and wizened he looked, she could understand why Clara ran away. He cleared his throat.

"Yeah, well whatever you're selling I ain't buying, lady."

"No problem. And there's me thinking if you helped me, I could pull strings for what you're facing to get you a lighter sentence for cooperating. Foolish really, when you don't know what I want help with." She picked up her file and rose from her chair, then turned to face the door. "Pity really, they're talking out there about putting you in the general prison population to teach you a lesson. I could have helped with that."

She hadn't quite reached the door, when he called her back. She'd had a good idea that last statement would get his attention.

"Wait. No promises, what is it you want to know?"

She turned and walked back over to the table, slapped the file down, and took a seat.

"You have a friend over at Hunter's Lodge. Joseph Ackerman. I'm looking for background information on him."

"That douche bag. He ain't no friend of mine. He owes me money. A lot of money."

"Would that be the money for you marrying his daughter, Clara?"

"No law against that. Besides, she's over eighteen. I'm

240

reckoning they worked me over for the money. Ten thousand's not to be sneezed at, is it?"

She opened then closed her file

"We have Clara locked up. I wish I could say the same for her dad."

"Serves her right. Little bitch. Who else have they turned over?"

If he was the murderer, he was acting smart, talking as if Ackerman was still alive. She was hoping for an emotional response, but his expression gave nothing away. She let his question ride.

"I know you were there with him this weekend from a witness at the church, and your text message says that you were to meet up with him on Saturday. We can have your movements checked from data extracted from your cell phone, so I'd be exact with the timing if I were you. Lie to me and I'll let the guys out there ship you to wherever they want. For now, explain how you think they worked you?"

He scrunched his eyes.

"Whoa, roll back a minute. I had nothing to do with the church thing. I wanted none of it. I'm guessing it was all an act they'd worked out. Soon as we got back to his house and I got out of his pickup, he drove off. He'd no intention of giving me the money back. The wedding thing was all a sham on their part. I didn't even get to touch her."

"So what did you do?"

He was clearly rattled, but thankfully for Bossé, Rhymer ran off at the mouth.

"What the hell could I do? I had a business to run. I drove around looking for him for hours. When I couldn't find him, I drove back home."

"What time?"

"Around nine thirty in the evening, why?"

"You're missing something out. You sent him a threatening text at eight thirty."

"Oh, that. I was trying to flush him out. It didn't work."

Bossé wiped the smile from her face and leaned toward him.

"Here's what I think. You drove around, and not finding him, you parked out of sight, then you broke into his house to look for the money. He came back and you chased him down to the barn. Then you tortured him to find out where he'd hidden the money, but it didn't work, so you killed him. Isn't that right?"

He looked like a scared jack rabbit caught in the headlights. Then his attitude changed.

"Don't talk shit. If you've found my fingerprints from his house, then all it does is to prove I was there. I ain't denying that I was there. I swear I didn't kill him. Besides, some young guy at the church threatened to kill him and threw a hammer through his pickup window. Maybe you should talk to him. To hell with you anyway, lady. I'm not saying anything else without a lawyer."

"What did this young guy look like?"

Rhymer ran his finger and thumb across his lips as though he were fastening a zipper. The message was clear and the interview was over.

"Fair enough. It wouldn't make much difference to you if you admitted it and told the truth. At your age you'll be dead before you'd see the light of day by the time your sentence for downloading porn runs out, especially when it's tagged onto your existing sentence. Enjoy living in the general prison population," she said, picked up her file and left him to stew.

Deputy Morris met her in the corridor as she exited.

"Nothing more I can do here until forensics report back on the tests on his vehicle and clothing," she said.

"Yeah, I heard. At least he isn't going anywhere," Morris said. "You know he won't be going back to prison straight away. We'll be sending him to the county jail to await arraignment for his current charge. So you weren't wrong about him being in the general population. It's not as though these charges are for molesting anyone. He can ask for segregation, but there's no guarantee he'll get it. Maybe he'll crack and call you."

Bossé glanced at her watch and wished she had access to a time machine, so that she could fast forward to Hunter's End in the morning. Bossé knew that she would need to find out who

242

threw the hammer. Watching television in a hotel room wasn't exactly her idea of a pastime. It was times like those that she wondered if it would be better to have a husband to go home to, but that was a nonstarter. Five years on from her bitter divorce and she still didn't have it in her to trust anyone. The only consolation, she thought, was that they didn't have any kids. She sighed.

"I won't gamble on a phone call. Besides, I don't want him confessing to something that he hasn't done to get segregated from the run-of-the-mill prisoners. We'll see what the forensic report says. He'd have to tell us details only the murderer would know for a confession to work."

With five persons of interest, she knew the hard work was just beginning, and at some stage she'd have to speak to Gilbert Rhodes with a progress report. She took her cell phone from her purse and switched it on. There were five missed calls from Rhodes, two from the office, and one from John at forensics. Her finger hovered over the screen as to who to phone first.

Chapter 49

Checkmate

Bossé arrived back at Hunter's End and entered the sheriff's office. She took a seat, feeling guilty at having turned off her phone the night before. Bossé powered it up to an instant buzzing, with four missed calls and one text message showing on the screen. Gilbert Rhodes was three of the missed calls, and her boss the other, but she ignored them and opened the text message from John at forensics.

"I have some results. J."

She phoned him back right away.

"It's Alana, what have you found?"

"The blood type from the weapon, Clara's clothing, and backpack, they're all O negative, extremely rare. It matches the blood sample I took from the victim."

Bossé took a deep breath, and then blew a rasp through her closed lips.

"Ouch, that doesn't bode well for her with the blood on her knife, never mind her clothes. If the DNA matches, that's your evidence right there."

"There's more, but I'll not use tech speak. The autopsy revealed he had advanced throat cancer. His blood alcohol level was off the scale, and they found he had a disc hernia at L-four and five near the base of his spine. The bear trap severed his spinal column at the neck and pierced his carotid artery. He will have died before he bled out."

"So he'd probably have died of cancer anyway if they'd have left him be?"

"Looks that way. There had to have been extreme anger there for whoever killed him to have sliced his gut open after he was already dead. One other thing, well two actually. We tested the rope pulley. It definitely had a faulty ratchet. It worked correctly on weights up to one hundred and ninety-five pounds. Anything over that and it slipped when you let it down, but then the ratchet grabbed it again. That's why he was left hanging. The victim weighed in at two hundred and twelve pounds. And finally, a dried scrape sample I took at the barn revealed the possibility of deer blood. Under the microscope. I found parasites normally associated with deer. Also, the blood on the apron was a match with a deer."

"So the pulley was likely used for hanging a deer to bleed out some time before the murder. What do deer weigh?"

"Depends. If it was female, say sixty-five to two hundred pounds. A buck would be anything up to three hundred pounds."

"When will you have the DNA?"

"I should have the DNA results soon. I've had Gilbert Rhodes pushing for them. I'll let you know as soon as I have the results."

"Thanks, John."

She hung up. Bossé pictured the scene. As much as the evidence appeared to have Clara in checkmate, it still didn't let her other suspects off the hook. Apart from the victim having his gut sliced after the event, she wondered if it could have been an accident. They'd only lived there for two weeks, so unless the deer Ackerman had shot on Hunter's property weighed over one hundred and ninety-five pounds, Clara wouldn't know that the pulley was faulty, but then neither would any of the other suspects. She imagined that the way he was found indicated someone had tortured him for either information, or a confession, or maybe even just to scare him. Then the rope had slipped and in their anger, they had sliced him open.

She didn't think Clara would need information or a confession to have been motivated to scare the crap out of him as revenge. Jordan, his friends, or Nat could have been motivated to get him to confess for abusing Clara, and maybe they intended to hand him over to the sheriff. Rhymer on the other hand would need information. In his own words, he'd said that Ackerman didn't want to give him the money back. There was ten thousand reasons right there to torture him, and every reason to lash out in anger when he didn't get what he wanted.

Her cell phone rang. Gilbert Rhodes' name popped up on the screen. Bossé chewed on her lip as she picked up her phone and answered.

"You're hard to get hold of."

"Yeah, busy interviewing suspects," she said.

"Suspects! No need for that. We have to send the files and relevant documents for discovery to Clara's attorneys tomorrow. I don't need any red herrings from wild-goose chases on file that the defense can jump on. You can wrap it up there. We have everything we need apart from the DNA results, but his blood type and forensics to date will do for now. The psychiatrist's report has her cleared for trial. She's talking normally to the patients, and they're shipping her back to the county jail. She's just refusing to talk to anyone in authority. Your note on the file about her claiming Ackerman abused her is motive enough, never mind her stealing his money. I'm guessing that the defense will ask for a plea bargain once he sees what we have. I might even offer one, in view of the abuse she suffered for us to get a guilty plea."

"Whatever. I can't halt what I'm doing. I'm going to type up what I have so far and add it to the file today, and then I'll be continuing with my investigations."

"How many lines of inquiry do you have for other suspects and how strong are they?"

"Besides Clara, I have five, one of them very strong and one who disappeared on the night of the murder."

"Damn it. That's all we need."

"It is what it is. Incidentally, there's a chain of command. In future speak to my boss if you want briefing on where I'm at with the investigation."

He ended the phone call abruptly. Bossé couldn't have made her intentions more clear. She didn't care if what she had said caused friction with the DAs office, not when she had it in mind that this was to be her last case. All the same, the conversation with Rhodes had her ruffled. A shot of caffeine was called for, so she set about making coffee. She cursed when her phone rang again. This time her boss's name appeared on the screen.

"Hi, what is it you want?"

"For you to return my calls for a start."

"Oh, yeah, sorry. You were next on the list to phone."

"Well, I'm talking now, so there's no need, is there? What's all this about five suspects?"

She held the phone away from her ear. Rhodes had obviously been bending his ear, and by his tone, she guessed he was about to twist hers. Bossé gave him a rundown of events, and then poured coffee.

"Not much you can do then, only come back here and to get back to your other cases. I'll arrange for a warrant to get Rhymer's cell tower locations so we can see his movements, but other than that, I can't see what more you can do, only wait to see if the APB you've put out on Jordan Hunter comes up with a result. His friends are lawyered up, so you'll get nowhere with them, and as for this Nat MacCaffrey, he isn't really in the frame apart from having a thing for Clara."

Bossé picked up her cup and took a long swig. She could sense his game. He wanted everything to come to a halt until after the discovery session with Clara's defense lawyer, and until the DNA results had arrived, so they could put it to bed. Rhodes had gotten to him. It was looking to her as if they were both pinning their badges on a plea bargain. She'd worked with him long enough. It was time to play him back at his own game.

"You're dead right. I'm in a blind alley with it just now. I wish I could get back. Problem is my car engine is playing up. I was just about to get the local garage to try and repair it. Doubt they'll fit me in today. I've just worked four days straight, so I'm due a couple of days off. I can spend the rest of the day typing up what I have."

He didn't answer right away. She could hear him sucking air through his teeth at his end.

"What's wrong with your car?"

"How in hell's name would I know? Maybe it's the thruster for the widget thingamajig under the hood. All I know is that it's running rough."

"Very funny. Just get back here as soon as you can."

With the call closed, she snickered. She didn't mind telling white lies to suspects about what she knew or didn't know about events to get them to talk, but this was the first time she'd used lies on a colleague. Still, it wasn't exactly a lie. Her engine did have a flat spot when it hit sixty, but then it had been like that for more than a month. She decided that she'd get it serviced to cover her ass. Bossé locked the office door and walked over to the garage. When she arrived, she was surprised to see Nat under the ramps working on a vehicle exhaust. He wiped his hands on a rag.

"How can I help you, detective?"

"My car needs a service. It's sluggish at picking up speed when it hits sixty."

"No problem. I'm not the mechanic, but I can book you in." He ambled over to the counter and opened the reservation book. "There's a spot at three o'clock tomorrow, How's that?"

"Fine." He was doing that blushing thing again. "That your car?" She pointed to the one on the ramp.

"No, it's a customer's car. I can handle some jobs, but not all of them."

"Is this where you work full time?"

"No, I help my uncle out when he's busy. I'm a handyman full time, but I've helped my uncle out part time since I was old enough to pass him a wrench."

"Listen, while I'm here, I need to arrange to talk to you over at the sheriff's office about what happened at the church with Clara."

"Sure. I finish here in around an hour when my uncle gets back, if that's okay with you?"

"Sounds good," she said, and then set off back to the office.

As she stepped off the sidewalk, Bossé looked over her shoulder. Nat was looking her way and talking on his cell phone, and then he turned his back to her. As she arrived at the office, the detective in her couldn't help but wonder if he'd worked on his dad's brakes just before he died when his car ran off of the road.

Chapter 50

Clandestine Witness

Bossé had only just put the key in the lock at the sheriff's office, when Mrs. O'Ahern walked past her. She stopped and fidgeted inside her bag.

Not even looking at Bossé, she said, "I need to talk to you in private, but not here. Father David is out for an hour. Meet me at the cottage." She carried on walking on over to the cottage.

Intrigued by the clandestine manner of her delivery, she didn't want to make her offer look obvious to prying eyes. Bossé closed the office door behind her. She sneaked a look through a gap in the blinds. Satisfied no one was paying any attention in her direction; she exited the office and walked over to the cottage.

"Is there a problem?" Bossé said when she met Mrs. O'Ahern in the living room.

"Depends on your interpretation of what I'm hearing. Don't let my surname fool you. I'm an outsider, considering I've only lived here for four years. Word's spreading that no one has to talk to you about what anyone saw and heard at the church. I'm not prepared to say who, only that I clean for a few retirees and I've overheard conversations."

"Is that coming from the MacCaffreys or the Hunters?"

"The MacCaffreys, but they still want them to say Jordan made a death threat that day at the church. I know different. Jordan wasn't the only one who made threats that day. Nathanial MacCaffrey threatened to kill him. I heard him clear as the day."

She went on to explain all that she saw and heard. Bossé wondered why the townsfolk didn't just let it lie and say nothing, especially seeing as how Clara was charged with his murder. It sounded as though the town were using the murder to get even with the Hunters.

"Why are you coming forward?"

"Guilt. It was me that pointed Clara's dad in the direction of the church. Maybe if I hadn't, none of this would have happened. Clara was such a sweet girl. So naive. It's hard for me to believe that she could have done such a thing."

"Is the sheriff involved in these rumors?"

"I'm not sure. The sheriff is a sort of outsider herself seeing as how she's law enforcement, but she's still family. From what I've heard, her family turned against her when she married a Hunter and she left town. Only came back three years ago to take the job as sheriff. It looks as though her family have let the past stay in the past."

"Are you sure that you have that right? Wouldn't she be Mrs. Hunter?"

"MacCaffrey is her maiden name."

"Divorced?"

"No. Suicide. Her daughter disappeared from outside her house twelve years back. Apparently her husband never got over it. Turned to drink and drugs until he couldn't take anymore."

Bossé thought back to MacCaffrey's odd reaction at Hunter's Lodge when they'd opened the case and they found the children's clothing, together with the knife and duct tape. She thanked her and set off back to the office.

The Sheriff's SUV was parked outside when she arrived. MacCaffrey grunted a begrudging good morning as Bossé stepped inside the office.

"Anything new transpired?" MacCaffrey asked.

She hesitated answering, not knowing if she could trust her with all the latest information.

"John phoned with the blood tests. The victim's blood is a rare type and it matched the samples taken from Clara's clothing and the weapon."

Bossé looked for a reaction. A smile curled on the sheriff's lips.

"There you are then. Cut and dried as I said. I guess you'll be wrapping it up and going home now?"

There wasn't time to answer as the office door opened.

"Ah, Nat. You're on time," Bossé said. "Take a seat."

"Why the need to interview him now? You have the blood test results," the sheriff said.

Bossé hadn't told the sheriff she had asked Nat to come in for an interview. It seemed fortuitous to her that the sheriff arrived after she had seen Nat talking on his cell phone.

"Still have loose ends to tie up to get the full picture."

Sheriff MacCaffrey tutted. Nat took off his hat and took a seat at the desk opposite Bossé.

"So, Nat, why don't you start from where and when you first met Clara?"

Nat ran through an encounter when he'd come across their vehicle stuck in a drift.

"How did they seem to you? Any tension between them?"

"She never spoke. I asked her out to a local dance to meet the others of her age in town, but her dad answered for her. When I asked her, he seemed annoyed. He said they'd be away on the Friday and he slammed the pickup door, then drove off."

"When did you see her again?"

"I didn't exactly see her, only through the window at the lodge. It was two days later. I called to see if I could sell him some tire chains. He was out and Clara said that she didn't open the door when her dad wasn't there."

"Sensible. So how come you took her to the dance?"

"I called back when her dad was there and did an exchange for the tire chains for some tools. While he was in the barn, Clara asked if I'd take her to the dance, but not to tell her dad."

"So I guess you were sweet on her?"

"Hold on a second." Sheriff MacCaffrey rose from her chair. "What sort of a question is that? He was just being polite. It's his nature. He's already said he asked her to come to the dance to meet others of her age."

Bossé was taken aback by her interference.

"If you don't mind, Nat can answer my questions."

"He doesn't have to say anything. What are you driving at anyway?"

"It's okay, aunty, I can answer. It's like she said. Clara was new in town and I was just being polite."

"Then why did your ex-girlfriend end up fighting with her?"

"She got the wrong idea that's all, and so did I, when I saw Jordan touching Clara. It was all a misunderstanding. We made up after and I helped Jordan to rescue her from marrying that old pervert and we took her to the church. It was Jordan that was sweet on her."

He went on to give his account of what happened at the church. Bossé tapped her lips with her finger when he finished.

"You're missing something."

His cheeks reddened.

"Look, he's told you everything. I'm sure he has some work to do."

Bossé glared at the sheriff, and said, "I haven't finished yet." She turned her attention to Nat. "Why not tell me about the hammer you threw at Ackerman's pickup? The one that crashed through the back window and the threat you made to kill him."

Nat threw a glance at Sheriff MacCaffrey.

"He doesn't have to answer that. What's the point? You have your killer."

"You're right, he doesn't have to answer. I've had a witness fill in the blanks for him. I'm also not stupid. He didn't have a claw hammer on his tool belt when we arrived at the lodge, but he had it after I saw him lean into Ackerman's pickup."

"Don't answer her."

"Like I said, he doesn't have to, but maybe he can tell me his movements on the night of the murder?"

"Go ahead, Nat, tell her. I'll call Clarissa," the sheriff said, and opened the office door.

A young woman with blonde hair climbed out of Nat's vehicle and entered.

"I was with Clarissa all night," Nat said. "Ask her."

"That's right, I was with him all night at his house and we got engaged," Clarissa said, and held out her hand to show Bossé the ring.

"It was all thanks to Clara." Nat said. "When I spoke to her at the church, she made me see sense. See, we'd split because I asked Clarissa to marry me, but she wanted to go to college. Anyways, we worked it out and we'll get married after she's finished college."

"Well good for you, congratulations," Bossé said. "I guess that'll be all then."

Sheriff MacCaffrey had a smirk a mile wide as she ushered them out of the door. Bossé didn't buy his alibi. It all seemed so contrived with Clarissa waiting in the wings to save the day.

Her cell phone rang. John's number appeared on the screen. Bossé stepped outside the office and answered the call.

"I have a DNA result," he said, "but it poses more questions than it answers."

GIRL AT THE WINDOW

Chapter 51

Clara's DNA

Bossé wondered what John meant by the DNA result posing a problem.

"So go on, what are we dealing with?"

"Clara's DNA isn't a familial match with the victim's markers. So unless she's adopted, we have no proof of who she is."

"Then who the hell is she?"

"That's all down to you. Maybe you should ask her? What I can tell you is that Clara has DNA markers which indicate that one of her parents and her ancestral lineage is Native Indian, and indigenous to Alaska."

Bossé's mind went into turbocharge mode, snatching at scenarios from when John had said that she could have been adopted, to her thinking Ackerman could have abducted her as a child, or her being someone he picked up along his travels. Rhymer could have been right. They could have worked together at rolling victims over with such as a marriage scam.

"You there?" John said.

"Yeah, sorry. Just trying to get my head to absorb the implications. I'll go back out to the lodge and see if we missed some adoption papers."

Bossé ended the phone call and stepped back into the office. Her stomach knotted.

"Where can I get a sandwich?"

"The grocery store," Sheriff MacCaffrey said, not even lifting her vision from the file she was reading.

Bossé ambled over to the store. There was no sign of Jordan's friends. She ordered an egg salad sandwich and coffee, and then took a seat.

"You'll be that detective," the woman behind the counter said. She lifted the hatch and walked over with her order. "I don't know what you said to Jordan's friends, but it's a relief they're not hanging around outside, so thank you. Did they tell you about the day they went out to Hunter's Lodge to torment Mr. Ackerman?"

Bossé had taken a bite of her sandwich and shook her head. The woman took a seat opposite.

"They were buzzing when I heard them talking all excited about them going to the lodge with Jordan, and throwing snowballs with stones at the house. Ackerman fired a warning shot at them." She sat back with a smug smile on her face.

She'd confirmed what Jake Hunter had said, and the info about the provocation fitted in with the reports on their antics in town. When Bossé added the altercation at the church in the mix, there was motivation of a feud right there, for both revenge, and to teach Ackerman a lesson, but she thought it could have gone wrong when the ratchet failed.

"Jordan threatened to kill him after the fracas at the church you know. I wouldn't be surprised if he was somehow involved."

"And you heard that?"

"Yeah, the whole town probably heard it. A customer called me outside onto the porch."

"I might need a statement later. And you are?"

"Susan MacCaffrey. This is my store."

That fact didn't surprise her. Nor did the fact that she had not mentioned Nat making the same threats and launching his hammer at the pickup. It was when she had leaned forward and added into her script that Jordan had called out death threats that Bossé had switched off. Bossé drained her coffee, thanked her, and then walked outside. Looking at the distance to the church, she doubted that Susan MacCaffrey had heard anything. The sheriff's vehicle had gone from in front of the office. Bossé guessed that the sheriff had achieved a result she was there for in shepherding Nat through his interview, mission accomplished.

She hurried across Main Street and climbed in to her car. Turning the key in the ignition to fire up the engine, Bossé drove to Hunter's Lodge. She stopped at the gates to remove the tape, and then drove on into the drive.

The first thing she did when she entered was to look in the pantry. The cuts of meat hanging there seemed to be an almost complete deer. She envisioned the joints of meat she bought at the supermarket. Maybe seventy-five pounds including the rest of the carcass, she thought. A thorough search through all the papers in the office proved fruitless. Bossé exited and walked across to the woods. She was looking for a bullet embedded in a tree trunk, but found nothing. Instead, she found empty beer bottles and marihuana stubs scattered around a tree trunk. She lined up her sight from where she had found the items to Hunter's Lodge. The front door and upstairs windows where clearly visible.

Jake Hunter stepped out from behind a tree trunk and she put her hand to her chest. It didn't go unnoticed that he was carrying a rifle.

"Damn it. You scared the living daylights outta me. I never heard your footsteps."

"People never do, especially the critters before I put a bullet between their eyes. This is my property. You need a warrant to start searching around. I suggest you put those things back where you found them."

She knew the items were worthless. He was right though. Any court would throw them out as any type of evidence without a warrant. Besides the elements would have destroyed any DNA to prove who had handled them.

"Why would you want me to get a warrant? A little bird told me in town that Jordan and his friends were tormenting Ackerman when he fired a round to scare them off. I'd say those discarded stubs and bottles go some way to proving this is where they hung out that day."

"A little bird! That would be the MacCaffreys. I'll have to see them about that. So they're trying to have my son and my nephew tied in to this are they? Jordan might be the runt of the litter, but don't be thinking that you can drag my family into this. Stay off of my property. I wouldn't want to go mistaking you for a deer."

"Is that a threat?"

"Call it what you like, but let's just say it's a friendly warning."

Bossé turned and walked to the barn, the hairs on her neck bristling knowing he was behind her with the rifle. Stepping inside, she looked around, hoping to find anywhere he might have stashed something that could identify Clara. She rummaged everywhere, but found nothing. One last look around and her eyes set on a bow saw hanging on a nail. Next to that were two knives and rows of other tools. She took out her cell phone and took a picture.

Pondering on events, she exited and climbed into her car. Bossé reversed, when she heard a crunch under her car. She climbed out to find that she'd run over a branch. A little shoving and tugging and she managed to free it and threw it to one side. When she glanced at the tree line, she noticed Jake Hunter still there watching her. For him to put family before any animosity he had with Jordan, together with the veiled threat he'd just made, she wondered if she should add him to the top of her list of suspects.

Chapter 52

Rhymer Sings

The sheriff was in her office when Bossé arrived. She took a seat at her desk and opened her laptop. The atmosphere was sour, but she knew that it was all in her mind. Bossé still hadn't forgiven her for interfering with Nat's interview. She wondered if she should cut her some slack seeing as how he was a relative. She set about typing her notes following her visit to Hunter's Lodge.

"Find anything interesting out at Hunter's Lodge?"

The drums had obviously been beating for her to know that's where she'd been. It reminded her of just how tight knit the town was.

"No. Just trying to find some ID for Clara. I was hoping to find adoption papers."

"Adoption! Why's that?"

She didn't think there was any harm in telling her. Maybe, she thought, it would be a chance to break the ice.

"The DNA results show there isn't a match between Ackerman and Clara."

"What? You saying they're not related?"

"Looking that way."

The sheriff chewed on her lip. She looked rattled.

"You've had a message from Deputy Morris. He wants you to call him back."

She passed her a note with Morris' number. Bossé dialed the digits.

"Detective Bossé here. Is that Deputy Morris?"

"Yeah, you've had a break. Rhymer has been shanked by one of the prisoners. I've just interviewed him at the hospital. He's forgone his Miranda and sixth amendment rights to an attorney. He's singing like a canary to make sure he gets returned to the segregation wing."

"What's he saying?"

"He's saying he kicked the door in at Hunter's Lodge to look for his money and searched everywhere, but he swears he didn't find it, and that he didn't encounter Ackerman. When he pulled out of the drive, a two-tone SUV followed him at speed and tried to bounce him off of the road, but he managed to swerve to avoid them, and their vehicle careened, then stalled. He couldn't make out the color or make, except to say it was dark at the bottom and light on top."

"Did he get a look at them?"

"No, apart from he thought he could make out three outlines of people in the vehicle."

"Did he mention the time?"

"Around nine thirty in the evening. He said that he intended to hang around to wait for Ackerman, but the incident scared him off. I have a signed statement."

"Good, e-mail me a copy." Bossé hung up. "Well, well, Rhymer's singing."

"What's he saying?"

Bossé gave her chapter and verse of the conversation, but missed out that he'd said the SUV was a two-tone with three occupants.

"You can't trust anything he says. Not if he's desperate for segregation. I'd say it changes nothing. Besides, every man and his dog have an SUV around here. It probably skidded on the snow trying to overtake him."

She was right, but all the same, she thought it odd for her to say that, apart from Nat drove an SUV. She wondered if it was her way of deflecting attention from him, and she'd been strung a pack of lies about his alibi. The only things she could confirm about what Rhymer had said, was that the time fit the profile of tower pings from his cell phone, and the mode of entry was only what the person who had broken-in would know. Without a firm time of death, there was still no way of saying that he didn't murder Ackerman.

"I still think that you're wasting your time here."

"Yeah, well, it ain't over until it's over. I still think there's something I'm missing at the barn."

"What's there to miss? Seeing as how they didn't have video cameras in the barn, we only know what I found, and that was Clara with the weapon."

"I don't know, I still think I'm missing something at the scene."

"Yeah, like you've gotten some gray matter missing. I just think you're wasting your time. Anyone with shit for brains can see she's guilty," she said, and rising from her seat, she grabbed her coat from the back of the chair, marched to the door, yanked it open, and then closed it on the heavy side as she left the office.

Bossé was taken aback by her attitude, thinking it unprofessional at best, and rude at worst. The office phone rang and she answered.

"Detective Bossé, please."

"That's me."

"Park ranger's office. Our officers have located Jordan Hunter. County deputies are on their way to pick him up and bring him to Hunter's End for questioning. No one has approached him yet."

"Where is he?"

"They've located him at his dad's hunting lodge."

The last thing she wanted was an attorney or the sheriff interfering with an interrogation.

"Tell them not to bring him in, but to keep him under surveillance. I'll interview him there. Give me the GPS coordinates."

It was only a seven-mile drive out of town. Her mind was doing that thing again as she drove out of town and along the highway, darting in a multitude of directions as to how to conduct the interview. His two-tone SUV was the ace up her sleeve, but she knew she would have to be careful how she used it when she talked to him.

Bossé arrived and pulled over behind the patrol SUV. Behind their vehicle, she noticed the park ranger's jeep. Two deputies walked over to her as she climbed out of her car.

"The rangers are on foot and they're staking out the cabin. We're in radio contact. We can either walk, or you'll have to take a ride in our SUV off road to the cabin, but then he'll hear us coming."

"We'll walk. I have some rubber boots in the trunk."

Bossé changed her shoes and they set off walking between the tire ruts along the inclined trail. She huffed and puffed, laboring all the way to the tree line at the cabin.

"He's likely armed, so let's do this textbook style," Bossé said.

One of the deputies pulled his mic to his lips. Jordan's two-tone was parked to one side of the cabin. Smoke rose from the chimney.

"We're going in, watch the back," the deputy said.

Taking up their positions at the door, guns drawn, one of the officers rapped on the door then moved to one side.

"Police, open up."

The door opened right away. Jordan was standing there, his hands held high, and with a scared shitless look on his face.

"I'm unarmed. What do you want? I've not broken any laws."

Bossé holstered her pistol and stepped forward.

"Just some questions," she said, and then smiled. "No need to be alarmed. We were just being careful. You can drop your arms."

"Come in," he said. "Not much room in here."

There wasn't a table, just two chairs in front of the wood stove. One officer stayed at the door, the other walked over and stood in front of a rifle mounted on the wall. On one of the chairs, Bossé noticed an outdated newspaper with the headline about Ackerman's murder. She picked it up and signaled for Jordan to take a seat.

Bossé tossed him the newspaper.

"That front page article is why we're here to ask questions. Hopefully you'll help us with our inquiries. You're not being charged with anything, but I need to tell you that you don't have to speak without a lawyer present." She went on to recite his sixth amendment rights.

"I don't need a lawyer. I'll help you all I can. Especially if it helps to clear Clara. I can't believe she did it. If she'd have done as I asked her, none of this would have happened and she'd be with me now."

"If you really want to help her, best you start at the beginning when you first met her right up to you leaving town. Don't leave anything out, because there are some things I know already."

He didn't leave anything out as far as she could make out, filling in quite a few of the blanks. When prompted, he even gave an estimate for the weight of the deer near to her own estimate that he'd seen strung up in the barn, and which Clara had been in the middle of dissecting. That snippet troubled Bossé. The revelation that the maps in her backpack were ones that she took from her dad got her to thinking. She wondered why he had needed to mark the dots and numbers on the map.

She was about to throw him a low ball to ask about where he was on the night of the murder in his vehicle, and who he was with, when he freely admitted that his friends and him had tried to stop Rhymer leaving and to give him a beating.

Bossé had nowhere else to go with the interview. She sucked in a deep breath and let it out in a sigh.

"So to finish off, tell me how you met up with Clara to murder her dad?"

Chapter 53

Revealing Interview

Bossé didn't have to wait for a reaction from Jordan. It was instantaneous, with a look of shock and horror. Contrived or otherwise, she couldn't be sure. He rose from his chair, a pained expression on his face. The deputy stood forward and placed his hand on the butt of his pistol. She could see that Jordan's action was more out of anger at the accusation she'd put to him, rather than an aggressive move. She showed the deputy her palm.

"Hang on a damned minute. You can't think... Wait, you do, you think I murdered him with Clara?"

"Well, did you?"

"Don't be stupid. I didn't know he'd been murdered until I bought the newspaper when I went to buy provisions."

"So are you saying that the last time you saw Clara was at the church."

"No that's not what I'm saying. I tried to phone her lots of times, but Father David's housekeeper said she wasn't to be disturbed."

"What does that mean when you said it's not what you're saying? Did you see her after the incident at the church or not?"

He dropped his backside on his chair again. His fingers trembled.

"I saw her earlier today at the jail. Her attorney was there before me."

Caught off guard with that revelation, she pushed back in her chair.

"How is she?"

"Not how I thought she'd be."

"What does that mean?"

"She's loving it. As she says, after she had her evaluation

and she'd arrived back at jail, they've given her more freedom. She's made friends, she can read books, and watch television, and she gets three meals a day made for her. To her it's a step up from how she'd lived her life before. It's lucky I bumped into her attorney when we signed in."

"Why's that?"

"Because she wouldn't answer his questions. He wasn't in there five minutes before me. He came out into the waiting room and asked for my help. Said he had something important to put to her if I could get her to speak to him. He went back in after me once I'd explained to Clara that he was there to help her. Luckily, I got her to agree to talk to him."

Bossé Imagined that it was the DAs plea bargain that he wanted to put to her. It ran through her mind that if she was happy in there, she might plead guilty just to get to stay in the system. Worse, she might plead not guilty in the hope of never getting out, for if the verdict went against her, and for Clara to get the full sentence.

Jordan shuffled on his chair and clasped his hands together. He was obviously wrestling with something. She had it in mind to ask him if she'd confessed to the murder, even though it would be hearsay, when Jordan interrupted her thoughts.

"Listen, you said I have rights. I've told you everything, but I'm not saying anything else without I've spoken to someone. Not if you think I was involved."

There was nothing more she could do. As he'd said, he'd told her everything, which was a lot more that she already knew about events leading to the murder. He hadn't seemed to have held anything back, short of a confession. Jordan saying that Nat and he were sort of love rivals for Clara's attention had contradicted what Nat had said. She shrugged her shoulders.

"Yeah, that's right; you don't have to say anything. But if you decide there's anything else you can recall that you've missed, phone me at the sheriff's office."

Bossé looked over at the deputy and swayed her head in the direction of the door. She rose from her chair and they set off back to their vehicles.

Driving back to Hunter's End, her mind rolled over everything that Jordan had said. She couldn't rule him out, but there just wasn't any evidence to prove he was involved. She turned on her headlights as dusk turned to night, then slapped the steering wheel as she hit Main Street. Bossé cursed that they couldn't pin down the exact time of death.

An antiquated fire engine flashed by as she pulled over at the sheriff's office. She thought it quaint that someone's arm was reaching out of the side window pulling on a cord to ring a bell, and shook her head. No sooner had she climbed out of her car than she could smell the smoke. The sheriff charged out of the office door, slipping on her jacket as she headed for her vehicle.

"What's happening?"

"Fire over at Hunter's Lodge."

"I'll follow you."

Both the barn and the lodge lit the night sky, with a pall of smoke rising above the flames as she approached. She parked behind the sheriff on the road. The firefighters already had the hose rolled out, but the pump was silent and they weren't attempting to douse the fire. Instead, they were huddled around the mayor who was wearing a fire chief's helmet. He poured coffee from a thermos flask, and they each took sips and passed it around.

"Why aren't you fighting the fire?" Bossé said.

"Calm down. We don't exactly have a fire hydrant here. Best let it burn out. All we have is what's in the tank. Time to make a move is if the sparks hit the pine trees," the mayor said.

There was a sudden loud crash. When she looked over her shoulder, the lodge had collapsed in on itself, sending a mass of sparks into the air.

"Right, boys, get the pump running and douse the trees," the mayor called out.

At the nozzle end, someone turned.

"We're ready," he said.

Bossé caught sight of him from the glow of the flames. It was Nat. She looked on as the hose filled out as if it was a shed snakeskin coming to life until it hit the nozzle.

269

The barn soon followed the lodge, collapsing and sending more sparks billowing into the sky. Bossé turned to the sheriff.

"This has to be arson, don't you think? Someone must have wanted the murder scene destroyed."

"There you go again, jumping to conclusions. It could have been an electrical fault. Looks like the fire started at the house and sparks probably jumped to the barn. If it was arson, every crook for miles around would know it was empty. As I said before, we've had a run on break-ins in the area. They could have set it on fire to cover their tracks. Whatever, this is local business."

Bossé ignored her bad attitude. The fire crew turned their attention to what was left of the barn and the lodge, until all she could see was smolder and steam rising from the debris.

"Can I borrow your flashlight?" Bossé asked the sheriff.

"Sure," she said, and lifting the flap on her jacket, the sheriff took her flashlight from her belt and handed it over. "What are you looking for?"

"Tracks."

Bossé headed over to the tree line with the sheriff in tow, scanning the ground around her. She arrived at where she had found the stubs and the beer bottles. They were gone.

"Have you found something," the sheriff asked.

"No. I'm not exactly a scout when it comes to looking for tracks." She handed her the flashlight. "Like you said, this is local business. I'll head back to the office."

"I'll follow you, not much I can do here until daylight," Sheriff MacCaffrey said.

Bossé had a different destination in mind before heading for the office, and she slowed as she passed the drive for Hunter's Farm. She could see the outline of the farmhouse, but it was in darkness, so she accelerated. She noticed the sheriff catch up with her in her rearview. Outside the office she saw a red pickup and parked behind it. Bossé sidled off of her seat and glanced sideways at the driver as she walked by. She wondered why Jake Hunter was parked there, and if he'd had word that she had interviewed Jordan. Bossé tapped on his window and it rolled down.

"I guess you don't know anything about the fire at Hunter's Lodge?" Bossé said.

"Why should I?" He held up his palm. "You may as well talk to the hand, lady. I ain't got anything to say to you, except I'm here to have a word with the sheriff in private," he said, then climbed out of his cab as the sheriff pulled up behind her car and exited her cab, together with Nat and the mayor.

"Be my guest," Bossé said.

She'd had enough for one day and walked on over to Father David's cottage. Father David wasn't there, but Mrs. O'Ahern was busy making a meal in the kitchen.

She climbed the stairway to her bedroom, stripped and took a shower. Feeling refreshed, she walked over to the window with a towel wrapped around her. Over at the community center, people crowded around the door. There wasn't as many as the night before. Nat was there with Clarissa. The sheriff followed behind them with Jake Hunter at her side. The attorney who stopped her interview, he was talking with Jordan's friends who were loitering behind the others. The mayor was standing to one side with Susan MacCaffrey, and a few others that she didn't recognize. Bossé dressed, and then rushed down the stairway and into the kitchen.

"Is there a council meeting?"

"No, it looks like a meeting of the clans to me," said Mrs. O'Ahern, and then laughed.

"Damn it, I wish I was a fly on the wall. I don't suppose you've been invited?"

"I wish that I was summoned to attend. It isn't every day you get to see them congregating together. Something is afoot, that's for sure."

"Was the woman with the wheelchair at yesterday's meeting Nat's mom?"

"Yes, why?"

"I think I'll go and talk with her. She's not there with him now. Where does Nat live? This is too good an opportunity to miss."

Chapter 54

Out of Step

Mulling over her visit with Nat's mom the night before while sitting alone in the sheriff's office, Bossé felt as though time was running out to get anywhere before the trial date. Nat's mom said that Clarissa and her son hadn't been there at her house when she'd gone to sleep at ten in the evening on the night of the murder, but they had both been there when she awoke the next day. If they stuck to what they had both said that was an end to that line of enquiry. The only chink in their armor was that his mom didn't find out about the engagement until the same day as she interviewed Nat. She thought that odd, but no doubt they could come up with some cockamamie story for delaying telling her.

The office phone rang and she answered.

"It's John. The DNA results have come in. All the samples connected to Clara on the weapon and clothing have come back as a match to Ackerman's DNA, but the other results I've had back are more sinister. Those tests on the clothing we found in the suitcase, they all have different DNA, but the semen stains match Ackerman's markers. Six of them are a match with missing children on the national database. The most recent is from a girl that went missing in Alaska two months ago near the border with Canada. The oldest is from ten years ago in California."

"Have you informed Brennan, my boss?"

"Yeah. Just before I phoned you."

"Send me the database results on those missing children by e-mail. That one you mentioned in Alaska is around the time they left there for Colorado."

"Your call."

She didn't wait for Brennan to phone after she hung up. She dialed his number and waited for him to answer.

273

"Hi, it's Alana. John said he'd just phoned you. I'm going to have to go and visit Clara. She could have information on those missing girls."

"Information! She could be in cahoots with him on some of them. It doesn't get away from the fact that the evidence says she murdered him, especially now we have the DNA results."

"Give it a rest, one of the missing girls is from ten years ago when she was only eight years old. There's reasonable doubt on the murder case and you know it. By the bucket load I'd say if you've read my updates. I just got your e-mail about the medical treatment she had at the county jail. I'm thinking she's a victim in all this. First of all she was limping when they processed her, and the doctor had to give her opioid tablets, with muscle relaxants for sciatica. So I fail to see how she could have hoisted him on the pulley. Then there was a bump on the side of her forehead. That could have been someone striking her in the barn. Also, did you see the photos of identifying marks? Besides the birthmark, I guess you saw the scars on her ankles?"

"Yeah, I saw them. You're sounding like a defense attorney."

"I only want to get at the truth. The way I see it, those scars were probably caused by shackles. We're going to need the DA to hold off on this one and ask for an adjournment. Hell, we don't even know who she is. We might have to cut her a new deal for her cooperation into these missing children, never mind the existing plea bargain for the murder of Ackerman. She had either an accomplice, or accomplices, or maybe even she walked in on the murderer and she's innocent. We can't even rule out Rhymer. His motivation and opportunity is strong. Last thing I want is another innocent person doing time if she accepts the plea bargain."

"Ah, now I understand where you're coming from. Come on, it's the jury's decision if she pleads not guilty, not ours. The fact is, we've already put the offer for a reduced sentence and we can't take it back. The DA put it to her defense for a guilty plea after he'd read your report on the alleged abuse that you discovered, but he hasn't got back to us. I'd need to run any further meeting with Clara through her attorney with the DAs approval. I doubt the DA will think it's a good idea without her attorney present. Rhodes will probably cite *Massiah v The United States nineteen sixty-four.*"

"Yeah, well if he does, throw *Texas versus Cobb two thousand and one* right back at him. No way is it a *Massiah violation* of her sixth amendment rights. We'd only be asking about her dad's crime, not the one she's been charged with. It's completely separate. Who is her defense attorney?"

"Richard Parker. He'll go ballistic if we go ahead and interview her without him there."

Bossé sighed, having crossed swords with Parker on cases before.

"Oh, yeah, I know him. So what if he does go ballistic if we're within our rights not to have him there."

"Whatever, don't go speaking to him, or to Clara. Like I said, I'll run it by Gilbert Rhodes, but any meeting without her counsel could be argued to be intertwined, with both cases overlapping. That would screw up any charges against her if she was involved with him in some of the kidnappings."

Bossé sensed her anger bubbling at his indifference to her request.

"Intertwined. It's a complete separate inquiry. Go and look up *Texas versus Cobb,* and I'm sure you could argue with him. Anyway, what about the rights of the children and of the parents to have closure? They should let her go on the basis that she's done society a favor if she did murder him."

"Whoa there, calm down."

"Calm down, you're telling me to calm down. I'll tell you when I'll calm down, after I've fully investigated every lead to a conclusion one way or another, and after I've resigned."

Bossé was deafened by the silence waiting for a reply. There wasn't any way of taking the words back. Her fingers holding the handset trembled, when his voice exploded.

"Whoa there, where did that come from? It sounds like you're over emotionally involved. You've let the Jeremiah Coulter situation get to you, haven't you? Do you want me to put someone else on the case? In fact, no, I'm thinking that isn't even an option, and I'm closing the case down as of now. I want you back here as soon as they've repaired your car. Besides, I've phoned the FBI. They're going to take over any investigation into the missing children."

She looked up at the ceiling. Bossé knew she'd stepped over the line. There was no playing him this time, only to call his bluff.

"Fine. If that's what you want. I'll mail in my resignation," she said, then slammed the handset back on the cradle.

She dropped her head into her hands. Bossé grimaced at the thought that she hadn't even told him about Hunter's Lodge and the barn that had burned down. Bossé thought he was right, and that maybe the Coulter case had colored her judgment. The door burst open. In marched the sheriff and on over to her desk. She leaned over with her hands on the desk and put her nose right up to Bossé's nose. Bossé reared backwards, still rattled from her conversation with Brennan.

"Why the hell have you been to see Nat's mom? Did you know she has cancer?"

MacCaffrey had chosen the wrong time to lay down the law. Bossé was still seething and the sheriff had taken her emotion up a notch.

"What the hell has it got to do with you why I went to see her? Oh, yeah, before I forget, it's your sister-in-law, and Nat's your nephew. But then it's as someone said earlier, you MacCaffreys all piss in the same pot around here. I have a murder investigation on my hands here, so back right off, lady. She seemed fine to me."

The sheriff slapped her hands on the desk, then turned and walked over to the mailbox. Any hope she had of getting on the right side of her had just evaporated. MacCaffrey sifted through the mail and tossed an envelope onto Bossé's desk.

"That one's for you," she said, then exited the office in the same kind of whirlwind as she'd arrived.

It wasn't stamped, all it had on the envelope was her name in childish writing. She opened it, read the content. Dropped it on the desk. Pushed back on her chair.

"YOU ARE NOT WANTED HERE. GET OUT OF TOWN WHILE YOU CAN," it read, with letters cut from a magazine.

Bossé rose from her chair and pulled at the slats on the blinds, wondering just who out there wanted her gone. She noticed Jordan was in town. His SUV was parked outside the grocery store. He was goofing around with his two friends on the porch. Nat's vehicle was parked outside the garage, and the sheriff was over at the mayor's funeral parlor. She turned and walked back to the desk. Bossé got the feeling that it wasn't a question of who had sent the threatening letter, but that the whole town had a secret and wanted her gone.

She shrugged as if a ghost had walked through her body. Bossé thought back to her argument with Brennan. If only he had said from the outset that the FBI had been called in to deal with the missing children, Bossé felt that she wouldn't have blown off steam. Maybe then, she could have handled the sheriff's anger with a touch of diplomacy. She had a decision to make. Walk away, or to stay and tough it out, and to hell with the town and her boss.

Chapter 55

The Set Back

The following day, early morning, Susan MacCaffrey was behind her counter when Bossé entered. She ordered coffee, and then took a seat. Bossé placed her folder filled with empty statement sheets on the table. Deep in thought, she gazed out through the window. Bossé had spent the evening trying to decide what she would do with the little time she had left. The hour was fast approaching when her car would be repaired and she would have no option but to return home. She had filed all her reports. All that was missing was a few signed statements and she'd be done.

She knew that if Clara didn't accept the guilty plea bargain, the DA had what he wanted to try the case. If she did plead not guilty, then at least she thought that she had done her best to follow every lead, and she could resign with a clear conscience. The defense attorney would have what he would need after full disclosure of her reports, and maybe he'd have a PI pick up the baton to beef up the defense. It would be up to him to throw doubt into the mix with other suspects, and to put forward a different scenario as to what took place. The deputy had witnessed what Jordan had said when she had interviewed him. Mrs. O'Ahern had agreed to come over to the office to sign a statement after work, but she thought that the more statements she could get on file the better.

"Are you sure you don't want anything to eat with your coffee?" Susan MacCaffrey said, as she placed a mug on the table.

"No, I've had breakfast. Really, the main thing I called in for is to ask you for a signed statement about Jordan making his threat outside the church, and what you overheard about when they went to the lodge to rile Ackerman."

"Oh, that. I'd been meaning to talk to you since we last

spoke. I can't do that, sign a statement that is. Last thing I want is to sign something I'm not sure about exactly what I think I saw and heard. The more I've thought about it, the more I'm wondering if maybe I added in what I heard at the church from what others were saying. And to be honest, I could have misunderstood what was said about them going to Hunter's Lodge, because I had customers to serve at the time." She didn't wait for Bossé's reply and stepped over to her counter.

Bossé folded her arms and leant them on the table, fixing her gaze on the steam rising from her coffee. Someone had gotten to her, she thought, and recalled the Hunters meeting with MacCaffreys at the community hall the night before. She pushed the coffee to one side, rose from her chair and set off outside.

Knocking on doors up and down Main Street proved fruitless. It was the same story. No one admitted to hearing or seeing anything happen outside the church. She was about to give up when she noticed Jordan's SUV park outside the grocery store. He climbed out of the cab with his two friends and they took a seat on the bench outside on the porch. Over at the sheriff's office, she noticed a guy in a suit with a white shirt and tie. He was trying to look inside through a gap in the blinds and tapping on the window.

"Hey, can I help you?" she called out, and stepped over to the office. "I'm Detective Bossé."

"Pleased to meet you," he said," and offered his hand. "FBI Agent Jason Crook."

Bossé stifled a snicker that someone in law enforcement carried the burden of the surname of Crook. She shook his hand.

"Yeah, I get that all the time, you can call me Jason."

"Great, you can call me Alana, then we're even."

Bossé unlocked the door and they stepped inside. She took a seat at her desk and he pulled up a chair. He looked quite distinguished, with dark hair, but greying at the sides. She thought he was the sort that she'd go for if they met under different circumstances.

"I'm only here to talk about the missing girls, so I won't be stepping on your toes during your investigation into the murder of Ackerman."

With the matter of factness of his delivery, she doubted he was having the same thoughts.

"You can do what you like," she said. "My case has been closed down. I go back home today. Before we start, I'll check my e-mails."

"Sure."

She opened an e-mail from Brennan. Clara's attorney had rejected the plea deal and he'd be entering a not guilty plea. Most of his e-mails were less formal and he usually typed his name at the end. Bossé typed out an e-mail with details of the fire at Hunter's Lodge without typing her name and pressed send.

She opened an e-mail from John and downloaded the image attachments, then attached a USB cable to the office printer. Bossé returned to her desk and took a seat. The last one rolled out of the printer as Sheriff MacCaffrey returned, walked over to the machine, and picked up the copies.

"This is FBI Agent Jason Crook. He's here to investigate a connection between Ackerman and some missing girls."

The sheriff turned, and said, "FBI! Pleased to meet you."

Crook rose from his chair and they shook hands.

"I need something from my car," he said.

"Could you pass me those copies?" Bossé asked MacCaffrey.

The sheriff picked them up out of the tray and sifted through them as she walked over to Bossé. MacCaffrey's eyes were moistened. Bossé guessed that she wasn't the only one that was emotionally involved, especially with the sheriff having lost her own child. Bossé thought she'd try and put an end to the animosity they shared for each other as a parting gift.

"Listen, I heard about your child and what it did to your husband. I'm so sorry. I suppose those images have brought it all back?"

The words to answer wouldn't escape the sheriff's lips. She nodded her head and pulled a handkerchief from her pocket.

"Damn it, why did Ackerman have to bring it all to my town?

Do you have any kids?" she asked Bossé.

"No. I don't have any family around either. I was an only child. Mom and Dad have passed on, and I got divorced a while back. I put work first I'm afraid. Dad was from France and Mom was from Angola. They came to the US before I was born."

"So that's where the name Bossé came from? I guess that with you having no family that's why you can't understand family sticking together."

"Probably."

Crook returned and took a seat.

"If you're looking into those girls going missing, you need to start here," MacCaffrey said, and walking over to the wall, she stabbed her finger on the map. "When Clara was talking, she said they lived near a small town called McCarthy. She reached out and picked up the printed images. Shuffling through them, she picked one out and slid it over to Crook. "This one went missing around the time that they left Alaska. She lived around forty-five miles from McCarthy."

The landline rang and the sheriff answered the call.

"Sorry, I have to go out, I'll be back later. I hope you do a better job with these children than you did for my daughter," MacCaffrey said, and walked outside the office to her vehicle.

"What was all that about?"

Bossé explained the situation to Crook about Sheriff MacCaffrey's daughter going missing. He stroked his chin.

"Just thinking. The best place to start is to question Clara," Crook said. "There's no doubting Ackerman was responsible for kidnapping six of the girls from the forensics on the clothing, and he wouldn't have kept those other six dresses if he wasn't responsible for those ones either. What we need to find out is where he could have disposed of them for the parents to have closure."

Bossé's eyes had sparkled at the mention of interviewing Clara, but then her composure hit south at knowing their hands would be tied behind their backs to go down that avenue.

"There's a problem with talking to her. For one, we don't

know if she is his daughter. Their DNA doesn't match, so unless she's adopted, they aren't related, unless she's a stepdaughter. I'm waiting for clearance to question her from the DA. My boss is worried the missing girls' case is too intertwined with the charge against her, and interviewing her could violate her sixth amendment rights as a *Massiah violation,* especially if her attorney isn't present. I've also just heard that she's pleading not guilty, so talking to her could screw up the case."

Crook leaned forward and smiled. As she looked into his eyes, for a moment Bossé was in another place.

"You can wait all you want. I can't see the connection. It's a completely separate investigation. I don't need permission from anyone. Besides, what planet is your boss and the DA on? How could there be a violation if we don't discuss anything to do with the case against her. If she did slip up and give something away, all it means is it couldn't be used in court, or they'd throw it out as evidence. It wouldn't stop the trial. I take it they have their evidence to have charged her?"

"Yeah, she was found at the scene with a weapon. The DNA seems to tie it all up, but there is another problem in interviewing her. She took some goading from a friend to even talk to her attorney. She clams up with anyone in authority."

"Then we need to talk to her friend."

Chapter 56

Timely Intervention

Crook heaved his briefcase onto the desk, opened the catches, and then took out a file.

"I'm ahead of the sheriff on this one. This is the file on June Morris that went missing in Alaska a few months back. We've matched up a sketch of a person of interest that was seen in the area, with the copy of Ackerman's photo on his carry permit that you sent through to your office." He opened the file. The sketch of the person of interest was the first page. "It's not definitive, but if you mask off the headwear it's close. However, what's more than a coincidence is that I've just had a message from forensics at the garage. They found a trapper's hat with the same color and pattern of the one in the sketch. It was in the pocket of a white waterproof jacket under the seat."

"Well, I'd say that was definitive."

"It will be when they've checked some hair samples they found. There's no DNA to match with June on the clothing, but we identified the dress is hers with a search of the database from the pattern, and the label is a match. Regardless, there's no doubting Ackerman's DNA was on her dress, and seeing as how he lived in the area, that nails him down for that one."

"May I?"

"Feel free," Crook said.

Bossé turned the pages and winced at the photos of the six girls that DNA tests had identified.

"So that leaves five of the items of clothing unmatched to any missing girls?"

"So far. We have matches on the database from descriptions of the dresses in the case, but there are multiple matches. What we need to know from Clara is, where and when they lived in different states, or any long journeys he took. Then we can narrow it down as to who the clothing belongs to in the suitcase. Problem is that it's likely some of them went missing before she was born."

Bossé turned the page in the file and noted a list of the missing girls that had been identified, together with the different states they had lived.

"Is there a pattern as to how they were taken?"

"Only that they were girls that were allowed to play out on their own. All of them had playgrounds nearby that they frequented, but they were all taken from the streets near their home."

Bossé sighed. She didn't envy him the task of finding the bodies.

"I guess we'd better talk to Jordan then, but I wouldn't hold out much hope of his help. Not after I told him that I suspected him of being involved in Ackerman's murder."

"I thought you said that they had their evidence on Clara and she was caught there at the scene."

"Like I said, they have, but that hasn't stopped me following up other leads. If it wasn't for the circumstances of the sheriff finding Clara at the crime scene, I'd have had six suspects and an open case. Still, that all ends today now they have the DNA results, especially on the weapon."

Bossé thought Crook was disinterested in knowing any more when he changed the subject.

"Where does Jordan live?"

"We don't need to go to where he is staying. He's outside the grocery store."

"Then let's not waste time. All I need you to do is to introduce me and I'll do the talking."

"Well, good luck."

They rose from their chairs, walked out of the office, and stepped across Main Street.

Jordan and his friends were horsing around outside the grocery store, but they stopped as soon as Bossé and Crook arrived. She looked directly at Jordan.

"FBI Agent Crook here needs a word with you in private."

Rick and Drake laughed. "They have crooks in the FBI?" Drake said.

"You two beat it. It's Jordan I want to talk to... in private," Crook said.

"They ain't going anywhere, and I don't have to talk to anyone." Jordan turned to Rick. "Pass me Abe's card."

Rick dug into his pocket and handed Jordan a folded card which he passed on to Crook.

"You can talk to the man on the card. I ain't gotten anything to say."

"Listen, I just need your help and it has nothing to do with you or the charges against your friend Clara. Still, if you're not man enough to stand on your own two feet, call your attorney guy," Crook said, and returned the card to Jordan.

Jordan puffed out his chest.

"If it's not about her dad's murder, what's it about then?"

"I'm not talking in front of your friends."

"Yeah, well, I ain't talking in front of her," Jordan said, and sent Bossé an evil stare.

"If you don't mind," Crook said, and glanced at Bossé.

Bossé got the message, and rolled her eyes, but before turning on her heels, she noticed Susan MacCaffrey at the store window.

"You two scram. I shouldn't be long," she heard Jordan say as she walked across Main Street to the office.

Crook was only five minutes behind her. He said nothing, but walked over to the sheriff's desk and snatched the handset from the cradle. It was obvious from what he said on his phone call that Jordan had agreed to help, when she heard him make an appointment to interview Clara with Jordan present.

"Do you want me with you?" she asked, when he ended the phone call.

"No, this is outside your remit. I'll take it from here. I doubt I'll be back."

Crook grabbed his briefcase and walked out of the office. She watched him through a gap in the blinds as he climbed into his car, then he set off across to the grocery store where Jordan was waiting in his SUV. Jordan pulled away first with Crook following. Bossé looked at her watch. There was just enough time to read through her files and to type out her resignation and to send it to Brennan in an e-mail, before she'd be ready to collect a statement from Mrs. O'Ahern.

They hadn't been gone more than thirty minutes and she was about to press send on her resignation e-mail, when screeching brakes outside caught her attention. She rose from her chair and looked out through the window. Jake Hunter's pickup was parked outside the grocery store. He slammed his door when he climbed out of the cab and hurried inside the store. She noticed Rick Hunter and Drake as they ran across Main Street and followed him into the store. A few minutes later, Jake Hunter looked pissed, when he marched out of the store and across Main Street toward the sheriff's office. Bossé half-expected that in his mood, it would be a less than friendly encounter, and thought it better to have some distance between them. She took a seat at her desk and waited.

As expected, he hadn't calmed down on his way over. He had a face like thunder when he barged into the office. He walked over and thumped the desk with both his fists.

"What the hell does the FBI want with Jordan? Where is he?"

"Nothing to do with me. I only introduced them. Apparently they want his help? None of my business. Phone the nearest office in Denver. Maybe they'll know," she said. Bossé doubted Crook would have phoned in his movements.

"If this is any of your doing, lady, there'll be trouble. You're not wanted in town. I suggest you get the hell outta here while you can."

Jake turned and stormed out of the office.

At three fifteen, Mrs. O'Ahern was late. Bossé wondered if she had missed her and decided to see if she was still at Father David's Cottage.

Father David was reading a book when she arrived.

"Is Mrs. O'Ahern still here?"

"Sorry, she's gone. Said she had to visit a sick relative. Sheriff MacCaffrey phoned and had words with her, and she left shortly after."

"Did she say when she'll be back?"

"No, I told her to take as long as she liked."

"Do you have a contact number?"

"Yes. She doesn't have a cell phone though, only a landline."

He gave her the number and she entered the digits, then pressed the call icon. A recorded message answered her.

"Sorry, I'm not at home. I'm away on vacation. Please leave a message and I'll get back to you when I return."

Bossé held back the hell and damnations out of respect for Father David. In the same way she thought someone had gotten to Susan MacCaffrey, she felt as though there was more to Mrs. O'Ahern leaving town than a sick relative. Except, no one knew that she was going to give a statement, and she doubted Mrs. O'Ahern would have told anyone. Then she recalled penciling in her appointment in her diary that she'd left on her desk. 'O'Ahern—Statement' she had written. Only one other person could have seen the entry, and that would be the sheriff, but to do that, she had to have noseyed around and opened her diary at the page. The question she asked herself was, *why?*

Chapter 57

Standing Down

Bossé had left Father David in peace to read his book. She looked out through her bedroom window. It looked like the gathering of the clans once again over at the funeral parlor. Jake Hunter was remonstrating with Sheriff MacCaffrey, with the mayor and Susan MacCaffrey standing back with their arms folded. Hunter turned to Drake and Rick. He seemed to give them a mouthful and they sloped off. Then Jake Hunter marched to the garage with the sheriff in his slipstream. Nat greeted them at the entrance to the garage with Clarissa at his side. Hunter vented his anger on them judging by the way that he was throwing his arms around in the air. Nat and Clarissa took the verbal pasting with their heads bowed, until Tiff MacCaffrey walked outside the garage and stepped between them. Hunter turned to the sheriff and gave her one final poking-finger rebuke on her shoulder.

Sheriff MacCaffrey just seemed to take it from Jake Hunter, and then she watched him as he hurried back to his pickup. He climbed inside his cab and drove off at speed, his back tires burning rubber. Bossé noticed the sheriff put her arm around Clarissa as if comforting her. Nat took over and guided Clarissa back into the garage with his arm around her shoulder.

Sheriff MacCaffrey stood akimbo, faced the road and shook her head, then stepped off the sidewalk and walked over to her office.

Bossé wished she'd had super hearing to have known what was said. At the same time, she imagined it was about Jordan driving off with the FBI, but what it had to do with Nat and Clarissa, she couldn't work out.

She walked away from the window and thought back to having endured a mouthful of Jake Hunter's venom in the office. It hadn't struck her at the time, but as she thought about it, Bossé took out the threatening letter from her purse. The letter was almost word for word what he had said to her. She decided the sheriff needed to know, and hurried down the stairway, and then stepped out of the door. Closing in on the office door, Bossé was worried that she hadn't told Brennan about the letter should anything happen to her.

The door was locked when she arrived. She put the key in the lock and pushed the door, but it was stuck.

"Sorry, I fastened the catch," Sheriff MacCaffrey said as she opened the door. She looked flustered as she stepped over to her desk and took a seat. "How was your day?" she said, in an unusually friendly manner.

"Pretty uneventful." Bossé got the feeling that MacCaffrey was acting shady, and decided not to tell her right away about her thinking that Hunter had sent her a threatening note. Sheriff MacCaffrey's cheeks blushed.

"Listen, I was looking for a pen when I noticed you'd typed out your resignation. I take it you'll be leaving us?"

Bossé had forgotten all about her resignation letter and realized that she hadn't had the presence of mind to switch off the power. She dropped her backside on the chair at her desk. She didn't believe the sheriff for one minute that she'd been looking for a pen. Her screen should have been in slumber mode, but it wasn't. Bossé saved her e-mail to draft, then powered her laptop down and closed the lid, wondering what else she might have read. Bossé didn't want to tell her that she would be leaving as soon as her car was repaired.

"No, I'm not resigning just yet. You know how it is in this job. I had a mini crisis, but I'm over it now."

She noticed the sheriff frown, then she smiled.

"Yeah, I get them. How did it go with the FBI?"

"Oh, him. I simply briefed him on the Ackerman case and he took off."

The sheriff sucked on her bottom lip, then said, "But you talked to Jordan with him. What business did he have with him?"

"Not a clue. He said he wanted to talk to him, so I introduced them. He made it clear it was none of my business. Is that what

Jake Hunter was asking you about over at the funeral parlor?"

"Well, yeah."

"I guess he'll have to wait for him to return then to find out. But why he'd be interested after Jordan and he didn't get along beats me."

"It's like I said before. You not having family, I guess it's hard for you to understand."

"There is that. What's more important to me is that Jake threatened me. He used the exact same words earlier in the office to what was in a threatening letter you gave me, remember—the hand written envelope?"

MacCaffrey rolled her eyes.

"Oh, dear. You never said the letter contained a threat."

"I'm telling you now in case anything happens to me."

"Do you want me to speak to him?"

"No, I'll talk to my boss and see what he has to say." Bossé took the letter from her purse and placed it in a plastic cover, then walked over the copier and set it to digitize. "It's on your hard disk now, so you can print a copy. I'll use your computer to send it as an attachment to the office if you don't mind, then I'll get John to check it out. With a little luck, forensics will pull either a fingerprint or DNA from the surface."

She looked disinterested. Mentioning forensics didn't seem to trouble her in the slightest.

"So where are you at with your investigation? I've had word that Clara is pleading not guilty and they're going ahead with the trial. I guess it ends now, right?"

"Depends. I'm not finished with it yet, especially if they find her not guilty." Bossé said, knowing she was lying and that she had only delayed sending in her resignation and she'd be leaving town.

"Yeah, but even if they find her guilty, they'll probably give her a token sentence, surely. Especially now they know Ackerman had a history of abusing her, and that he kidnapped children. She'll be out in no time. She's done society a favor."

It was sounding as though she'd changed her tune and she was now displaying some sympathy for Clara. Not surprising to Bossé really, seeing how her child had been kidnapped.

"She could have done that anyway by accepting the plea bargain. Have you ever stopped to think why she'd plead not guilty?"

Her cheeks flushed.

"You're the detective. Most of my work involves traffic violations. I only know that I found her at the scene with a weapon."

"Yeah, well I only know I'm missing something. It wouldn't surprise me if there was someone else involved seeing as Hunter's Lodge and the barn were torched."

The sheriff opened her top drawer and pulled out a large buff envelope.

"Read this. It's a county fire officer's report. He reckons it was electrical and sparks spread it to the barn."

MacCaffrey developed a self-satisfied smug look on her face. Bossé pulled out the report and stopped reading when she noticed the fire officer's name—Neil Hunter. The phone rang and MacCaffrey answered.

"Yeah, she's here. Do you want to speak to her— what?— okay, I'll tell her."

She placed the phone on the cradle.

"Who was that?"

"Detective Brennan. He said to tell you he'll expect you in the office tomorrow. He has a new case for you. So I guess you will be leaving us after all?"

Nat walked in through the door and dropped Bossé's car keys on the table.

"It's ready. I've parked it outside. It just needed new plugs."

"How much?"

"Just the price of the plugs. I won't charge for my time without a receipt. Cash if you have it." He handed her a note with the price.

"Sure."

Bossé fished in her purse and paid him. It wasn't worth asking for a receipt to submit for expenses, not with it being her last day. She had every intention of resigning and taking her vacation time as notice

"It'll be nice to have my office back," MacCaffrey said.

294

"I bet it will."

Bossé picked up her laptop and diary and walked over to the door. The sheriff opened the door for her. She didn't look back, but turned left in the direction of Father David's cottage. She was pleased to be leaving the town behind with a clear conscience that she'd done everything she could to investigate all angles, and with no one talking, all leads were at a dead end anyway.

Bossé stepped into the cottage and walked through into the living room.

"Just called to say thank you for letting me stay here and to collect my overnight bag."

"It's a pleasure."

She handed him an envelope.

"There's a little something in there for your collection box."

"That's very kind of you. Have a safe journey."

She shook his hand, then walked out into the hallway and picked up her bag.

"Let me get the door for you."

Bossé arrived at her car and stored everything in the trunk. She opened the door and had one last look around. The blinds twitched inside the sheriff's office. She shrugged her shoulders as she climbed inside and fired up the ignition.

Bossé smiled as she hit the highway, her thoughts turning to what sort of other work she would like to do, or if she should take time out to travel. The heavens opened. Rain hit the windshield in a deluge. A semi-truck's trailer and container loomed large as it jackknifed in front of her. She jammed her foot on the brake pedal. There was no pressure, the pedal having no effect. Then smack, she hit the trailer with a deafening crunch.

Chapter 58

Car Wreck

Bossé yanked at the steering wheel a split second before she had hit the semi. The trailer careened at a forty-five degree angle across the road. It all happened as if in slow motion, but she was helpless to do anything. She hadn't come to a full stop, but scraped alongside the chassis, metal to metal screeching as if both vehicles were screaming in pain. Both of her passenger windows imploded, showering her with shards of glass. The chassis was guiding her to a metal crash barrier. She gripped the steering wheel in readiness of the inevitable and closed her eyes.

Bang. With the severity of the impact, the airbag inflated in an instant, knocking the wind from her, leaving her with the sensation that she was in a spacecraft without gravity, floating, and then tumbling. There was a sudden jolt to her entire body. The next she knew she was upside down and with an awareness of spinning, then light faded to dark.

"You okay, lady?" she heard a faint voice calling out. "Hang on in there. We'll cut you out in no time."

Still upside down, her ribs hurt like hell. All she could see were peoples' legs moving around outside her window. Her first thoughts were to move her fingers and to wriggle her toes. She sighed with relief that her limbs responded and appeared to be intact. Bossé expected 'no time' to mean seconds, desperately hoping for relief from the pain in her ribs. She could hear the whining of the cutting machine and its blades slicing the metal, but it seemed to her to go on forever. They used the cutting machine to cut the seat belt. Arms grabbed a hold of her. Slowly they extracted her and lay her down on a folded gurney. Paramedics pushed the fire officers out of the way. The rain burst had thankfully slowed to a fine drizzle. Someone held an umbrella over her.

"Any pain?"

"My... ribs. I... I can... hardly breathe."

One of the medics placed an oxygen mask over her mouth as the gurney rose and rumbled on the asphalt and on into the ambulance. She was aware of them fussing around, pumping up a strap on her arm to check her blood pressure, while someone attached probes to her finger and chest.

"She's stable."

"Any ID?" Someone asked.

"Here."

A highway patrol officer's face loomed over her.

"Detective Alana Bossé. Just blink if that's you."

Bossé blinked.

"Please, leave her. She's going into shock. We need to get her to hospital."

Bossé ripped off her mask and grabbed the police officers arm.

"P... Please. My purse and items in the trunk. H... Have them sent to the hospital."

"Sorry you have to go," the medic called out.

She gripped the officer's wrist tighter.

"You have to get forensics to check the brakes and a letter in my purse. P... Promise me."

"I promise."

She let go of his wrist and her arm fell limp by her side. Her entire body shivered. The medic gave her an injection, then draped a thermal blanket over her and replaced the mask.

"Okay, let's go."

Her surroundings blurred. A pleasant numbness sensation relieved her of the excruciating pain. The sounds of the medics calling out vital statistics faded into the background. Bossé knew she was slipping into unconsciousness. Her last thought was to pray to God that she'd live to see another day.

Chapter 59

Discharged

The forty-eight hours in the hospital had driven Bossé to despair. At last the doctor appeared. He picked up the chart from the bottom of the bed.

"Good news. You can go home now once the nurse has given you your medication. From what I hear, you were lucky to have survived with only bruised ribs and a cut on your hand. The MRI scan is clear, so no worries there. Take two weeks on sick leave and you'll be good as new."

Bossé doubted that she would ever be as she was before until she found out what or who caused her brakes to fail. The car wreck had been a defining moment, leaving her determined more than ever that she was done with working in the homicide division.

The doctor had no sooner left than her boss Brennan swaggered into the room.

"How are you?"

"You took your time. You're my first visitor apart from the patrol officer who brought my personal items. As it is, I've been told to take two weeks sick leave and then I'll be fine."

"Good. Maybe it's a blessing in disguise to give you time to think straight. I spoke to the sheriff at Hunter's End. I thought you weren't serious about resigning?"

She was aware of a blush developing at the thought MacCaffrey had told him about her e-mail. In her mind, the two weeks sick leave had bought her time to investigate in her spare hours just who had made an attempt to kill her.

"Tactics. I didn't trust the sheriff and I wanted her to think my investigation was over."

He didn't take a seat, but paced around the bottom of the bed. Brennan stopped and turned.

"Yeah, we should talk about that. I had a meeting with

Gilbert Rhodes yesterday. He said to commend you for tying up all the loose ends on any other suspects. He's satisfied he can discount them all if challenged by the defense in court, and he's looking forward to proving his case. He wasn't happy at the FBI interviewing Clara, but as they apparently didn't discuss the case against her, he can't see there being any objections brought up at the trial."

Bossé scoffed. "But what about the attempt on my life. Doesn't that worry you there could be more to this than just Clara?"

"That's the other thing I'm here for. Sheriff MacCaffrey executed a search warrant at Hunter's Farm. They didn't find any magazines with letters cut out, and the sample of his handwriting that she collected didn't match what was on the envelope."

"What about forensic tests on the letter?"

"Sorry, they couldn't get a print or DNA."

Bossé sucked on her lip. The fact that she hadn't been there to carry out the search annoyed her.

"I don't really care what Gilbert Rhodes thinks, and the threat on my life proves there's more to this case than we know. It's as if the entire town wanted me to drop all investigations. Someone in town knows who sent that letter."

She clenched her fist. The anger she felt touched every nerve ending in her body.

"Calm down before you burst your stitches. It wasn't exactly a threat on your life. The sheriff said you'd ruffled a few feathers in town. Listen, about your accident. We've had a report back on your vehicle."

"And?"

"The brake line under the chassis was compromised. A twig had pierced the pipe. Examination shows it was stuck there, lodged between the exhaust and the pipe. With the exhaust vibration, they think it probably worked loose enough to allow a small drip and an airlock."

Bossé recalled tugging out the branch from under her car at the barn. It dawned on her that maybe her judgment had been clouded as to how she had conducted the investigation, with the release of Jeremiah Coulter constantly bugging her. In a way, she thought it was a relief that her brakes failing was a coincidence, and the two weeks sick leave would give her chance to consider her options going forward, and to go back to letting the trial take its course.

Brennan looked restless. She was aware he wasn't one for small talk. The lull in conversation created an awkward silence.

"So is that it?"

"Yeah, listen I have to get going. You know how it is. I'll see you when you're back at work."

"No problem."

He'd not brought flowers. There hadn't been any sign of concern. Bossé knew that she wasn't anyone to him, only that she made the numbers up in the office to get the jobs done. The only concern he probably had, she thought, was to find out if she was serious about resigning. Bossé climbed off of her bed, pulled out her overnight bag from the side cabinet and dressed. She dropped her backside on the side of her mattress and waited for the nurse to arrive, when in walked FBI Agent Crook. His cheeks reddened as he pulled a bouquet of flowers from behind his back and handed them to her.

"Sorry I didn't call earlier. I did phone to ask how you were, but you were getting a scan at the time. I saw about the crash on the news. I'm surprised you're up and about. Listen, I came to thank you for pointing me in the direction of Jordan. I feel I owe it to you to fill you in on what I found."

Bossé felt touched by his concern, and the flowers, considering she didn't really know him.

"So how did it go with Clara?" she asked, and breathed in the scent of the flowers.

"Difficult. She can't remember dates, only seasons. Alaska is where they've lived the longest. From her childhood memories, I get the feeling that Clara is one of his victims, but for some reason he kept her as the ultimate trophy. Saying that, there were many occasions that he took her to local parks when she was a child. It's likely he used her to seek out some of the victims who were alone and appeared most vulnerable.

That could be one reason he kept her alive, besides her saying that he sexually abused her right up to her being eleven, then the abuse stopped. Not sure if that was because she no longer held any attraction to him at that age, or if it was because around that time, she started to cook and clean for him.

"Maybe he developed a bond?"

"Maybe. It's happened before with kidnappers and victims. I've sent the background of what I gleaned to our profiler. We'll see what he says. She can recall him bringing children back to the house and he told her they were cousins, but he'd lock her up until he'd taken them away. I really can't see her as a willing accomplice in all this. Especially after what she said and the venom with which she said it. She's lucky the interview wasn't recorded and I can't put it in my report, but then if anyone used it in the trial it would be thrown out by the judge anyway."

"What was that?"

"I can't tell you."

"I swear, I won't tell anyone. Besides, I've been ordered off the case, and it would be hearsay anyway."

He stroked the stubble on his chin.

"Clara said that there wasn't a day gone by this last few years with him that she didn't want him dead."

Bossé sank her head into her hands, then lifted her eyes and looked directly at him. It was looking as though Clara was guilty after all.

"But did she admit to killing him?"

"No, Jordan stepped in and stopped her saying anything else and he told her not to go there. He said that he'd ask her to stop helping me if I used it against her. To be honest, I need her help and to unlock her memories, so I agreed to ignore what she'd said. One of the descriptions of a dress that one of her so-called cousins was wearing has narrowed down one more of the victims. She seemed to have been as upset as anyone could be to learn about those missing girls. I've arranged to go back later to have another interview, but she says that she'll only talk to me with Jordan present."

Bossé's heart felt for the victims and the pain the parents

must have suffered.

"Is there anything I can do to help?"

"Not really. But here's my card. If you can think of anything, phone me. In fact, when you're feeling better, maybe we could go out for a meal. You know, to talk about how the trial and my investigations are progressing."

"Err... Yeah. Fine."

"Good, I'll be going then."

As he turned and walked away, Bossé couldn't be sure if he'd just hit on her for a date, or if it was for a meeting that would turn out as starched as his shirt collar. Whatever, she curled her lips into a smile.

The nurse arrived and gave her some medication. Bossé couldn't wait to get past the triage and through the front door. Outside the main door, she clutched her bouquet of flowers and her overnight bag and looked around for a taxi. A seventy-nine gold Pontiac Firebird pulled up and parked over a sign on the asphalt marked out for ambulances. She could just about see someone behind the tinted window wave their hand for her to come over to them. Whoever it was rolled down their window.

Chapter 60

Good Samaritan

It came as a surprise to Bossé that Father David was the driver of the Firebird.

"Do get in before I get a ticket. I saw you hobbling about when I arrived and I was about to take a space in the parking lot," he said.

"I didn't have you down as a muscle-car enthusiast," Bossé replied, and taking a seat, she placed her overnight bag on her knees, balanced her flowers on the bag, and hugged it as he set off.

"It's my only vice. Nothing I need to confess to God about," he said, and then laughed. "I didn't expect them to discharge you so soon after I saw the photo of your mangled wreck in the newspaper."

"Sorry for the wasted journey."

"No, not at all. Where can I take you?"

"I live fifteen miles north from here. You could drop me at the bus terminal."

"I saw you limping. Will you be okay on your own?"

"It's a case of having to I'm afraid."

"Then why not come back to town and stay with me until you're feeling better. I know Mrs. O'Ahern isn't there, but I can rustle up some meals."

Bossé didn't reply right away, but gave his offer some thought. It was times like those that she wished she had family, especially after having had a concussion.

"You're very kind. I accept."

"Good. I'm looking forward to having your company. I've enjoyed out chats. Will someone else take over making inquiries in town?"

"No, the case is closed. It's all down to the trial now to decide Clara's fate."

"Not wishing to interfere, but what made you think others could be involved?"

"It wasn't a question of that to start with."

Bossé explained about Jeremiah Coulter, the effect it had had on her, and how she was resigning.

"You've not heard then?"

"Heard what?"

"It was on the radio news when I drove over to visit you. He's been arrested for attempted rape and his victim might not survive the ordeal."

"What!"

She pushed back in her chair. The first case against him was for the murder and rape of a victim. She was thinking that he could have had a partner who left his DNA on the victim from the original case, which would vindicate her. They arrived at the outskirts of Hunter's End. Bossé shuddered as they drove past what was left of Hunter's Lodge.

"I have to be honest and say that it looks bad for Clara. I just feel I'm missing something and others could be involved. It looks as though her dad was involved in the disappearances of quite a few children. What makes it worse is that we don't know if Clara could be one of his victims that he let live."

"Well I'm sure God will provide the answers."

"I hope so. Not sure what I'll do with myself after I've resigned."

"Have you done much traveling?" Father David asked.

"Not really. Been to Florida once. Vacations out of the state are not my thing."

They cruised along Main Street, and then he stopped and parked his car outside the garage at his cottage. He reached over and pulled out a map out of the glove compartment.

"I've just about visited every state in the old boy," he said, and patted his steering wheel. "I just need to get to Alaska during my vacation for my final journey and I can mark it off," he said, and poked at Alaska with his index finger. "Maybe you'll get the travel bug when you resign?"

"Maybe, though I don't know what I'll do yet. I've thought about a new career with anything from being a PI, to opening a flower store. It's a little late to be thinking about starting a family, but I might consider finding a partner. That frightens me though. Even more so, I'm afraid that I'll find myself alone when I hit old age. A companion would do, though maybe not living under the same roof."

Father David laughed.

"Oh, I wouldn't let it frighten you. The trend is for many to live alone now. And of course, I live alone, but then I have my parishioners and God as my companions. But yes, I'll admit, it is a worry as to who will look after me when I get aged and frail. I'm sure God will provide the answer. He'll have it all mapped out."

She had heard him say that God will provide a few times. Bossé was just thinking that she wished she had his faith, when a thought hit her as if someone had switched on a light bulb at those last words he had uttered.

"Father David, you're a Saint. You might just have been the conduit to the answer the FBI is looking for to find the resting places of those missing children."

"Well I wouldn't go that far. I've been called a few things in my time, but never a Saint. What is it I've I said?"

"I'll tell you as soon as I find out if my hunch is right."

Chapter 61

Devine Intervention

Bossé couldn't wait to get to the sheriff's office. She left her overnight bag and the flowers in the hallway, stepped outside and closed the door, and then hobbled along the sidewalk.

"I didn't expect to see you again," the sheriff said as Bossé entered. A pained expression rolled over MacCaffrey's face.

"Call it fate."

"Are you sure you should be working? Brennan told me the case was closed. You look white as a ghost."

"That case might be closed, but there's a question of the missing girls. How I feel is nothing that work won't cure. Tell me, have you sent Clara's backpack for storage?"

"Not had time."

"Good. Could you get it for me, only I'd be struggling with the stitches on my hand."

MacCaffrey ambled through to the locker room, and then returned with the backpack.

"How do you think that what she has in here could help?"

"Divine intervention, you could say. That and someone saying that your life is mapped out for you. Could you pass me the map from the left side pocket?" She handed the map to Bossé and she spread it out on the desk. "What do those marks say to you on the map?"

"Not got a clue."

"Well I'll tell you. I'll bet they're all the places where Ackerman has encountered those children that are missing. I'll need to use your computer."

"Feel free."

Bossé used the office computer to pull up her e-mails. She opened John's e-mail with the list of the ones whose DNA matched the clothing.

"Listen. I'll call out some states and towns. Put thumbtacks on the map on the wall at the locations, and then we'll compare them with Ackerman's map. We'll start with the one in Canada that I know of," Bossé said.

She called out states of the other six and printed off the details. They poured over the map. MacCaffrey checked them off one at a time.

"What have we got?" Bossé asked.

"Six of them match the states marked on the map. There's no match for the one who went missing from Youngstown, Ohio."

Bossé studied the map.

"There. That one there matches with what I think is the date in the middle of those numbers. But it's across the state line in Pennsylvania. None of these marks on the map are an exact location of where the children were last seen. But looking at those numbers it's clear what they are. The numbers in the middle are the dates they went missing, and he's used the dates to separate GPS coordinates. The numbers on the left must be north and the ones on the right must be east."

They exchanged glances.

"Are you thinking what I'm thinking?" Sheriff MacCaffrey said.

"If you're thinking these marks are the burial places, then yes. I need to contact Agent Crook."

Bossé took Agent Crook's card from her purse and dialed his cell phone number. While she gave him the details, Bossé noticed MacCaffrey typing away on the keyboard. She had almost completed the call, when MacCaffrey rose from her chair and walked over to the printer.

"You'd better take a look at this. Poor innocent girl. It's her all right. I'd stake my life on it."

"Sorry, can you hold?" Bossé asked agent Crook, then turned to MacCaffrey. "Who are you talking about?"

"Take a look for yourself. It's from the details of the second mark on the map in the northern area of Alaska. Look at the date." She dropped a copy of the image in front of Bossé, then reached into her desk drawer and gave Bossé a second image. "Tell me that's not her."

Bossé compared the image of the three-year-old child from

the Missing Persons web site to the mug shot of Clara.

"Madison Jackson! You think that's Clara? Her DNA shows markers for someone native to Alaska. I would have been expecting a native name."

"And you need to ask that? Prob'ly a union between her ancestors and settlers. Ask Agent Crook to check if there's any DNA sample on record at the Missing Persons Unit, over at the Alaskan Bureau of Investigations, then they can compare it with Clara's sample."

MacCaffrey seemed knowledgeable as to whom to contact considering she claimed to be only concerned with parking tickets. As far as she knew it was the Missing Persons Bureau at the Department of Justice that dealt with such things. She relayed the message.

Crook said, "For someone on sick leave, you've done excellent there. I don't know what to say, except I'll contact all the offices in the various states and have those GPS coordinates checked out. I should be able to tie up all the ones where we didn't have DNA samples from those dates and the states you've given me. I'll also have the one you think could be Clara checked out and get back to you as soon as I know something."

When Bossé hung up the phone call and turned to face Sheriff MacCaffrey, she was in tears. She pointed to the notes on identifying marks under the image of the child. "Look at those details of the birth mark on the child's butt. Sorry, I need to go home. This has all been too much. I'm just thankful Mary isn't among them, so at least there's a chance my daughter is still alive, though I doubt it. I'll leave you the keys. I'm telling you, that is definitely Clara."

MacCaffrey rose from her chair and hurried out of the office. Exhausted and aching in every limb as her medication wore off, Bossé took a seat at the sheriff's desk. MacCaffrey had left the drawer open in her hurry to exit the office. Bossé picked up the mug shot of Clara. There was no doubting that Clara had a similar birthmark listed. She reached out to put it back in the file at the top of the drawer. When she opened the file, her jaw dropped as she flicked through the contents, then she stopped to study an image of the crime scene from an angle that she hadn't seen before.

Bossé shuffled from her chair and walked over to the window. When she looked out of the window through a gap in the blinds, she saw the sheriff pacing up and down outside the grocery store. She'd obviously decided not to go home. She took off her hat, then slapped her thigh and entered the store. A short while later, she exited with Susan MacCaffrey and they walked into the Funeral Parlor. It wasn't long after that Nat pulled up outside the parlor in his SUV. He climbed out of the cab with Clarissa. Jordan appeared from an alley and joined them. All three of them looked to be in a heated discussion, and then they entered the parlor. To top it all off, Jake Hunter's pickup screeched to a halt behind Jordan's vehicle and he followed them inside.

Bossé scratched her head, wondering just what was going on over there. Her legs ached and she limped over to the desk and took a seat. She picked up the image of the crime scene again and stared at it, wondering just why the sheriff would have not sent it with the other photos she had taken. Over at the photocopier, Bossé took a copy of the image, then placed the original back in the file and closed the drawer. Every bone in her body ached with her medication losing its effectiveness. She set off back to the cottage, where she hoped to study the image in private to see if she could work out if it held any significance.

Chapter 62

Tick Tock

Sitting at the dining table eating her evening meal with Father David, Bossé's cell phone rang.

"Sorry about this, please excuse me. I have to take the call. FBI Agent Crook is on the line." She pulled the phone to her cheek and stepped into the hallway. "Alana here."

"Hi, I thought you should know, Madison is Clara, The DNA records confirm it without any doubt, but that's all the good news I have I'm afraid."

"Poor girl. What she must have gone through. So she was abducted from the age of three?"

"Looks that way. Her father isn't listed on the birth certificate, just her mom. Her mother died in a car wreck with her six-year-old son eleven years ago. I have Madison's and her mother's birth certificates, together with a copy of her mother's death certificate. I'll send you copies of them for your file by e-mail, and I'll send copies to her defense attorney. I think it's best if he tells her. He'll likely use that as mitigating circumstances if she's proven guilty when it gets to sentencing."

"I think you're right on both counts. Any news on those GPS coordinates?"

"Yeah. It's not good news. I've had a phone call from our field office in Pennsylvania. I hope you're ready for this. The local police have uncovered a shallow grave of a young girl at those GPS coordinates you gave me."

"Oh, no."

"Yeah, that's how I felt. At the same time at least the parents get closure and the chance to put her to rest. After finding this one, I'm expecting the rest will prove to be the same."

"Yeah, I guess."

"You okay?

313

"Yeah, I'm fine. I was in pain earlier, but I've taken more medication. The only thing that's bothering me is something I've found that concerns my case, but I'll not trouble you. It could be nothing."

"You can tell me, I might be able to help."

"No it's okay. I don't want to go jumping to conclusions. I'll deal with it on my own for now. It could be nothing."

"Your call. Maybe we could discuss it when we go for that meal. I was thinking Saturday if you think you'll have fully recovered by then?"

"There'll not be much to talk about now both cases are almost at an end."

"Well, that's not the only reason why I wanted to ask you out. We could leave work right out of the equation. I'd prefer that anyway."

Bossé held the phone away from her ear. She couldn't believe what she had just heard.

"Am I getting this right? Are you saying it's a date?"

"Well, yeah, you okay with that?"

"Err, yeah, fine."

"Good. I'll speak to you anyway when I know more about the other missing girls and we'll make arrangements."

They said their goodbyes and Bossé returned to the dining table, took a seat and she turned to Father David.

"I don't believe it, I've just been asked out on a date at my age."

"Good for you, make the most of it," he said, and took a sip of his coffee. "You look troubled. In fact you've looked troubled ever since you arrived back here earlier."

"I'll be fine."

"I have a good ear for listening."

Bossé didn't want to go over what she had just been told. It was distressing enough. Nor did she want to talk about what she had found in the sheriff's file.

"It's okay. It's something I have to work out for myself."

She made her excuses after finishing her meal, then rose from the dining table and hobbled all the way to her bedroom. Bossé rolled over onto the bed, slipped the crime scene image from her pocket and stared at it. Drowsy with the medication, she dozed off, when the next thing she knew, her cell phone rang on the nightstand and she answered."

"It's Ann MacCaffrey. I need you to meet with me at my office, now."

"What time is it?"

"Eleven."

"I'm on my way."

Bossé thought it must be urgent to want a meeting at that time of night. She picked up the copy of the crime scene image, and then did a double take when comparing it with the image she'd taken on her cell phone at the barn. What she discovered sent her mind into overdrive on her way to the sheriff's office. When she arrived, the sheriff ignored her, rose from her chair, took her gun from her holster and removed the clip and put both on the desk.

"I'm pleased you phoned, there's something we need to discuss," Bossé said.

MacCaffrey blanked her. Her eyes looked distanced as if showing that she hadn't acknowledged Bossé's arrival. MacCaffrey took off her belt, walked to the coat stand and hung it over a hook. She sighed as she walked back to her desk, where she took a seat, unpinned her badge from her coat and put it in the drawer.

"What is it you wanted to discuss?" MacCaffrey asked.

"I was going to ask you the same thing."

Bossé reached inside her jacket and pulled out the image of the crime scene at the barn and held it up for her to see.

"I'd like an explanation as to why you didn't send this with your report? It took some working out what significance it held. If I'm not mistaken, there's a knife missing from the wall mount next to the bow saw, and I'm sure when forensics get to work on it, that lump in the pool of blood is that knife. The other images you took and sent in, the knife was on the wall mount."

MacCaffrey looked indifferent to the revelation and shook her head. She pulled open her drawer and retrieved a bunch of papers.

"All you need to know about the image is in there. I'll sign them and you can witness them."

Bossé couldn't work out what she was getting at; other than she had acted strange from the moment she had set foot into the office. MacCaffrey worked her way through the papers signing them, and then pushed them over to the edge of the desk.

"It's all in there. It's my confession. I killed Ackerman. Clara walked in on me and I struck her with my flashlight."

"What! You? But why?"

The revelation had knocked Bossé off her stride. She had every man and his dog as a suspect in town, but it had never occurred to her that the sheriff could be responsible.

"You've looked in my file as I've noticed, so you'll be able to work it out. There's a copy of his identikit sketch in there. I did some checking when I found out from Clara where they'd lived before. I checked to see if there had been any crimes reported in the area around the time they left. They sent me the details in the file about the abduction. I needed to know if he had been involved in kidnapping Mary. I was going out there anyway to arrest him for assaulting Father David. I overpowered him in the barn and strung him up. Lowered him an inch at a time toward the bear trap. I didn't mean to kill him, the pulley slipped. In anger I slit him open with the boning knife."

"But why confess now?"

"Because when I realized Clara was one of his victims, I couldn't let her stew in jail if they found her guilty. Hell, what happened to her could have been what happened to my daughter. I've been fighting the guilt all along for setting her up with her dad's murder as it is."

Bossé pushed back in her chair and thought for a while. There was a chance that she was confessing just to get Clara off the hook, seeing as how she identified her situation with the possibility that her daughter could have ended up in the same circumstances. It wouldn't have been the first time someone had taken the guilt for someone else and made a false confession. She shook her head. The hidden crime scene image discounted that, and only the killer could have known about the faulty pulley. Then there was the fact that she'd destroyed any evidence of her involvement by washing her clothes and cleaning out her car. Getting Nat to clear the area in the drive had been a smart move. She realized the John had been right about plowing up the area and destroying the crime scene. She'd likely cleaned the murder weapon and hung it back on the wall. Bossé wondered if the sheriff could have set the barn and lodge on fire after she had said she was missing something at the crime scene.

"I guess I'd better lock you in a cell and ask someone from the county over to come and collect you."

"Guess so."

It all seemed to her to be something of an anti-climax. But then she thought it was always like that when faced with a confession. Bossé was just relieved that she'd kept digging, or maybe she wouldn't have discovered that Clara was abducted, and MacCaffrey would never have confessed and she'd have left Clara to face the trial. Thinking that, she allowed herself a smile at the thought of Gilbert Rhodes having to drop the charges against Clara. Not having met Clara, she made a promise to visit her if it was possible after her release.

Chapter 63

Gone With a Bang

Bossé escorted Sheriff MacCaffrey through to the cell and locked her in there. Dumbfounded as to how things had worked out, she returned to the office and dropped her backside onto the sheriff's chair. She pulled MacCaffrey's statement toward her, and then read through it, noting that she had started by saying that she understood her rights and that she was foregoing them. After witnessing all the pages, Bossé set about digitizing the statement and sent e-mails with the confession attached to Brennan, Gilbert Rhodes, and to Clara's attorney. She doubted they'd get to see the statement until the morning, so she knew that all she had to do was to phone for someone to collect Sheriff MacCaffrey and then she could hit the sack.

Her shoulders drooped, together with her entire innards, when the duty sergeant told her that no one was available until the morning. Bossé trudged through to the cells. MacCaffrey was holding the bars on the door and smirking.

"They'll pick you up in the morning," Bossé said.

"I could have told you that they'd have no one available tonight. There's a phone number in the card index on my desk for a sworn-in deputy in town. He covers for vacations and emergencies. Gordon O'Neil. You can ask him to guard me overnight."

Bossé stepped back into the office. She dialed O'Neil's number and made arrangements for him to come in and to guard the prisoner. It was a relief in her condition that she wouldn't have to sleep on a cot in the next cell to MacCaffrey. She didn't have long to wait for him to arrive and she handed him the keys, then walked to the cottage.

Father David had already turned in for the night when she arrived at the cottage, and she tiptoed up to her bedroom. Laid on the top of the bedclothes, Bossé's mind wandered. She decided that Coulter's re-arrest changed nothing and that she would still resign. Bossé thought that she could now see why MacCaffrey was defensive of Nat when she had him as a person of interest, and why the MacCaffreys had joined forces with the Hunters, after she had turned her attention to Jordan as a suspect. With her marrying a Hunter, Sheriff MacCaffrey had her feet in both clans in town, and as she had said, with Bossé not having any family, maybe she couldn't understand the bond that glued family together.

With her eyes heavy, her last thought was that, but for the confession, she would never have been happy with the outcome left as it was, regardless of what happened at the trial. All her suspects had motive to want Ackerman dead, and anyone of them, or all of them together could have been involved.

A loud crashing sound brought Bossé around from her sleep, followed by something metallic being dragged along the road outside for a few seconds. Bossé strained to hear anything else, but other than the sound of a car driving away there was silence. Still groggy, she rolled over and snuggled her head into the pillow, wondering if someone had been drinking late and hit an A frame advertising board outside one of the stores. She tossed and turned for maybe half an hour, when her curiosity got the better of her. She rolled off of the bed, drew back the curtain and peered out over Main Street. The light was still on in the sheriff's office, and but for the streetlights, all the houses and stores were in darkness. She noted the time at four thirty and climbed back onto the bed, disgusted that she hadn't had the motivation to undress before falling asleep.

Bossé tossed and turned with intermittent broken sleep. An annoying buzzing sound grew louder. The clock on the nightstand displayed the time at six thirty. She sat upright to the thundering sound of helicopter blades circling low overhead. She rolled off of her bed and looked out through the window. The deputy was pacing up and down outside the office, talking on a radio mic. A police chopper banked and headed in the direction of the highway, then circled low over a wooded area off to the right. She slipped on her shoes, opened her door, then made her way outside. The chopper was looking for someone that much was obvious.

"What's happened?" she asked the deputy as she arrived at the office.

"She's gone."

"Who's gone?"

"Sheriff MacCaffrey."

Bossé's jaw gaped.

"How in hell's name did that happen?"

"I had a phone call to attend a car wreck on the highway. Woke her to ask what I should do, and she said she'd be fine on her own and to go and attend. It was only a damned hoax call. When I returned, I didn't even know she'd gone. Didn't want to disturb her again. Half an hour ago, when I went to check her cell, she was gone."

"What time did you get the hoax phone call?"

"Around four. The chopper is out looking for her and they're arranging to set up a perimeter on the roads out of here."

Bossé followed him into the office and on through to the cells. There was no glass in the window frame, and the iron barred framework to the outside was gone.

Deputy O'Neil unlocked the back door. They followed scrape marks on the asphalt and found the barred frame twenty yards down an alley across from the backstreet. Bossé inspected the bars. It didn't take a forensic examination to see from the scratches and the bent bars that someone had fastened a cable attached to a vehicle, and yanked it out.

"Someone must have heard this and seen something," she said, aware that her cheeks were flushing at not having investigated the noise she had heard.

"Guess they would, but there's no one come to me and said anything."

Father David came up beside her.

"I heard all the noise and you hobbling down the stairway, what's happened?"

"Sheriff MacCaffrey has escaped."

"Escaped!"

"Yeah, she confessed to killing Ackerman, so I locked her in the cell. You were in your bedroom when I returned so I couldn't tell you."

"Oh, dear."

"Yes, oh, dear. Someone in town has helped her to escape, no doubt about it. I don't suppose you would tell me if any of the townsfolk confesses to helping her?"

Father David lifted his shoulders then let them drop. He bent his head and looked at Bossé over his half-rimmed spectacles.

"Well, no. That would be between me, the confessor, and the Lord," he said, and snickered. "I'll see you for breakfast at nine, and then we can talk," he said, then he turned and walked in the direction of his cottage. Bossé shook her head. O'Neil tapped her on the shoulder.

"The sergeant from headquarters phoned me earlier to say a search team would be here around nine. What should I do?"

"I'll wait with you until they arrive, then I'm gone and it's not my problem anymore. I'm supposed to be on sick leave."

Back in the office, Bossé lifted her feet onto the desk and pushed back in her chair. Exhaustion finally overcame the flood of adrenaline that she had experienced and she dozed off.

"Detective Bossé, it's almost nine," she heard, and a finger prodding her shoulder. She opened her eyes and O'Neil stepped back as she swung her legs from the desk.

"Thanks. I'll leave you to it and go for breakfast."

She walked out and onto the sidewalk, yawned and stretched her arms. Looking out over Main Street, stores were opening. Susan MacCaffrey was outside her grocery store with Jordan, Rick, and Drake. They were exchanging conversation, when they all burst into laughter as if they'd shared a joke. The mayor stepped outside through his doorway and leant an advertising board against the wall outside his funeral parlor, and then he waved at the crowd outside the store. Nat's SUV appeared and he parked up next to the garage. He climbed out of his cab and gave a thumbs-up sign in Jordan's direction. She half-expected Jordan to return a one-fingered salute, instead he returned the gesture with a thumbs-up sign of his own.

She was even more surprised, when Jake Hunter's red pickup pulled up alongside Jordan. Jake climbed out of the driver's side and walked over to Jordan. If they would have started a fight, she decided it was none of her business. She needn't have worried. Jake put his arm around Jordan's shoulder, gave him a squeeze, then removed his arm and ruffled his hair.

Jake looked over at Bossé and waved, instead of as she expected; him marching over and chewing her head off over the search warrant on his property.

She waved back, then turned and walked along the sidewalk to the cottage, shaking her head at the thought that it was game set and match to the town.

Epilogue

Clara's Domain

The Final Reveal

5 Years later. Sheldon Point Alaska. 62.06 °N, 163.30 °W.

Population 192. Number of registered sex offenders - 0

The glass fogs with the vapor from my breath. I draw a heart with my fingertip on the windowpane, and then glance out through the window at my domain. There isn't anywhere out there that I can't travel alone if I have a mind to go out without someone breathing down my neck. Strangely, after all I went through, I no longer desire to go out alone. It looks as though God did have a purpose for me after all. Despite the freezing cold, I can feel the warmth in the bulge of my stomach as our baby moves around. I say our baby, Jordan is out there in the yard feeding our thirty-two huskies that we rent out as dogsled teams to mostly tourists and hunters. Arranging tours in the wilds are what keeps the pantry stocked; that and a little hunting to keep the dogs and our bellies full. They're all shuffling about on the top of their kennels, wagging their tails, and waiting to be fed.

There is no danger out there as long as we keep our wits about us, and the huskies warn us if wolves or bears stray too near our house. We live on the outskirt of town. It's better that way. No one asking too many questions. I take a seat on the

325

sofa next to Drake, my pet husky, the runt of one of the litters. He snuggles up close. Just like the blackbird back at Hunter's Lodge, he can't talk, and I share confidences with him as I am about to do now. Really, we don't need to talk to each other, because I'm sure he can read my mind, but anyway, he's a good listener.

Mom, as I call her in the company of strangers, or should I say Sheriff Ann MacCaffrey, she lives with us here. Besides helping with the dogs, she tends to growing vegetables and salads in our greenhouse that Jordan built. Bless him; he can turn his hands to anything.

It was sad to learn that my real mom and brother had died. Maybe with that situation, and Ann losing her daughter, I guess that's how us living together has worked well, with the both of us being surrogates to each other. It helped that I had a copy of my real mom's birth certificate, and she took her name, which coincidently, she had Ann as her middle name.

As soon as they dropped the charges against me, I was released. The sense of freedom as I hit the sidewalk caused me to have a mini-meltdown. I was afraid and relieved in good measure. Jordan was there with Detective Bossé waiting for me. She never said, but I could see it in her eyes and a shake of her head that she had sort of worked out the truth before she gave me a big hug.

We stayed at his dad's hunting lodge for three months to get to know each other, just like he'd said that day in church. It took a while before Jordan told me the truth of everything about Ann confessing and escaping. He had to really. The family arranged a phone call from a payphone in Florida to Susan MacCaffrey. She talked loudly about the phone call within earshot of the new sheriff, saying it was from Ann, and to create a diversion while we made the drive to the Canadian border.

We all sort of bonded on the hike through Canada until we made it to Alaska, and well, the rest is history. Turns out, the MacCaffreys and the Hunters had arranged her escape on that day before she had made her confession. Jordan's dad was pleased, because he thought that Bossé would have never let it drop. He hid Ann at his farm for three months for her protecting Jordan while waiting for it all to die down in the news.

Father David visited last year when we got wed. The town's church is nothing like his, more of a dilapidated shed with a sloping wooden cross on the tin roof, surrounded by overgrown grass and weeds. He said something about visiting for the wedding would kill two birds with one stone so he could mark it off on his map, but then he said that he was not sure it counted, since he hadn't driven there, whatever that meant.

It was great to catch up on all the gossip. We didn't have to worry about him going to the police. He knew exactly what had happened before Bossé left town from Ann and others visiting the confession booth. It wasn't just that, besides his doctrine to keep what's said in the confession booth a secret, Ann said the town had their own hold on him for his indiscretions with Mrs. O'Ahern. She used that, together with a threat of going to have words with the Bishop to get her to leave town for a while, so she wouldn't have to make a statement about what she saw and heard that day outside the church.

Father David told us that Bossé married some FBI guy and she was now running a flower shop in Denver. It was the same FBI guy who interviewed me in jail. He is the one credited with finding all the bodies of you-know-who's victims. Sorry, but I can't speak his name. From what Ann has said, the credit should have gone to Bossé and her.

The sad part was that Nat and Clarissa never got married. She committed suicide a year after we left, but we were told it had nothing to do with them not getting married. She'd dropped out of college and returned home. It was all down to the guilt and depression for what took place the barn that night according to Nat. It was just fortunate that she didn't leave a suicide note to spell out what happened. Nat moved out of town when his mom died of cancer shortly after, and hasn't been heard of since.

Jordan always said that Clarissa had a temper as I had witnessed firsthand that night at the Halloween dance. Nat and

Jordan only wanted to frighten him, to teach you know who a lesson, knowing that the sheriff would likely arrest him shortly after they'd finished with him for at least assaulting Father David.

Clarissa grabbed the rope on the pulley from Nat and it slipped. She couldn't hold his weight. Jordan wasn't sure that she wanted to stop him slipping. And well, that's what killed him when he hit the bear trap and the pulley grabbed the rope. Nat and Jordan were rooted to the spot with shock. Not Clarissa. She grabbed the boning knife from the wall peg and slit his gut open. Turns out an uncle had abused her as a child when she lived in California, and she was carrying that anger with her.

Clarissa dropped the knife and Nat grabbed her hand, pulling her to leave through the barn door. Jordan followed them, and then they all stopped, caught in the sheriff's headlights at the entrance to the drive as she exited the lodge after finding it ransacked, and she was about to drive off. They were all doused with blood splatter, so there was no hiding that something untoward had happened. It was around the time I was trudging across the fields. Ann had a good idea that he was involved in abducting a child in Alaska, and she was going to question him about it after arresting him for assaulting Father David. She thought it was divine retribution when she marched them into the barn and found his body strung up. She told them to get the hell outta there and she'd clean up.

It wasn't long after that I turned up as Ann was about to leave. Said she stayed there in the darkness, hoping that whoever or whatever it was scratching around would leave. Of course, I didn't leave, more fool me. She said that she panicked and struck me with her flashlight. Before I came round, and seeing me with my hunting knife in my hand, that's when she had the bright idea to arrest me as soon as I stirred, for her to rescue Nat from prosecution. It took a while to forgive her, and that's the God's honest truth. Hell, I even thought I had done it, and my mind was hiding it from me until the day they set me free. If it wasn't for Jordan convincing me to plead not guilty,

I'd have accepted the plea bargain. When he eventually told me what had happened, I was too head over heels with him to give him a slap. Besides, if it had been in my power, I'd have bestowed them all with a medal.

Anyway, he told me that he arrived back at his dad's around midnight. He thought his dad would be in bed, but he wasn't. Right away, he knew Jordan had been involved in something serious, when he saw his clothes covered with blood. He didn't ask him what he'd been doing. All he did was to order him to get changed, and then his dad burned his clothes in the wood stove and told him to get the hell outta town.

Just goes to show, that whatever problems family have, sometimes blood turns out thicker than water. In the case of the town, I doubt the Hunters and MacCaffreys will ever break their newfound bond and they'll take the secret to their graves.

His dad nearly messed it up when he sent Bossé a threatening letter for her to leave town, and later he burned down the lodge and the barn. Luckily, they asked Ann to carry out the search warrant, and she burned the magazine with the letters cut out in the same wood stove that his dad had used to burn his clothes. Then she wrote out a sample of the words from the envelope to pass off as his writing and saved the day.

I guess I owe Bossé a debt of gratitude. But for her digging, no one would have found out I'd been abducted as a child. That's what prompted Ann to act when she identified my situation with the possibility that her daughter could be in the same position. It was no longer just a question of protecting her nephew by implicating me.

Ah well, that's enough of that, no point dwelling. Time to prepare the stew, it's expected, though fortunately, it's my decision and not drilled into me. Besides, Mom, my white knight, and my baby need nourishment.

SCORPION BOOKS
THRILLERS WITH A STING IN THE TALE

Other books by Declan Conner

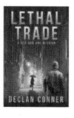

Made in the USA
San Bernardino, CA
04 May 2018